VANISH

Eden House Mysteries #3

Bill Kitson

Published by Accent Press Ltd 2015

ISBN 9781783753499

Prologue

November 1965

As the set drew to a close, the group began to play the opening chords of their latest hit, still at number one in the charts after five weeks. Although it was cold and foggy outside, the auditorium was packed, sweaty, and deafening. The sound of the group onstage, relayed by huge banks of speakers, was soon surpassed by the shouts, cheers, and most of all the piercing screams from the audience: most of the crowd that had flocked to see the group were teenage girls, desperate to get close to their idols. Behind the group, depicted in garish neon, their name: Northern Lights.

It was 1965, the heyday of rock.

Four encores later, still deafened by the shrieking adulation of their fans, the band made their way off stage. They headed down the warren of Newcastle City Hall's corridors to their dressing room. A phalanx of security guards surrounded them and ushered them inside; two remained standing like sentinels outside the door. One of the roadies greeted the triumphant musicians and told them they had to wait for the limo that would take them to the hotel following the final gig in a long and exhausting tour.

After what seemed an age, the senior roadie appeared, to summon them. 'There's a right scrum outside the stage door,' he warned them. 'I reckon there's even more heat outside than there was in the theatre.'

He turned and gestured towards the auditorium, and as he did so realized something was wrong. 'Where's Gerry?'

he asked.

The band members looked around, as if expecting to see their lead singer lurking in some dark corner. Then they looked at one another in perplexed surprise. A babble of denials followed.

'What you're saying is, nobody's seen him since you left the stage, right? Well he can't be waiting in the car, can he?'

'Probably found something he fancied and stopped off for a quickie,' the drummer suggested, accompanying his comment with a lewd gesture.

'I doubt that.' The roadie motioned to the security men. 'Go check in and around the auditorium. I suppose it could be like he says and some tasty bit of jailbait has waylaid him. Don't disturb him if he's having a knee-trembler though. Way he's been behaving lately, you're liable to finish up with a black eye.'

As they began their search, one of the group's most ardent fans walked nervously towards the river, glancing over her shoulder from time to time. Her instructions were clear, but as she waited by the riverbank, Julie Solanki was uneasy. The area was deserted, dimly lit; the large amount of money she was carrying made her feel highly vulnerable. She heard footsteps, but as the approaching figure appeared out of the gloom, Julie realised it wasn't the dealer she had been sent to meet.

She saw the distinctive jacket and was about to greet him; to congratulate him on the group's performance, when he turned abruptly and headed towards the Tyne Bridge. Julie was surprised. He must have seen her, must have realized what she was doing there. After all, he'd been the one who passed her the message from the dealer. Before she could ponder this, a car drew up alongside her. Seconds later, the deal was done. As Julie set out to deliver the drugs, she caught a fleeting glimpse of two figures, their faces seemingly averted, also heading for the Tyne Bridge. They vanished into the shadows. It would be years before she had cause to remember them.

It was over half an hour later before the men reported back.

'We checked onstage and around all the ground floor. We also did the balcony and the foyer. We even checked every cubicle in the bogs, both men's and women's. God, they're in a ruddy awful state, some of them! We thought he might have slipped into one of them if he wanted to get his end away, but no luck – for us or him,' he ended with a grin.

'I went down to the stage door, and when I could make myself heard above the wailing throng, I asked the others if they'd seen Crowther,' his colleague added. 'I thought he might have slipped out without anyone noticing him, but they said he definitely hadn't been through there.' He grinned. 'The fans would have eaten him alive if he'd ventured out that way.'

'I can think of worse ways to go,' the drummer commented.

'The thing is,' the first security man told them, 'nobody's seen him. There's no trace of Crowther in this building, and I can't see any way he could have got out of here. He's vanished. Utterly and completely vanished. Into thin air.'

Chapter One

December 1981

'I want you to find a dead man.'

Those were the words Lew Pattison spoke the first time we met. It was a clear, cold winter's morning, the sunlight making the frost on the fields sparkle like thousands of tiny diamonds, and Eve and I were returning from our morning stroll. Since Eve had moved from London to join me at Dene Cottage in the Yorkshire Dales, it had become a ritual we both enjoyed and gave us the chance to discuss our plans for the day. On this day, as with many in the immediate past, these centred on our plans for the extension to the cottage.

When we reached the brow of the hill that marked the boundary of Laithbrigg village, we were surprised to see a car parked in the lane in front of the gate. Not just any car, either; the gleaming paint and sleek, majestic lines of the bodywork proclaimed it to be no less than the ultimate in luxury, a Rolls-Royce.

'Wow! That's some piece of metal.'

'I wonder who it belongs to. Do you think it's someone visiting us?' Eve asked.

'If so, they must be friends of yours. Nobody I know could afford the wing mirror off a car that expensive.'

As we approached, the driver stepped carefully out, obviously wary in case his expensive, highly polished leather shoes came into contact with anything untoward. I was still admiring the man's smart, tailored business suit, which seemed totally out of place in our surroundings, when Eve recognized our visitor.

'It's Lew Pattison.'

'See, I knew it had to be one of your plutocratic friends. Who's he?'

'Alice's husband. You remember me telling you about Alice Pattison, the barrister? She and I were friends in London; she represented me at my appeal.'

Long before we met, Eve had been found guilty of attempted murder after stabbing her violent partner with a carving knife. The conviction had been overturned on appeal, when Eve's counsel had been able to produce evidence and eyewitnesses who testified to the man's long-term abuse, which had culminated with him scalding Eve with boiling water. It was in an attempt to escape this torture that Eve had retaliated.

'Lew, this is a pleasant surprise,' Eve greeted Pattison, before introducing me. 'How's Alice? Is everything all right?'

'She's fine. She sends her best wishes. She wanted to come along, but she's in court all this week.'

'How did you know where to find us?'

'It would be hard not to. You two seem to be international celebrities. I read about your exploits when I was in Rome last week. Even there the papers and the TV bulletins carried stories about you both. I had to come to Yorkshire on business, so I thought I could kill two birds with one stone, so to speak, because I have a favour to ask.'

'Why don't we go inside and have a cuppa, then you can explain why you're here,' Eve suggested.

A few minutes later, when we were seated in the lounge, Pattison explained. 'It was seeing the newspaper article that prompted the idea. I talked it over with Alice, and she reminded me of that other business you were involved in, at some castle or other? It seems you two have a talent for detective work.'

'We don't go seeking it,' Eve protested, 'it just seems to find us! Adam's an author, and nowadays I'm learning to be a housewife, editor, and critic, and before long I plan to be a building site foreman, all rolled into one. We've had plans for an extension approved,' she added by way of explanation.

'I understand, and I won't be offended if you refuse, but I do need some help, and you'd be ideal. For one thing, I know I can trust you, and you living here makes it even better.'

'Why not tell us what it is you want us to do?' I suggested.

Pattison paused and took a deep breath. 'It's a long story, but basically … I want you to find a dead man.'

As an explanation, Pattison's opening statement was more baffling than revealing. I blinked, and to cover my surprise, which I could see was mirrored by Eve, I said, 'There are lots to choose from. Graveyards round here are full of them.' Pattison gave me a pained smile, so I continued, 'I assume you have someone specific in mind.'

'First of all, I should explain my background. Eve knows a bit about me, I guess, but not too much. I'm in the music business. At least, that's my main sphere of operation, although I've diversified in recent years. I started out as a roadie in the sixties, and then became a manager for several groups and solo artists. It was a golden time for British pop music, and the whole thing blossomed from there.

'Currently, one of my brightest stars is a young girl with a great future. She's only sixteen, but she's already had a couple of hit singles. There are more songs waiting for her to record that I'm certain will make her a megastar. It's one of those songs that's the problem. The girl's name is Trudi Bell. You may have heard of her.'

I certainly had, and I could tell from Eve's expression that she had too. 'Last week,' Pattison continued, 'we received a registered letter at my office addressed for her attention. Inside was some sheet music, plus a demo tape. That's by no means unusual. Fans often send in stuff, imagining they've written the next number one and asking their favourite pop star to record it. I had it down as just another of those losers until I scanned the dots.'

'Sorry, you've lost me.' I could tell by Eve's expression that she didn't understand either.

'I meant, when I'd read the sheet music, it looked really good, so I played the tape. As soon as I heard the melody, I knew the song would be just right for Trudi. Whoever composed it knew exactly how to tailor a ballad for someone with a voice like hers. That made me curious about the songwriter. I was convinced it had to be someone with a profound knowledge of music.'

'I take it you'd no clue as to the identity of the sender,' Eve said.

'No, there wasn't a letter or anything.'

'What about a return address on the envelope?'

'There was, but it wasn't much help. It simply said, "John Smith, c/o Barclays Bank, Harrogate".'

'So the composer wishes to remain anonymous. Where's the problem with that?'

Pattison turned to me. 'Adam will understand, being an author. It's all to do with copyright. Unless we can get the writer's signature on a contract we could lay ourselves and Trudi open to huge claims if the song does become successful.'

'I get that, but I still don't see where the hunt for a dead man comes in,' I said.

'I listened to that demo over and over. All the time something was nagging at the back of my mind. You know how it is when you see someone in a street and recognize them, but can't put a name to the face? Well, it was a bit like that, or when you read something and feel sure you know the author, even if you can't remember their name.

It's pretty much the same with musicians. If you hear something, you can often tell who it is playing or singing, even before they announce it.'

'That's true,' I agreed. 'I only need a few bars to recognize Miles Davis, for example.'

'That's exactly what I mean. I was still struggling with it when, quite by chance, I heard a record from 1964 on the radio. That was when I knew who the player was. I knew without doubt that not only had he played, but also that he'd composed the song on that tape. There was only one problem. It couldn't possibly have been the man I had in mind, because he died in 1965.'

'Maybe he recorded it before he died and someone else sent it in?' Eve suggested. 'His wife, perhaps, or a close friend.'

Pattison shook his head. 'He wasn't married, had no family, and precious few friends. Apart from that, back then it would have been reel-to-reel tape, not a cassette. Besides which, it was in stereo, not mono.'

'OK, so who is this mysterious composer? I take it we're discounting it being the work of a ghostwriter.'

Pattison groaned. 'It didn't say anything in that newspaper article about your weird sense of humour.'

Eve snorted. 'If you think that's bad, wait until he really gets warmed up.'

Pattison leaned forward and set his mug down carefully on the coaster. 'What do you know about Northern Lights?' He must have anticipated my reply because he added swiftly, 'I'm talking about the pop group, not the Aurora Borealis.'

The name was familiar enough. 'I seem to remember they were tipped for stardom. As I recall some people reckoned they might be as big as The Beatles or The Rolling Stones, but then something went wrong and they were never heard of again. Wasn't there some sort of scandal?'

Pattison looked at me mockingly. 'I thought you used to be a reporter?'

'Not in those days. Back then I hadn't reached such heady heights.'

'I used to manage Northern Lights. You were right; they would have been huge if they'd stayed together. Looking back, I think it was inevitable that they would have split up sooner or later. What happened in 1965 just made it sooner.'

'What was their problem?'

'You name it and you'd probably be right. Back-biting, jealousy, petty squabbles, professional rivalry, women – all fuelled by booze and drugs. At the root of it all was the fact that the group had split into two factions. Everyone knew that but for the genius of one of their members, they'd still have been playing pubs and working men's clubs, earning a pittance and struggling to get gigs.

'It was like that before Gerry Crowther joined them. He had a good singing voice and he was an exceptional keyboard player, but his genius lay in his talent as a songwriter. Crowther composed all their hit singles plus every track on their LPs. He was both talented and prolific – and most of the others hated him on both counts.'

Pattison paused and took a sip of his tea, which must have been cold by then. 'Crowther actually chose the most famous line-up. He knew he could mould them into a unit capable of producing the sound he wanted. In the process he insisted they replace some members of the original line-up. Several of the others protested, but deep down they knew they would have to go along with Crowther's ideas if they wanted to succeed. You'd think that would make them grateful, but in fact it seemed to make them resent him even more.'

'What happened to cause the split?' Eve asked.

'Northern Lights were playing their final gig of the tour

in Newcastle in November '65. At the end of their set, the group went back to their dressing room to unwind and waited for their transport. After a while, someone noticed that Crowther wasn't there. When they couldn't find him everyone went into panic mode. Eventually, the truth came out: it seemed Crowther had walked from the venue to the Tyne Bridge and jumped to his death. He was seen near the bridge by one of the group's fans. It was a long time afterwards that his body was recovered from the river. There was no possibility of a mistake. They even recovered his trademark leather jacket.'

'Was it very distinctive?'

'Unique around the north-east, I reckon. It had the name and image of Crowther's hero, Buddy Holly, on the back.'

I blinked with surprise. 'I've got one of those. I've had it for years. Mind you, I got mine in New York, not Newcastle. And you must have got it wrong. If Crowther died in 1965, someone else must have played on the song.'

'I didn't get it wrong. I'm convinced I didn't. I'm sure it was Crowther who wrote and played that music. No one came close to his style.'

'If you're right, whose was the body in the river? And how did they come by Crowther's jacket?'

Pattison shrugged helplessly. 'I've no idea. That's why I need your help.'

'Accepting that you believe Crowther is alive, why ask us to find him? Isn't that the sort of job a private detective would be better at?'

'Or the police perhaps,' Eve added.

'The police won't get involved. As far as they're concerned, Crowther's dead. Even if he didn't come to any harm and simply vanished of his own volition, they won't be interested. It isn't illegal to disappear. As for private investigators, I've very little confidence in their ability. There are other reasons for asking you as well.'

'Such as?'

'Back then, I got a firm of private detectives involved and details of Gerry's disappearance appeared in the press within a couple of days. At that point we were trying to keep it under wraps. The leak must have come either from my office or the enquiry agent. I'm still not sure which.'

'What are the other reasons?'

Pattison spoke slowly, choosing his words with great care. 'There are aspects to this case that I wouldn't want to entrust to them. Like I said, there was a lot of strife within Northern Lights. Crowther only had two allies within the band: Neville Wade, the drummer, and Billy Quinn, the lead guitarist. After Gerry disappeared, Quinn's behaviour changed. He became introverted, morose, with hardly a word for anyone. Soon after Crowther's body was recovered from the river, Billy was killed in London. At the time, I thought he'd simply made a bad mistake, but now I'm not sure. So, I thought that the best chance of finding Gerry without anyone getting wind of what's going on would be to involve a complete outsider, and someone who had no previous connection either with me or Northern Lights.'

'So you picked us because you want to avoid anyone learning that Crowther's potentially alive? That's the only reason?'

'Not quite. For one thing, Crowther was born in this area. Well, West Yorkshire to be exact. I particularly remembered because the place name was so unusual that I'd to ask him how to spell it. It was Mytholmroyd.'

I smiled and corrected Pattison's pronunciation. 'If everyone believed the suicide story, they must have thought Crowther had a reason. Do you know what that might have been?'

Pattison was silent for a moment before answering.

'Musicians are an odd bunch. A few are normal, level-headed individuals. I'd have put Crowther in that bracket, but towards the end he became more … difficult, shall we say. About a month or two before he vanished his behaviour changed abruptly. I got reports back that Crowther had started drinking. He certainly wasn't a teetotaller, none of them were, but I'd never seen him drink much.'

'And you've no idea what caused the change?'

'No. I thought his death was the culmination of his downward spiral, and assumed that drink, drugs, or depression, or a combination of all three, had finally got the better of him.' Pattison smiled rather sadly. 'The three Ds that are the bane of performers everywhere. Now, I'm not sure what to think. If Crowther is still alive, then the mystery of why he vanished is greater than ever. Apart from that,' he continued, 'I have a piece of evidence to show you.'

'What's that?' Eve asked.

He produced a large registered envelope from his briefcase. 'This is the envelope that the music came in.' He pointed to the top right-hand corner. 'When Alice saw that, she convinced me to drive up from London to visit you. She said it was too good an opportunity to miss.'

The envelope bore the postmark of the village of Allerscar, no more than fifteen miles away from where we were.

Before Pattison left, we'd come to a compromise. Although we'd agreed to try and locate Gerry Crowther, as Eve pointed out, we couldn't consider starting to make enquiries for some months. 'You've asked at a very bad moment,' she told him. 'The builder starts work straight after New Year and Adam is working to a deadline. We'll have to refuse if you need something doing in the immediate future.'

'That's not a problem,' Pattison smiled. 'It isn't as if I need the music for Trudi to record next week. She has several more potential songs lined up, just not as good as that one. How does this sound: if you agree to take the case, I'll gather all the background material I can find together and when you give me the go-ahead, I'll send it up to you via registered mail. You can start by having a look through it all, and let me know if there's anything else you need. Then you'll be au fait with the facts. It'll take me quite a while to get all the info down on paper anyway.'

As we watched him drive away, Eve said, 'Lew's comment about "taking the case" makes us sound like real private detectives.'

'That's true, and I hope all the villagers saw Pattison's car outside our house. It'll do wonders for our reputation.'

'They'll probably charge us double for the work we want doing on the house.'

I looked at my intended with interest. 'Are you certain you weren't born in Yorkshire?'

'Now that we've decided to play detective, have you an idea where to start?'

'There isn't much we can do until Pattison supplies that background material. I have had one idea, though.'

'Only one? Adam, you're losing your touch.' Eve has a great talent for insulting me. What's more worrying is that I'm starting to enjoy it.

'I think a trip to Mytholmroyd sometime in the future might pay dividends.'

'Mytholmroyd? Why there?'

'That was where Crowther was born. He might have returned there after the supposed suicide. Alternatively, we might find someone who could give us a clue as to where he is now, and what he's been doing for the past sixteen years.'

Eve shook her head sadly. 'Your thinking might be good but your arithmetic is lousy. I counted three ideas, not one.'

'OK then, here's another idea for you. Your friend Pattison was a little less truthful in a couple of respects.' I closed the door and followed Eve into the study.

'In what way was he untruthful?'

'He said the police wouldn't be interested because no crime had been committed. That isn't really right. If Crowther didn't commit suicide that night, what did become of him? And if someone else's body was washed up later wearing Crowther's clothing, might that not make police suspect that Crowther might have been responsible for the unknown's death?'

'You think Crowther might have vanished because he'd murdered someone, and dressed the corpse in his jacket to make it appear as if it was him who had died?'

'It's a possibility, and I reckon that's the real reason Pattison doesn't want the police involved. The other reason might be connected to Quinn's death. Pattison merely said he was "killed". He didn't elaborate, which I found a bit suspicious.'

Chapter Two

Work on the extension went better than we could have hoped, helped by an unusually mild winter and spring. The end of May saw the new part of the building ready for occupation.

Our home was no longer small; the extension had changed the cottage into a house. It was with great ceremony that the plaque bearing the name *Eden House* was installed, replacing the previous Dene Cottage. I held Eve close as we gazed at the sign. 'Well, my little builder's foreman, you've certainly proved your organisational skills.' I smiled at her. 'Perhaps the next thing you can organise could be a wedding?'

'That'll have to wait a bit longer. You've another book to finish first, and there's that job we promised to do for Lew. Besides, who mentioned marriage? I happen to like collecting jewellery,' she said, staring at my mother's engagement ring on her left hand.

'If you're that keen on rings, then I'll buy you a gold one to go with it.'

It was early July before I had time to spare. Eve then phoned Lew Pattison to ask if he still wanted us to try and find the missing musician. He seemed pleased that we were ready to make a start and would get the paperwork sent through as soon as possible.

We had finished our evening meal when our phone rang. Eve answered it, and her greeting of 'Hi, sis,' told me it was her older sister Harriet who was calling; or Lady Rowe, to give her correct title.

Harriet was doing most of the talking, because all I heard from Eve were several monosyllables, followed by an, 'Oh dear, that's terrible. How is he?' She ended the call by saying, 'I don't know. I'll tell Adam, and see if he's got any bright ideas. It's unlikely, but you never know.'

'Problem?' I asked as she put the phone down. I can be very perceptive at times.

'And how! You know they're all supposed to be jetting off to the States?'

I nodded, and Eve continued, 'It looks as if the whole trip will have to be cancelled. Tony might have to go to that conference in New York on his own.'

Eve's brother-in-law, Sir Anthony Rowe, was scheduled to attend an international business symposium in New York, and that had been the planned springboard for a six-week holiday for the whole family, including Lady Charlotte, Tony's mother.

'Why, what's gone wrong?'

'Charlie has been sent home from school after spending two days in the sanatorium. He's gone down with a severe case of tonsillitis. He's got a high temperature and there's no way the doctor will allow him near an aeroplane until he's better. That means Harriet, the twins, and Lady Charlotte will all have to stay at home.'

Charles Rowe, Tony and Harriet's son, now fifteen years old, was a great favourite of ours. The solution seemed obvious.

'Tell Harriet we'll go across to Mulgrave Castle tomorrow, bring Charlie back here, and take care of him. That way the rest of the family don't miss out.'

'That's brilliant. But that would mean he has to stay here for over six weeks. Are you sure?'

I raised my eyebrows, shook my head, and sighed. 'I'm surprised you didn't think of it.'

Eve's response was an extremely rude gesture. She rang Harriet back, then told me, 'The rest of them are thrilled, and Harriet says even Charlie has cheered up a bit. He'd been very down at the thought that he might be responsible for everyone missing such a huge treat.'

Next day, we arrived at Mulgrave Castle to find the Rowe family in the throes of last-minute packing. This was postponed as they greeted us, then Eve and I went to collect our patient.

Charlie had developed from an energetic, cheerful, slightly impudent child into an intelligent, athletic, and humorous teenager, with none of the behavioural problems normally associated with that age group. When we first met, I had been impressed by his ability to judge people; since then I'd realized that he was extremely mature for one so young. This, together with him being tall for his age, tended to make people treat him as an adult rather than a teenager.

Although he had every right to be depressed at missing out on his holiday, he seemed to be taking the disappointment stoically. Or perhaps he was simply too poorly to care. One glance as his flushed face and the lacklustre expression in his eyes told us he was far from his normal self, even before he attempted to speak. The result of that was a barely audible croak. With Eve talking to the patient, I bent to pick up the cases Harriet had finished packing. As I did so, I glanced at the poster on Charlie's bedroom wall. I blinked with surprise and straightened up. 'I didn't know you were a fan, Charlie.'

He nodded, which it seemed was easier than talking. Eve looked at the poster. 'That's Trudi Bell, isn't it?'

The young pop star was certainly a very attractive girl, and there was no doubt that Charlie was smitten. 'What a strange coincidence,' Eve told him. 'Adam and I were only talking about her yesterday. Her manager is a friend of ours. Perhaps we might be able to arrange for you to go to one of her concerts.'

Having wished the Rowe clan a safe journey and

promised to take good care of the heir to the baronetcy, we returned to Eden House with our guest. It was indicative of how poorly he was that after ordering him to bed, Eve went up to give him a dose of the medicine prescribed by their doctor, only to find Charlie fast asleep.

'What shall I do?' she asked me.

'Leave him be. Sleep and plenty of fluids will do him as much good as the medicine.'

Charlie's condition had improved only marginally a couple of days later, when we took delivery of a large and extremely heavy parcel. Bored with staring at the wallpaper in the spare bedroom, Charlie spent his waking hours watching cricket on TV in the lounge.

'There seems little to choose between the two,' Eve commented.

'At least the TV picture keeps changing.' Charlie's reply was the first sign that he might be on the mend, even though it came out as somewhere between a growl and a squawk.

As an antidote to boredom, I explained what the parcel contained. 'I think Pattison's sent every file from their office, judging by the size and weight of it.'

'Can I help?' Charlie enquired.

Eve looked as though she was about to veto the idea, but I thought it would do Charlie good; and bravely told her so. 'Why not let him, Evie, there's plenty of work there for three of us.'

As I explained later, 'Charlie has a keen and enquiring mind. Moreover he loves mysteries. I could tell when he was listening to the story of Crowther's disappearance that he was intrigued, and when I mentioned Trudi Bell he could barely contain his excitement. It will take his mind off his illness, and prevent him moping.'

'OK, I take your point, Adam; I just don't want him to make himself worse.'

'I don't see that sitting in the study reading files is that much different from sitting in the lounge staring at the telly. If Boycott's batting it'll certainly be more exciting.'

'I'll take his temperature before I make my mind up. If that hasn't dropped, I'm not allowing it.'

Although Charlie's temperature wasn't back to normal, it had reduced sufficiently to satisfy Eve. 'OK, Charlie, you're in, but the minute you begin to feel tired you stop, got it?'

'Yes, Aunt Evie,' he muttered. He waited until her back was turned and then winked at me, mouthing the word 'fusspot' at the same time.

I turned away so that Eve couldn't see my grin.

Having unpacked the parcel, we surveyed the young mountain of paperwork it had contained. 'Where the heck do we start with this lot?' I wondered.

'I thought we could begin by looking through the ones about the band line-up as it was when Crowther vanished, plus the others who were there that night.' Eve said.

'That sounds logical, but what do you mean by "the others"?'

'The tour manager, the roadies, hangers-on, fans, groupies even, and pressmen.'

'It would help if Pattison had supplied an index. I don't suppose you've come across one, have you?'

I looked up to see Eve brandishing a sheet of paper. 'Oh, good; let's get cracking then.'

We spent the rest of the day going through the files. By the time we gave up, we had barely got halfway through the stack, but by then we all agreed that our brains couldn't absorb any further information.

We resumed the following morning.

'I think we should each take a third of those folders and read the contents. Then if we find anything interesting, we can bring it to the attention of the others.'

The file I found most interesting in the stack I went through was the one referring to a former band member, one of those ousted by Crowther's insistence on a change of style. His name was Wayne Barnett. I read some of the details out before passing the file to Eve.

'It doesn't sound as if Barnett went quietly,' she said.

'What does Mr Pattison say about him?' Charlie asked.

'Apparently Barnett tried to sue the group collectively and the members individually, plus Pattison's management company, claiming breach of contract. The actions failed, but Barnett wasn't prepared to let the matter rest at that. His resentment and bitterness boiled over into violence following a Northern Lights appearance in Stoke-on-Trent in the latter part of 1964. He took a sledgehammer to the group's bus and broke the jaw of one of the roadies who tried to stop him. He then got past the security guards and burst into the dressing room. Before the guards pulled him away he had Crowther pinned up against the wall and was trying to throttle him. Crowther escaped with nothing worse than a black eye and a sore throat.'

Eve paused. 'Now this is interesting. Apparently, Crowther refused to press charges for the assault and paid off the roadie who was injured. He also shelled out for the repairs to the bus. Why do that, I wonder?'

'Probably because he felt guilty that Barnett had lost what he must have seen as a golden opportunity for stardom. Nevertheless, it's intriguing. I bet Barnett didn't appreciate the gesture though.'

'Why do you say that?'

'Human nature, I suppose. If you hurt someone and they forgive you, it can make you hate them even more.'

Eve and Charlie went on to relate what Pattison had written about some of the other group members, both those that had left and those still playing when Crowther disappeared.

'There's not much info about a couple of them,'

Charlie said. 'There's a note saying both these blokes were sacked, as well as someone called Tony Kendall, but there's nothing in the file on him apart from an address in Newcastle and a phone number. There's even less information about Carl Long. All it says is "whereabouts unknown", which isn't much use. All the stuff about Long and Kendall dates back to the sixties. I'm surprised it isn't written in Latin, it's that old.'

'Don't be so cheeky,' Eve told him. 'Adam swears that a lot of people had started using English by then.'

'Oi, you two, show some respect for your elders and betters,' I told them. 'The one Lew seems to know most about is Robbie Roberts. Apparently he's become very rich and successful. He started a magazine, then went into property. His portfolio is handled by a property management company, because Roberts is no longer a UK resident. Lew says he's a tax exile.'

Charlie looked up. 'What's one of those?'

'I'm not sure of the precise details,' Eve told him, 'but I think anyone who isn't resident in this country for more than ninety days a year doesn't have to pay tax here. Those who want to keep hold of their ill-gotten gains move to tax havens, which means they only pay a very low rate of tax there.'

'It all sounds very dodgy,' Charlie commented, with the blunt innocence of youth.

'Extremely dodgy,' I agreed, 'but it's not something that's ever worried me. Not on the sort of money I was paid.'

Eventually, I suggested we call a halt. 'I think we ought to visit the former band members. We've got little or nothing from the files, perhaps talking to the guys who knew Crowther before he vanished will pay dividends.'

'So where do we start? They're not all exactly accessible. One of them lives in Australia. I can't see Lew Pattison funding a trip down under simply to spend ten minutes talking to an ageing rock guitarist.'

'OK, so we stick to the ones within striking distance.'

'And what excuse do we give for talking to them? We can't say we're looking for a man who has been dead for nigh on seventeen years, can we?'

'That's a good point, Evie. We'll have to think about that.'

There was a prolonged silence. This is quite unusual in our house, except perhaps on Armistice Day. Eventually, Eve broke it. 'I've got an idea.'

Charlie and I listened.

'We could tell them you're an author, they can check that out easily enough. That establishes your credentials, especially if we throw in the bit about being a former TV correspondent. We could explain that you've been commissioned to write a series of articles about sixties pop groups, either the ones who didn't make it, or the successful ones that split up. We could tell them it's intended to be a sort of "where are they now".'

'That might work, but the first question they would probably ask is, who commissioned the series?'

'We could say it was Lew Pattison.'

'If we tell them that, the first thing they'd do is check.'

'Then we forewarn him. Simple, really.'

Charlie and I stared at her admiringly.

'That's brilliant, Aunt Evie. You've thought of everything. Once we've done that, what do we do? Two of the people from Northern Lights live in Leeds, and that's where the eyewitness used to live.'

'Who are the musicians who live there?' I asked.

'Pete Firth is one of them, he played guitar. He's stayed in the music business, sort of. He works as a DJ at a disco close to Leeds city centre. The other is Jimmy Mitchell,' Charlie told us after looking through the folders. He read aloud, '"Jimmy Mitchell, the bass guitarist, joined the army but was dishonourably discharged for fighting with another squaddie. He was later convicted of assault following a pub brawl and went to prison. After his release he returned to Leeds. He's currently working as a mechanic in a garage.'"

'Sounds like a nice boy. I'm really looking forward to meeting him,' I said.

Charlie grinned and turned to another file. 'Not only that, but there's a groupie who saw Crowther after the gig. If we can locate her, she has to be worth talking to.' His enthusiasm was growing. 'And if we're going to Leeds,' Charlie concluded, 'what about the guy who used to be their drummer? He's a vet now, based in Harrogate. His name's Neville Wade.'

'We're probably better just turning up on the off-chance,' I suggested. 'A vet will often get called out on emergencies, so making an appointment would be difficult.'

'Hang on, what's all this "we" business?' Eve enquired. 'What makes you think you'll be going with us, Charlie? And who'd speak to us with a teenager in the room?'

'Oh, come off it, Evie. You can't leave Charlie kicking his heels here. He's missing enough fun already. Besides, he might pick up on something we miss.'

'Yeah, Aunt Evie. You could say I'm on a work experience course.'

Eve looked from me to her nephew and back. 'And which of you is going to explain to my sister that we're taking her son into possible danger?'

'Whoa, who said anything about danger? All we're going to be doing is talking to people in the most innocent circumstances. No way is there going to be the slightest bit of risk for any of us.'

One of these days, I'll learn stop making such rash predictions.

'OK, who's going to phone for the appointments?' Eve's question signalled her capitulation. Charlie grinned and gave me a thumbs-up sign, which fortunately his aunt didn't see.

Once we'd set up our cover story with Lew Pattison, the squabble over who should call the musicians was settled by Charlie. Eve had maintained that I should do it, as the author. My idea was that she should pose as my secretary.

'Why not take it in turns?' Charlie asked. He looked through the files again. 'There are plenty to go at. Two of the former members of Northern Lights are in or around Newcastle, as well as the ones in Leeds. Steve Thompson, the other vocalist and saxophone player now works as a bouncer in Newcastle. There's also the other guy, Tony Kendall.'

Eve made the first call, to Pete Firth. As she was talking to him, Charlie remarked, 'It's lucky Mr Pattison has all their details. Why is that? Do you know?'

'I think it's to do with sending them royalty cheques. Every time someone plays one of Northern Lights' records on the radio, the musicians on it will be entitled to a share of the royalties.'

Eve ended her call and reported her success. Just how successful she'd been we were not to discover until we arrived in Leeds.

She handed me the receiver and I tried to contact Jimmy Mitchell. I was nowhere near as lucky. After I put the phone down, Eve asked, 'How did it go?'

'There was no reply. Let's try the Newcastle ones instead. I'll start with the mysterious Tony Kendall.'

Like my previous attempt, my call was a short one, but this time the line had been discontinued. 'It may be disconnected,' I suggested, 'we could go to the address just in case.'

I handed the phone to Eve. 'You try Thompson. You seem to have more luck than me.'

Chapter Three

Charlie appeared next morning sporting a shirt and tie beneath his sweater and clutching a notebook and pen. 'Got to look the part,' he informed us as we climbed into the car. Eve shook her head and sighed.

The journey to Newcastle proved to be a waste of time and fuel, or so I thought at the time. Steve Thompson, the former sax player turned bouncer, provided little fresh insight into Crowther's character, his disappearance, or the reason he committed suicide. I sensed a deeper feeling of anger and resentment in Thompson, directed at Crowther.

The closest I got to a meaningful response was when I asked Thompson, 'Don't you think it curious that Crowther committed suicide when the group such a success?'

Thompson's reply, although not in itself informative, was accompanied by an expression that I couldn't identify. Eventually, I realized it was one of guilt and shame, but for what reason, I had no idea. I decided on an outlandish way to try and find out the underlying emotion.

'If he did commit suicide, that is.'

'You're not suggesting Gerry Crowther was murdered, surely? That's crazy. Why would anyone want to kill him?'

'Crazy, possibly, but why would he want to kill himself? He had everything to live for.'

'That idea's laughable. You should be locked up. Or is this going to be a work of fiction?'

'No, I merely put it forward as a possible alternative.'

'You're mad,' Thompson stammered, his eyes reflecting his anger. 'Of course he bloody topped himself.' I wasn't sure, as he spoke, whether Thompson was trying to convince me or himself. Something in his eyes told me we'd outstayed our welcome. I thanked him and we took our leave.

'What did you make of him?' Eve asked as we drove towards the address Pattison had given us for Tony Kendall, one of the guitarists who had lost his place in the original line-up.

'I wouldn't trust Thompson further than I could throw him. What's more, I'm convinced he's hiding something.'

'He didn't like it when we asked about Crowther. It made him very uncomfortable.'

We reached the address and stared in dismay at a large expanse of overgrown, weed-filled grass. 'What's happened?' Charlie asked.

'At a guess I'd say this is slum clearance. It's a shame there hasn't been any redevelopment. One thing for certain, we're going to have to look elsewhere for Kendall.'

Having failed to gather information in Newcastle, we hoped for better in Leeds. What we got was more than we bargained for. Eve insisted Charlie stayed home. The trip of the previous day had left him tired and she was concerned that he was not as fit as we thought.

The disco where Pete Firth worked was near the city centre. When we arrived he was waiting in the foyer. Firth was thirty-nine years old, but his appearance suggested someone older. The mane of black hair that had been a sixties' trademark, was tied into a ponytail which was liberally streaked with grey. The boyish good looks female fans found dangerously attractive were now etched with lines, suggesting that life had not been easy for the former guitarist. I wondered how much the ageing process had been accelerated by Firth's drug habit.

Pattison's background notes gave an air of authenticity to my cover story. Although knew the answers beforehand, Eve scribbled furiously on her pad. Whether she was transcribing Firth's answers or writing a shopping list it certainly made us look the part.

I asked Firth about Northern Lights, eventually broaching the subject of Gerry Crowther as a preamble to the key questions surrounding his disappearance.

'Crowther should have gone it alone.' Firth's voice was a deep growl. 'He was more suited to a solo act than as part of a group. Don't get me wrong, he was a brilliant musician and songwriter, but he was a complete misfit, an out-and-out loner. The problem was, I don't think he'd the guts to try it as a soloist.'

'You didn't get on well with him?'

'None of us did. Crowther didn't try to make friends. He never hung out with the guys and despite what you saw on stage, he'd no social skills. Onstage Crowther was totally different. Fans thought the sun shone out of his arse. They didn't know that it was all an act. Once the curtain came down he switched the act off. It was almost as if he'd exhausted himself performing and couldn't be bothered any more. He rarely went for a beer with the lads. He'd sit in the coach or limo waiting to go back to the hotel.'

Firth grinned and cast a sly glance at Eve. 'Some nights Crowther would have to wait for a long time, if one of us had found a tasty bit of crumpet to help us relax. That was his fault. I for one had no sympathy.'

'You say he often didn't go back to the dressing room? Was that what happened the night he vanished?'

I saw his expression change as soon as I mentioned Crowther's disappearance. He became guarded, withdrawn almost, and for a long time I thought he wasn't going to answer.

'I suppose so,' he said at last. 'At the time I couldn't fathom out how he managed to get out of that place without anyone seeing him. Mind you, my head wasn't always too clear in those days!'

'Now you've had all this time to think about it, have you any ideas as to how he could have done it?'

Firth's reply was swift, as if he'd been waiting for that particular question, and glib enough for it to have been rehearsed. That could have been for our benefit, or possibly the fact that he'd been asked the same thing many times. 'I'm not sure, maybe he paid one of the security men to look the other way. Who knows, and to be honest, who cares?'

'One thing I'm not clear about. Did you all go straight to the dressing room once the set ended?'

'Yes we did, we were exhausted. Besides which, some of us had made arrangements with fans to meet up at our hotel. I think you can guess why.'

That seemed to be it, but then Firth had second thoughts. 'No, wait, hang on there. Nev didn't go straight to the dressing room. He never did, but it was so much a part of the routine that it slipped my mind.'

'That's Neville Wade, the drummer?'

Firth nodded. 'Nev was paranoid about his drum kit. He wouldn't let anyone else touch it, even the roadies who'd been with us for ages. Nev always insisted on packing it himself before he loaded it on the van. He did it that night and then joined us in the dressing room.'

I moved on, changing the subject before Firth realized the possible importance of his remark. 'Do you think committing suicide was in character? It seemed a bit odd, with the group doing so well, and Crowther being hailed as a genius.'

'I don't know. Crowther wasn't the sort you could get close to. Maybe it got too much for him. The music industry is littered with the corpses of performers who couldn't handle fame and success. All I know is that Crowther had been acting weirdly for some time and that night in Newcastle ended things, not only for him, but for Northern Lights and the rest of us. If you ask me, I'd say that was Crowther being selfish right up to the end, but that's only my opinion.'

'I wanted to talk to the fan who saw Crowther near the Tyne Bridge that night. Julie Solanki, I think her name was. The reports I read mentioned that she came from Leeds, but I checked the phone book and there's no one of that name listed nowadays.'

Firth grinned at me. 'Ah yes, Julie Solanki. You looked under the wrong name, that's why you couldn't find her. You should have looked under the name Julie Firth.'

'You married her?'

''Course I did, I wasn't going to let any other bloke get his mitts on her. I know a good thing when I see it. Besides, I'd got her pregnant and there was the kid to take care of.' He glanced at the clock. 'If you want to talk to Julie, she should be home now. It's only a few miles up the road.'

Having persuaded Firth to ring his wife, we set off to meet her. Half an hour later we were seated in the living room of a small terraced house on the outskirts of Leeds.

Julie Firth had withstood the passage of time better than her husband, I thought. The walls and other surfaces were covered with photos: of Julie, Pete, and their children, and of Northern Lights. Among the photos were publicity shots of the band, both as a whole or individually. One of these caught my eye.

'Who is that?' I asked, pointing to the figure.

'Billy Quinn, the guitarist. Even Pete says Billy was a genius. Mind you, Pete could say that. There was no chance of him being jealous of poor Billy.'

'Why not?'

Julie coughed delicately, before looking at Eve. 'You'd

be safe alone in a bedroom with Billy' – she gestured to me – 'but you certainly wouldn't.'

'You're saying Quinn was a homosexual?'

'And how! Of course it had to be hushed up in those days, until the law changed.'

I looked again at the image. Quinn was seated on a stool, the sort popular with kitchen manufacturers and singers alike. Looking closely, there was a hand resting on Quinn's shoulder. I wondered if the image had been culled from a larger one. Pattison had sent us a lot of material, but some of Julie's collection was new to me.

I gestured to another frame. 'I haven't seen that photo before. Do you mind if I take a look?'

Julie nodded, and she and Eve continued chatting quietly. Although my attention was on the photo, I could hear Eve asking about Julie's family, obviously intending to put her at ease. The image that had attracted my attention was of Gerry Crowther. He was seated at the keyboard, his face half-turned towards the camera. I examined his features closely, noticing something that hadn't been apparent from any of the other images I'd seen of him.

'What a waste,' I said as I replaced the frame. 'His death more or less ended Northern Lights, didn't it?'

'Yes, Northern Lights died the night Gerry Crowther did. Even if they'd tried to continue, there was no chance after what happened to Billy.'

'I've heard he was killed, but nobody seems willing to give me details.'

'That's probably because of the circumstances. Mind you, it's almost all rumour. The story is that Billy went out on a blind date. He was assaulted and stabbed to death.' She stared fixedly at me as she said 'assaulted'.

'You mean he was raped?'

'Yes, but like I said, it was all hushed up. I think Lew Pattison made sure of that.'

I decided to change tack. 'You were close to the group. What did you make of them?'

Julie's answer revealed a total lack of self-consciousness. 'Apart from Pete, you mean? Neville Wade and Gerry Crowther were two of a kind. Neither of them mixed much with the others. Nev was usually too preoccupied with trying to get his leg over. But then I guess you could say that about most of them, with the exception of Crowther and Billy Quinn. I couldn't work Gerry out. He didn't seem interested in girls. Billy wasn't either, of course, but that was for quite different reasons.'

'OK, what about the other group members?'

'I went out with Jimmy Mitchell once, before I realized what a waste of space he was. Not only that, but I think I was too old for him.'

I raised my eyebrows in question and Julie nodded as she continued, 'Added to which, he'd a vicious streak in him. But he did introduce me to Pete and that was that. Pete couldn't keep his hands off me, and I didn't try too hard to stop him. I've no illusions about Pete, but in spite of his failings, and mine, we've been together a long time now.'

'What binds you?' Eve asked. 'Is it true love?'

Julie laughed. 'You could call it that, coupled with the fact that I threatened to cut his cojones off if I ever caught him with another woman.'

'I can see how that would concentrate his mind. Returning to the night of the Newcastle gig, you were the last person to see Crowther alive, weren't you? Did you have any idea of what he was planning to do?'

'Of course not; it didn't cross my mind until it was too late. I'm sure he recognized me, even though he turned and walked away, but that was typical of Gerry. I thought perhaps he was going to meet someone and didn't want me to know who it was.'

'He recognized you? You're sure of that?'

'Absolutely certain.'

I paused and lowered my voice to ask the next question. 'Why did you go down to the river? I'd have thought you'd have headed straight for the hotel if you wanted to see Pete.'

Julie looked uncomfortable, embarrassed even. She didn't reply immediately. 'Ah, well, I don't suppose it matters after all this time. Pete sent me to pick something up for him.'

Knowing Firth's history made it easy for me. 'I get it. You went to meet a dealer for him, is that it?'

'Yes, but you won't put this in your book, will you?'

I soothed her fears. 'I promise you there will be no mention of drugs. Did anyone else know you were going there, and why?'

It was clear that she had never given the matter any thought before now. 'Yes,' she said at last, 'Gerry Crowther knew, because earlier he'd passed Pete a message from the dealer and he was there when Pete asked me to go; saw him give me the money.'

'One final question, what prompted you to go public with your sighting of Gerry?'

'It was one of the guys in the group. We were talking about it in the hotel a couple of days later. At the time, Gerry was just missing. I mentioned seeing him by the river, and they suggested I tell the police.'

'Can you remember who it was? One of the group, you said.'

'I can't be sure. I think it was Neville Wade.'

We thanked Julie and asked if we could contact her if we had any further questions.

As she waited for me to unlock the car door, Eve said, 'That was brilliant. The way you got the information out of Julie, I mean.'

I looked at her suspiciously. Eve wasn't one for throwing compliments around, but this time her praise appeared to be genuine.

'I think we should head for home now,' Eve said. 'We've been far longer than we anticipated and Charlie will be getting bored. We can start again tomorrow.'

I agreed and we'd almost reached the other side of Leeds when Eve asked, 'What did you find so interesting in those photos at Firth's house? I noticed you spent a fair while peering at them whilst I was talking to Julie.'

'It was the one of Crowther that attracted my attention to begin with. I was struck by the pose, which was unusual. All the photos I've seen of him, all the ones Lew sent up had him looking to his right, towards the camera. The only one which shows his left side is the one on Julie's wall.'

'I take it there's some significance in that?'

I explained what I'd seen, and as she pondered it, I continued, 'As I was looking at the photos, I saw one of Billy Quinn. When I examined it closely, I found that one even more intriguing.'

'Why?'

'At first I thought the photo had been cut from a larger one, because there was obviously someone standing alongside Quinn. Billy was seated, but you could clearly see another person's arm and hand. However, when I looked at the edge of the photo, there was that white strip they always leave when they develop film, so obviously this was a single shot.'

'Could you tell who was on the edge of the photo?'

'No, like I said all I could see was the arm and hand. The hand was resting on Billy's shoulder, and Quinn was looking up slightly, as if he was speaking to his companion. The other point that seemed clear was the affection on Billy's face.'

'Are you sure it wasn't one of the other members of the group, or a female fan perhaps.'

'I don't think it was a female at all. The hand looked

too big, too masculine. That led me to speculate about the nature of the relationship.'

'Are you buying into Julie's theory that Quinn was a homosexual?'

'It's possible, but it would have been a closely guarded secret. Back then, homosexuality was a criminal offence and lots of prosecutions were brought against anyone caught in the act.'

'When did the law change, do you know?'

'I'm not certain, I think it was around '67 or '68, but I'd have to look it up. One thing's for sure: if people close to him knew Quinn was gay, they'd have gone to extreme lengths to keep it quiet.'

'It's a shame we can't find out who the man in the photo was. If we knew, we could ask him.'

'I would know him if he still wears the same ring on his left hand.'

'Was it very distinctive?'

'Unusual, to say the least. It was some sort of semi-precious stones, aquamarines or something similar, arranged in a large star shape inside a heavy gold claw setting.'

'Blimey! That would be striking even on a woman's finger. On a man, I'd say it would be unique.'

On the way home, Eve asked, 'Do you think it's wise for Charlie to know what these people are saying about Billy Quinn?'

Whilst I respected Eve's wish to protect her nephew's innocence, I doubted whether, after several years at boarding school, Charlie was as naïve as she believed.

We spent the evening telling him of our day's findings, omitting some of the juicier statements we'd heard. Eve was trying to be tactful regarding Billy Quinn's sexuality, but failed miserably.

'You telling me he was a queer?'

'Charlie!'

'Oh, come off it, Aunt Evie, I'm almost sixteen. I even know the facts of life!' I saw Charlie grin at me and wink. 'Especially as my bedroom is just across the corridor from yours and Adam's.'

Eve went scarlet with embarrassment. I don't think my loud outburst of laughter helped.

Chapter Four

Next morning we set out again, taking Charlie with us. Eve had added conditions. If he began to feel unwell he should say. 'Perhaps you ought to stay in the car when we talk to the men,' she suggested.

'Oh, Aunt Evie,' he protested, 'that won't give me much work experience.'

'If you want to come, get in the car!'

I'd tried to contact Jimmy Mitchell again the previous evening. At least someone picked the phone up this time, but after I introduced myself, they put it down again without speaking. From then on it was a continuous engaged tone. I gave up in despair. It was just after lunch when we reached the address. We hoped we would be able to fit in our planned visit to Neville Wade in Harrogate later that day.

The property was a brick-built semi, dating I guessed from around fifty years earlier. The front gate was open, which looked to be a permanent arrangement as it hung drunkenly from rusted hinges. The front garden showed a similar lack of care, and the building looked in need of urgent maintenance work. As we walked up the crumbling concrete path, I noticed that although it was a bright, sunny summer's day, all the curtains were closed, and no light showed through from behind them.

I rang the doorbell, but got no response. 'Perhaps he's at work,' Charlie suggested from the open car window.

After I failed to get any reaction to a second ring, Eve said, 'Let's try round the back. At least we can see if his car's there.'

We walked down the path alongside the building, which was in no better condition than the one at the front. A lane acted as a service road to all the properties, and beyond it was a row of detached asbestos-clad garages. Eve pointed to the small window in the door of the one directly behind Mitchell's house. 'There's a light on in there.'

The double doors to the garage were secured with a large padlock, which I found odd. Perhaps Mitchell had forgotten to switch the light off. Alternatively, there could be another entrance. I banged on the doors, but with no more success than with the front doorbell.

'Wait there, I'll have a look through the side window.'

The space alongside the garage was a tangled mass of knee-high weeds. Despite the gloom, I could tell that these were mostly thistles and nettles. I reached the side window, which was festooned with cobwebs. I cleared those that were on the outside and peered in. There was a Ford Cortina in the garage. The wheels had been removed and were stacked in the corner, leaving the car resting on its axles. I guessed that Mitchell was in the process of repairing the vehicle. However, the position of the car was unusual. Perhaps Mitchell had lowered the hydraulic jack for some reason, but I couldn't think what that might be.

It was only then that I noticed something protruding from underneath the front of the car. I recoiled, the shock of what I'd seen almost causing me to stumble and fall into the weeds.

I went back to where Eve was waiting to find Charlie standing alongside her, arguing. 'I was bored,' he grumbled.

Eve turned to me for assistance but I think she guessed from my face that I'd seen something amiss.

'Did either of you see a phone box as we drove here?' I demanded.

'There's one at the end of the street,' Charlie pointed to where we'd come from.

'Why, what's wrong, Adam?' The concern showed on her face.

'There's a car inside the garage, but that's not all.' I took a deep breath. 'There's someone trapped underneath it.'

'Dead?'

'I think they must be. I can't see how anyone could survive being crushed by that weight. We need to call the police.'

When we were sitting in the car, awaiting their arrival, Charlie began speculating about the accident, but Eve and I remained silent. It was only when he asked my opinion that I explained. 'It wasn't an accident, Charlie.'

'Why do you think that? You can't be sure?'

'Adam's right,' Eve told her nephew. 'Whoever is in that garage was murdered. The front doors are padlocked from the outside.'

'And there's no other way into the building,' I added.

'Good heavens, I didn't think of that.' Charlie sounded more excited than upset.

I still didn't respond, and Eve guessed I was holding something else back. 'Tell us everything, Adam.'

'I was thinking about my phone call to Mitchell, when whoever answered it left it off the hook. That person might well have been the killer.'

The cover story we'd agreed with Pattison about my researching a book came in very useful when the police asked why we'd visited Mitchell's house. It was getting late before the officer in charge yielded to Eve's pleas about her nephew's health and allowed us to set off back to Laithbrigg. Had he not recognized me, we might have been kept there even longer.

Having received confirmation that the victim was Mitchell, courtesy of a horrified neighbour, the officer,

Detective Sergeant Middleton, surprised me by asking me if I realized the implications in what we'd found. 'From what I've read about you two, I understand you're becoming experts,' he said, a trifle sarcastically.

I rose to the bait. 'You mean the fact that Mitchell was murdered?'

'What leads you to think that?'

'Oh, come off it, Sergeant; don't play the innocent with me. There can be no other explanation, unless you can demonstrate how the dead man padlocked the door from inside the garage.'

'Yes, I didn't think you'd miss that. What you may not be aware of is that his house was ransacked too.'

'Now that is interesting. Tell me, Sergeant; was the phone off the hook when you went inside?'

Middleton stared at me in astonishment, tinged with a little suspicion. 'How on earth did you know that?' he demanded.

I explained about my abortive phone call. Middleton seemed to agree with my theory, but added, 'We'll have to wait for the pathologist to determine the time of death, but you could well be right. I'll be in touch to arrange a formal statement.'

'You could save everyone time and expense by getting our local man to take it,' I suggested. 'His name's Pickersgill, John Pickersgill.'

As we drove back to Laithbrigg, two thoughts disturbed me. Had Mitchell already been murdered when I made the phone call, or had mentioning my name precipitated the attack? Was his death concerned with our enquiries? If Crowther was still alive, this disturbing development caused me to fear for his safety.

Along with that line of thought was another, equally troubling one. If the murder was an attempt to frustrate our investigation into Crowther's disappearance, might the killer not be tempted to more direct methods? I was concerned on two counts. The first was, how had the killer discovered what we were doing? The second, even more worrying: might their next logical step be to come visiting, to physically deter us from continuing with our enquiries? It did not take me long to decide that I would not share these ideas with either Eve or Charlie.

The discovery of Mitchell's body had delayed our visit to Harrogate even further. Next morning, Eve contacted Pattison to inform him of the development. As she was talking, I signalled that I wanted a word with him.

'What can you tell me about Billy Quinn's death?' I asked.

There was a long silence before Pattison replied. 'Billy was murdered in London. He'd been to a nightclub and his body was found in an alleyway nearby. He'd been stabbed several times. Police thought the motive was robbery.'

'I heard different. Someone suggested he'd been sexually assaulted.'

'That rumour was doing the rounds at the time, but I can assure you there's no truth in it. Why do you ask?'

'It seems a curious coincidence that one of the group closest to Crowther was murdered, and then as soon as we start asking questions, another one is killed before we had chance to interview him.'

After I'd rung off, Eve said, 'If Mitchell's death is connected to our search for Crowther, how did the killer know what we were up to?'

'There can only be two ways. Either there's a leak in Pattison's organisation, as he suspected originally, or one of the people we'd already spoken to told them. That means Thompson, Firth, or Julie.'

'Unless one of them killed Mitchell,' Eve pointed out.

'True, I hadn't thought of that. I can't see Julie as the type, nor does Firth really fit the bill. On the other hand, I could believe it of Thompson.'

We'd barely finished breakfast next day when the doorbell rang. I'd an idea of who our visitor might be even before I opened the door.

'Now then, Adam, what have you two got mixed up in this time?'

I stood to one side to allow him to enter. 'Good morning, Johnny.' I raised my voice. 'Eve, put the kettle on. The law's here.'

Eve appeared in the lounge doorway and greeted Johnny Pickersgill, our village bobby, who was also a good friend. She went into the kitchen, and after I introduced Charlie, I explained what had happened in Leeds. Midway through the tale, Eve reappeared with a mug the size of a small swimming pool, which she handed to Pickersgill. He eyed it approvingly, and listened to the rest of my tale in silence. It was one thing telling a stranger like DS Middleton our cover story, but Pickersgill knew us too well to be fooled.

'Somehow I can't imagine you writing a biography of sixties pop groups, Adam, so why not tell me your real reason for going to see this man Mitchell? What's really going on?'

I looked at Eve, who nodded, before explaining what Pattison had asked us to do. When I'd finished, Johnny scratched his chin reflectively.

'It sounds as if someone isn't too happy at the idea of this Crowther chap coming back to life. Let me know if there's any way I can help. I shall have to tell Middleton that you're looking into Crowther's death, of course.' Johnny smiled slightly and I knew full well that he wouldn't lie intentionally, just skirt the facts. 'For the meantime, I need your official statements.'

We travelled to Harrogate next morning. Two days had passed since we found Mitchell's body, but I noticed from the morning paper that the victim had still not been named.

As we pulled into the small parking area alongside the veterinary surgery, Eve pointed to the only other vehicle there, a tangible sign of Neville Wade's success. I looked at the car as we walked over to the surgery entrance. It was a newish-looking Triumph Dolomite Sprint, with Wade's initials incorporated into the registration number. I had to admit that the vehicle did look a little flash for a vet. 'Perhaps he's harking back to his rock 'n' roll days. Wade has obviously done better for himself than the other members of the group.'

Wade was of no more than medium height, with a cheerful, good-humoured expression that I guessed was as much professional as natural. The shock of blond hair that had been almost a trademark when he'd sat behind his drum kit was all but gone, save for a small fringe above his ears. It looked as if some demented barber had been overzealous when asked to provide a tonsure. I explained the reason for descending on him unannounced. He looked wary, but asked, 'What do you want to know about Northern Lights?'

As I took Wade through the band's history, it soon became clear that he had little regard for most of them. When I mentioned Gerry Crowther, however, Wade's attitude changed markedly.

'Gerry was the best thing to happen to Northern Lights, but I guess you've already worked that out. Despite that he was fairly bloody unappreciated by the others. They knew that he almost single-handedly took the group from an obscure outfit that I heard was on the verge of splitting-up, to chart-topping success around the world, but small thanks he got for it.'

Wade paused and looked from me to Eve and Charlie and back again. 'The rest of them were too busy feeding their own egos and imagining they had far more talent than they actually possessed, and being bitter and resentful about Crowther at the same time.' He took a deep breath that turned into a sigh of genuine sadness. 'Apart from Billy Quinn, that is. Billy was too gentle, too nice a person, and far too timid for all the backbiting that went on.'

'Were you surprised when Crowther disappeared, and when you learned that he'd committed suicide?'

'I wasn't at all surprised that Gerry wanted out, although the way he went about it was unusual, to say the least. As for the rest, I still don't … can't believe he committed suicide.'

'Why do you think he did it? Surely not simply because of discord within the band? There has to have been a deeper cause than that.'

Wade's expression changed; I could see the suspicion return. When he replied, his tone was hostile. 'Is that the real reason for this little chat about old times? Hoping to unearth a juicy scandal to sell your book? An exposé about sex, drugs, and rock 'n' roll would have far more potential than a history of 1960s bands. No matter that in the process you sully the reputation of someone who isn't able to defend himself.'

'That's not the case at all,' I protested. 'I merely wanted to get a rounded picture. There are lots of questions I'd like to ask. I resisted the temptation to ask the others them too.'

'What sort of questions?'

'Questions such as, did you help Gerry get out of the gig venue that night? There seems to be a bit of a mystery surrounding how he managed to get out of the town hall without anyone seeing him – or admitting they saw him. Might he perhaps have been hidden by someone? In the van that carried the instruments and stage equipment, for example?'

'How would I know? You'd have to ask the roadies that. They had control of the van.'

I'd been saving my bombshell until last. As I stood up

to go, I remarked casually, 'At least you're alive to answer my questions. It would have been terrible if I'd discovered your body as I did Jimmy Mitchell's a couple of days back.'

Wade stared at me, shock draining the colour from his face. 'Mitchell's dead?' His tone was incredulous.

'Yes, he was crushed to death by the car he was working on.'

'What a terrible accident.'

'It wasn't an accident. Someone let the hydraulic jack down and then left, locking the door behind them.'

I could tell Wade was still struggling to believe my story. We left at that point, but as we crossed the car park, I glanced back. Wade was watching us go, a world of trouble in his expression. *You, my friend*, I thought, *know far more than you're prepared to say.*

'Wade knows a lot more than he's prepared to let on,' Eve echoed my thoughts almost word for word.

'I got that impression too. Was there something specific that you picked up on?'

'For one thing, I'm sure he knows that Crowther isn't dead, or at the very least, suspects as much.'

'Why do you think that?'

'When you asked him about Crowther's suicide, he stumbled over his reply. His actual words were "can't believe he committed suicide", but I think he just stopped himself from saying, "don't believe he committed suicide", and there's a world of difference in the meaning, even if he only substituted one word. I believe Wade helped Crowther disappear. I also think he knows the reason for the vanishing act. Did you notice how hostile he became when you asked that question? Above all, I wouldn't be the slightest bit surprised if Wade knows where Crowther went after he vanished – and I don't think it was into the River Tyne, or anywhere near it.'

'He lied, too,' Charlie added.

'He did?'

'Either he lied or Firth did. You told me Firth said that Wade always loaded his drum kit – wouldn't let anyone touch it, but Wade maintained the roadies had done it.'

'Good point, Charlie, well spotted.'

We had decided to make a day of it, and visited the famous gardens at Harlow Carr, before adjourning to the equally well-known Betty's Cafe for afternoon tea, where Charlie gorged himself on their delicious choux buns, known to the locals as 'elephant's feet'.

Later, as we headed back to Laithbrigg, I suggested that we dine out rather than cooking at home. 'That's if you're up to it, Charlie,' I added.

'I'm feeling much better,' Charlie assured us. 'I think it's a great idea.'

'Where do you suggest, the Admiral Nelson?' Eve asked.

'We could, I suppose, but as we're passing the door, we could try and get a table at the Fox and Grapes near Allerscar. It's usually booked up well in advance but we might be lucky with it being midweek.'

It was early evening when we arrived at the steakhouse, but despite that the car park was already almost full. 'Gosh, what a lovely looking building.' Eve exclaimed.

I glanced sideways at the long, low frontage of the country pub, whose limestone walls were clad with ivy. 'Yes, and I'm told the food is equally good.'

As we walked across the car park our attention was drawn to the sound of a car engine. It sounded as if the driver of the vehicle was in a hurry. Driving at such speeds is unusual and fairly dangerous on the narrow, winding lanes of the dale.

We all turned in time to see the approaching car.

The vehicle was already almost level with the pub. The engine sound was distinctive; the livery even more so. The bodywork was bright yellow, the roof black. The combination had led a motoring journalist to describe the Triumph Dolomite Sprint as looking and sounding like a gigantic angry wasp.

Even at the speed the car was doing the numberplate was easy to read.

'That's Neville Wade's car,' Charlie exclaimed.

'It most certainly is. Where do you think he might be going, and in such a tearing hurry?'

'I can only think of one possible explanation,' Eve said. 'He's going to visit Gerry Crowther. But why drive here?'

'Perhaps Crowther doesn't own a telephone. If you intend to disappear completely, what use would you have for a telephone?'

'Which implies that Wade knew all along that Crowther is alive, and where he's living. Wade didn't actually deny knowing why he vanished. He dodged the question very neatly, by turning the tables and accusing you of muck-raking.'

'At least we know there's a chance that Crowther does live in the area, and didn't travel here specifically to post that music to Trudi Bell.'

On Thursday, we made the trip to the West Riding for our visit to Mytholmroyd. As we waited for Charlie to have a shower, Eve asked, 'How do you plan to locate anyone who might know Crowther's background?'

'If we go to the Register Office and get a copy of his birth certificate we'll know where his parents lived when he was a baby, and we might be lucky enough to talk to someone who knew him when he was growing up.'

'You're assuming that his parents stayed at the address on the certificate. It would be just our luck for them to have moved when he was three months old.'

'I love your unflagging optimism. I still think it worth a shot, unless you'd rather spend all day in bed making passionate love to me?'

'Mytholmroyd it is, then. I'll be very interested to see the place, if only to discover how to spell it.'

Chapter Five

We reached our destination by mid-morning. Mytholmroyd did not have its own Register Office so we'd had to visit Hebden Bridge to seek information.

I adopted the persona of an Australian seeking long-lost relatives, which convinced the registrar to divulge the information we sought. Eve, however, was less impressed. When we emerged from the office, she leaned against the wing of the car, helpless with laughter.

'What happened?' Charlie asked. 'What's so funny?'

When she recovered, Eve explained, before adding, 'That was without doubt the worst attempt at an Australian accent I've ever heard! You could have warned me. At one point I almost wet myself. And that poor receptionist, I'm not sure whether she thought she was dealing with someone with a speech impediment or an escapee from the nearest asylum.'

'It got us the birth certificate, didn't it?'

'Yes, but why did you have to go through that complicated rigmarole?'

'I wasn't sure if there were rules and regulations about giving out birth certificates, but I thought if I made it sound as if we'd come thousands of miles to look up a family member, we might get a more sympathetic reception. In the end, that lady couldn't have been more helpful.'

'That was probably because she wanted to get you out of there as fast as possible.'

'I wish I'd seen that,' Charlie said wistfully.

Courtesy of the certificate, we now had the address of Crowther's parents in 1942. Eve read this out as I started the car. 'It shouldn't take much finding in such a small town.'

Our luck was in when we pulled up outside the house. A young woman was pushing a pram down the short drive. Eve jumped out of the car and went to speak to her. 'That lady's only lived here a couple of years,' she reported back, 'but she says we should ask the man in the house directly opposite. He's lived here for over forty years.'

The elderly gentleman who answered the door was thin, tall, and smartly dressed. His snowy white hair was neatly brushed, and his eyes looked keen and alert. I launched into my cover story and asked him if he'd known Gerry Crowther.

He smiled wryly. 'I should do.' His tone was dry, the humour reflected in his eyes. 'Not only did he live opposite, but I taught him for four years.'

'Oh, I didn't realize you were a teacher! Would you care to tell us about him? This is Eve, my secretary, by the way.'

The old man bowed slightly towards Eve, a gesture of courtesy from a bygone age. 'What you actually mean is, can I tell you something about Gerald that you and the rest of the world don't know.'

I nodded. 'Something like that.'

'Gerald was a good pupil, easy to teach. He wasn't outstanding, except at music of course.' The smile flashed again. 'But you already knew that. He was polite and for the most part well-behaved. When I say for the most part, all boys get into some sort of mischief, but with Gerald it was nothing serious. He was a self-contained boy, who grew into a fairly introverted young man. I'm not suggesting he didn't mix with other pupils but he was at his happiest when he was alone with his music. He was quite a favourite with the girls, because of his musical talent, but he only had eyes for one. It was a typical childhood sweetheart thing, but whether it developed any further than holding hands or a kiss and cuddle, I couldn't say.'

'What about his parents?'

'Gerald's father died when the boy was only five. Cancer, as I recall. His mother had to struggle to make ends meet, but she did a very good job of raising the boy on her own, and Gerald was absolutely devoted to her. Gertrude died when he was eighteen, and he put the house on the market immediately after her death and moved away after the sale went through. Although he wasn't one to show his feelings, Gerald was prey to very strong emotions. I never saw him lose his temper, even when he was provoked, but he would go away and nurse the hurt. Although he may have appeared as cool and aloof to others, I think Gerald was deeply insecure.' The ex-teacher smiled sadly before adding, 'And I suppose his actions rather proved that, didn't they?'

'Were you surprised that he committed suicide?'

'Surprised and saddened, yes, but shocked, no. If something really traumatic had happened in his life, Gerald would only have two ways of dealing with it. One way was to lose himself in his music and let his emotions flow through that. There's one track on a Northern Lights LP that I feel sure is a dedication to his mother.'

The former teacher saw my look of surprise. He smiled, a trifle sadly. 'Simply because I'm over seventy years old doesn't mean I don't like pop music, and in Gerald's case I had a vested interest in it.'

'You said he had two ways of dealing with trouble. Music was one, what was the other?'

'By running away from it, but if the trauma was too great, by doing what he did.'

'You've been extremely helpful. One final question and then we'll leave you in peace. Can you remember the name of the girl that Crowther had a crush on?'

'I've been racking my brains as we were talking, but I simply can't bring it to mind. One of the penalties of age, I'm afraid.' He shook his head in self-mocking sorrow at his declining faculties.

'I guess it must be difficult to recall one amongst the many you taught over the years. Perhaps I could leave you my phone number and if you do remember, or if you can think of anything else that might help, you could let me know?'

He nodded his agreement, and as Eve was writing down the number he asked me, 'Whatever you do, please don't depict Gerald as weak, or belittle his character. I can only guess at the pressures the music industry puts on young people who are ill-prepared for the attention. It's hardly surprising that some of them cave in under such stress. Even without the emotional demands, there's the travelling and all the risk that entails. Take Gerald's hero, for example. Buddy Holly would have probably been alive to this day had it not for that ill-fated winter tour. I remember Gerald's distress on hearing the news. It was almost as if he'd lost a close personal friend or relative.'

'A lot of us felt that way about Buddy Holly,' I remarked. 'I was a great fan, no more than that, but I felt hurt by it.'

As we returned home, Eve said, 'There's your answer. Gerry Crowther was on the receiving end of some traumatic news, something too big for him to face, and so he cut and run. We're still no nearer to working out why he's chosen to emerge from the shadows after all these years.'

'Aren't we? I could be totally off target, but something the teacher said gave me a possible clue. What you have to do is link two facts together.'

I explained, and Eve and Charlie pondered the idea. 'You could be right, but how do we find out one way or the other?' Eve asked.

'There is only one way, and that's to ask the person concerned. However, we need to know all about them, and the only person who can tell us that is Lew Pattison.'

'I could phone Alice if you want? She could get the details from Lew. He's sure to have them to hand.'

'No, we'd need Lew to vouch for us before we ask the sort of questions we'd need to put. This isn't a matter of the group's history; it's something far more personal.'

Charlie remained quiet and after a while his aunt asked if he was feeling poorly again. 'No, nothing like that, Aunt Evie. I'm trying to remember something.'

When we reached home he vanished into the study, emerging several minutes later holding a press cutting. 'I don't know if this means anything,' he told us. 'But something came to me when you were talking to that teacher.' He held up the paper. 'This is the Gerry Crowther inquest report. The coroner recorded an open verdict. Is that something to do with suicide?'

'An open verdict simply means that they can't be sure what the cause of death actually was. In this case it could be any one of three things: accident, suicide, or murder. As to whether it's important, I guess that depends on which of the three it was.'

The following night, we all settled down to watch television. The theme from *M*A*S*H* signalled the beginning of *Top of the Pops*. The choral version of the theme music had been one of the surprise hits of 1980.

Eve sat alongside me on the sofa as we watched the opening of the show. My attention was slightly distracted by the gyrations of the female members of the resident dance troupe, Legs & Co.

'This song's quite apt, in an ironic sort of way,' Eve remarked.

The title, 'Suicide Is Painless', did indeed seem

appropriate to our investigation. It was a little over halfway through the show when the presenter told the studio audience and viewers, 'And now, here's a young lady we're going to hear a lot more of, a bright young talent who has already won acclaim from fans and music critics alike. Here she is, singing her latest hit ... let's hear it for Trudi Bell!'

Charlie, who had paid little attention to the preceding acts, sat bolt upright as the young girl's face came into close-up. Midway through her performance of the song, as the producer ordered a switch from one camera to another, I got a brief glimpse of the singer's left profile. I sat up abruptly, provoking a protest from my companion on the sofa.

'Did you see that?' I demanded, ignoring Eve's complaint.

'See what? I was watching Trudi.'

'Yes, but when they showed her left side, I noticed something strange. Watch closely, with luck they'll switch to that camera again.'

However, Trudi reached the end of her song, the music faded and as the presenter tried to make himself heard over the rapturous applause, it seemed that we were out of luck. 'Go on then, tell me, what was it you saw, or thought you saw?'

I explained, and although Charlie could see what I was getting at, Eve seemed unconvinced. However, she did agree that it was worth checking. 'Because if I am right,' I told her, 'I think it more or less proves my theory.'

'It isn't a theory; it's a wild idea based on what could be nothing more than coincidence.'

We didn't have to wait long for further evidence to back up what Eve had referred to as 'my wild idea'. Next morning, we were in the middle of breakfast when the phone rang. I went into the hallway to answer it, leaving Eve and Charlie to demolish the rest of the toast.

'Who was it?' Eve asked as I returned to the kitchen.

'The schoolmaster we met yesterday. He's remembered the name of the girl Crowther had a crush on.'

'Go on then, tell me.'

'The girl's name was Sheila Bell. Add the fact that Gerry Crowther's mother was called Gertrude, and I think it's safe to assume that Trudi Bell is Crowther's daughter, don't you?'

Eve looked at me sternly. 'You've got a very smug expression on your face. You're gloating because your theory's been proved right, aren't you?'

'A little bit, I suppose. The old man told me about Sheila Bell. Like Crowther, she lost her father when she was young, but in her case it wasn't that he'd died, he simply walked out on her mother. As the teacher put it, "That didn't mean Sheila was short of adult male relatives. If rumours are to be believed, she had plenty of uncles visiting the house".' I saw Charlie grin, an expression he changed quickly when his aunt glanced in his direction.

'He also said that Sheila was a very bright student, one of the best he'd taught. They wanted her to go on to university, but for some reason she dropped out of school. Her mother moved away, and he lost track of the girl.'

'That still gets us no nearer to finding Crowther. How do you suggest we go about trying to locate him?'

I blinked in surprise. 'That's strange; I was just pondering the same question.'

'What about asking at Allerscar post office? I don't suppose they get too many people sending registered mail from there, surely.'

'You don't know the sub-postmaster there like I do. He's a miserable, tight-fisted old so-and-so, who wouldn't give you the time of day unless you paid for it. I reckon you'd stand a much better chance of getting information out of the KGB.'

'OK, so if the post office is out, have you any other

ideas?'

'No, at the moment I'm right out of them.'

We were still no nearer a plan for locating Crowther when we retired for the night. However, next morning, Charlie had a stroke of genius. It came shortly after breakfast, when Eve had gone for a shower.

'Adam, the tape that was sent to Trudi Bell. That was how Mr Pattison recognized Crowther's keyboard style, correct?'

I nodded, puzzled as to what Charlie was driving at.

'If he's right and it was definitely Crowther on the tape, how did he do it?'

'Sorry, Charlie, I must be a bit thick this morning. How did who do what?'

'How did Crowther record the music? When he disappeared he had only the clothing he stood up in. He certainly didn't take his keyboard with him.'

'Yes, I accept that.' I was beginning to see where he was headed.

'Crowther would have needed access not only to a keyboard but also some recording equipment. At the very least he would have required a tape recorder.'

'I get you. He would have had to buy new equipment.'

'Either that or have access to a recording studio.'

'I don't think that's likely round here, Charlie. We might be able to track down where he lives from the place he bought the equipment. One of the music shops round here would be my bet. Let's see what your aunt thinks to your theory.'

I let Charlie pitch his idea to Eve. Her reaction was one of cautious approval. 'I think it's worth following up, Charlie, and as we seem to be stuck for any other options, I vote we give it a shot. There can't be that many music shops round here. What do you say, Adam?'

'What are we waiting for?' I went to my study and when I returned I plonked the Yellow Pages in front of

Charlie. He looked puzzled. 'There you go. As you suggested it, I think you should have the pleasure of finding some addresses for us.'

As Eve had suggested, there weren't too many shops in the area that stocked tape recorders, let alone keyboards. However, we'd drawn a blank with the closest ones, so we had to cast our net wider and wider. What had seemed simple when we started soon presented unforeseen snags. For one thing our vague description of the customer was almost twenty years out of date. Also, we might be visiting the shop on the one day in the week when the assistant who had served Crowther was on their day off. Nor did we have a clue as to what name he might have given. I felt sure he wouldn't have used his real name when buying a keyboard. That would have been too risky, especially when talking to someone in the trade.

'This is the next-to-last shop on the list,' I said, as we stood outside, 'and if we strike out here, I reckon we'll have to rethink Charlie's theory, because I've no confidence that Crowther would have used the other shops.'

The proprietor of the establishment, who I guessed to be in his late fifties, was certainly more helpful than some of his younger counterparts, although he was far more talkative, which made getting him to stay focused on our request difficult.

'We don't get many people enquiring about keyboards, let alone going ahead and buying them. The cost puts a lot off, and those that persist usually want them on the never-never. To get a cash purchaser is a rare event. Have you any idea what make of keyboard the person bought?'

'All we know is that the man lives locally, and that he's somewhere in his late thirties. At a guess, I'd say he knew exactly what he wanted.'

The shop owner thought for a moment or two. 'There

was one bloke, a year or so ago, who bought a Yamaha. I think he also bought a quality cassette recorder at the same time, as I remember. He was a cash buyer. He tried out the keyboard and he was a real maestro. In fact I wondered if he was a professional musician, he was that good.'

'Can you remember anything more about him? His name, for example?'

'Now there, you've got me. I have to admit I'm very bad with names. I seem to recall that he asked for the stuff to be delivered, but don't ask me where to, because I can't remember that either.'

'Is there no way you could find out; a receipt, for instance? I take it you do issue receipts?' Eve asked; her tone and expression pleading. It was a look I couldn't have resisted, and it seemed that the music shop proprietor was made of no sterner stuff.

'We do, but all that would tell me is that it was a cash sale.'

'Would you have ordered replacement stock?' I asked.

'Well, yes, I would. Why?'

'Don't suppose you have a purchase ledger, do you?'

'Of course I do, but what's that going to tell us? Oh, I see. If I check when I ordered one, then the sale would have been a little earlier than that.'

He thought for a little longer, then exclaimed, 'Deliveries! That would tell us.'

Eve, who seemed to have got his measure, leaned across the counter and placed her hand on his. 'Would you do that, for me?' she pleaded. 'Adam, you and Charlie go and pick out those LPs you wanted while this gentleman has a look.'

Eve's beguiling charm was too much for the shopkeeper. As Charlie and I wandered along the stacked shelves I could hear the conversation as Eve watched her new friend going through his books. I'd chosen one LP, and Charlie had picked four.

The owner paused and stared at an entry in his ledger for several seconds. 'I reckon this might be the man you're after.'

'What are the details?' Eve asked him.

'I'm not sure I should give you them, really.'

'Oh, I nearly forgot.' She directed her attention to me. 'Adam, didn't we want to look at a Teasmade for the new extension?'

I caught the look, or maybe it was a glare, she gave me. 'Er, yes, we did,' I replied through gritted teeth.

The owner looked at Eve, then at me. That was a mistake. He saw the pile of LPs we intended to buy and shrugged. 'I suppose it will be OK. 'The man's name is Hardin, and the address is Lovely Cottage, Fatted Calf Lane, Allerscar.'

Eve, who was taking notes, looked up. 'Is that Harding with a G or Hardin without?'

When the shop owner repeated the man's name, I stopped dead in my tracks and listened as he explained. 'Hardin, without a G. Mr Charles Hardin. I remember asking him the same question. He bought a Yamaha, a recorder, and reams of score sheets. I thought he looked vaguely familiar, and that name rang a bell too. Mind you, I was probably confusing him with someone else. If I'd to guess, I'd say this guy was a builder or a farmer, something like that. Certainly someone who works outside a lot.'

'That's definitely the man we're after,' I told them.

We thanked the shopkeeper and after paying for the LPs and the Teasmade, went outside. 'You seemed convinced this is the right man,' Eve looked at me, 'what makes you so certain?'

'The name he used; Charles Hardin. Even the shopkeeper thought it sounded familiar. So it should, especially to someone in the music industry.' I could see Eve and Charlie were still baffled. 'Charles Hardin,' I explained, 'Crowther's idol was Buddy Holly, and Buddy's real name was Charles Hardin Holley. Who else would Crowther use for an alias other than his hero?'

Chapter Six

One question was uppermost in my mind. Now that we had confirmation that Crowther was alive I was concerned as to the identity of the man whose body had been recovered from the River Tyne. There might be an innocent explanation as to why someone was wearing Crowther's jacket when their body was found, but I couldn't think of one. As I was trying to work out the best way to approach Crowther, Eve, and Charlie were looking through the collection of old photos of Northern Lights that Pattison had sent us. Their research threw up a possible candidate for the drowned man.

Before that, though, something quite unexpected happened which gave another interesting slant to the events leading up to Crowther's disappearance. I gave voice to the thought that had occurred to me. 'Do you remember the conversation we had with Pete Firth? Something Firth told us could provide a clue as to what happened in Newcastle. Firth said that Crowther's behaviour changed, which was more or less what Pattison said. I think his words were "Crowther actually became human for a while", or something close to that. Did you pick up on it, Eve?'

She shook her head.

'I think it might be worth having another word with Firth.'

'You'll have to wait until tomorrow.' Eve pointed to the clock. 'He'll be at work now.'

I got hold of the DJ the following morning, after Julie

had dragged him from his bed. Once he'd stopped complaining, I explained the reason for my call. Firth thought about the question for a long time before replying. 'Have you ever seen the film *Frankenstein*?'

'I have, and read the book,' I admitted, 'but that was a long time ago.'

'You could say that Crowther's behaviour was a bit like that. It was almost as if the electric shock brought him to life, and for a while everything was OK, but then the bump on the head changed him and he became a monster.'

'Whoa, hang on, you've lost me. What electric shock and bump on the head?'

'It was a few months before he topped himself. Less than a year, I'd say. We were playing a gig in Sheffield. The place was a bit ramshackle, but the booking had been made when we were struggling, and we didn't want to get a reputation for letting people down. There was something wrong with the electrics. During the rehearsal, when Crowther started to play he damned near fried himself and almost torched the building. I think if Nev Wade hadn't yanked the plug out of the wall Crowther would have died.'

'Nasty!'

'It was. Although Nev had cut the power, the instrument was in flames. One of the roadies rushed onstage with a fire extinguisher he'd grabbed from the wings, but all that was left was a charred and twisted lump of metal and plastic, all fused together.'

'Sounds as if Crowther had a lucky escape.'

'Yes, and it wasn't the first one either. He nearly got felled by a steel girder only a couple of weeks earlier.'

'What happened?'

'It was during a photoshoot for an album. Pattison had fixed a venue in Middlesbrough, on a building site. They were putting up a new industrial estate. As we were being set up by the photographer, a girder that was being swung into place on the roof behind us broke free and crashed to the deck only inches behind Crowther. If Nev hadn't seen it and pushed Crowther out of the way, he'd have been squashed flat, I reckon. The weird bit is, the driver was on his break at the time; they never found out who was operating it.'

'So that wasn't when Crowther got the bump on the head?'

'No, that came much later, in London. I never got the full story, but from what I was told, Gerry was attacked late one night; robbed and left for dead. There was some talk that a policeman disturbed the two attackers before they finished him off, but I couldn't swear to the truth of that.'

'And that was the bump on the head that caused his behaviour to change?'

'Actually, now I come to think about it, that wasn't the cause. It was the other accident that really triggered it off.'

'Another accident? He seems to have had more than his share of them.'

'I didn't think of it that way, but I suppose that's true.'

'What was the other accident?'

'It happened about a month, maybe two months, before he committed suicide. Crowther had started to unwind and enjoy life. He'd even got a girlfriend. I never got to know her name, but she was a smasher. Long black hair, lovely face, and superb figure.' Firth coughed and added quickly, 'Not a patch on my Julie, though. Anyway, Crowther had bought himself a sports car. I think it was an Austin-Healey. Brand new, and a real fanny magnet. One night he and the girl were travelling from Leeds to Harrogate when he went off the road. It was somewhere near that big stately home that belongs to one of the Royal Family.'

'Harewood House?'

'That's it. Anyway, the girl was lucky. She escaped uninjured, but Gerry ended up in Leeds General with severe concussion. We had to cancel a couple of gigs whilst he recovered. When he rejoined us, it was obvious he'd been badly shaken-up, and from there on in, we noticed the change. He was moody, barely spoke to anyone, and if you came up on him unawares he'd jump out of his skin. It was almost as if he was afraid of his own shadow.'

'What happened to the girl he was dating?'

'I've no idea. I never saw her again. I think maybe she'd blown Gerry out, because I caught him once, about a week before he died, staring at a photo of her, and I swear there were tears in his eyes. If she ditched him, I suppose that would explain his behaviour.'

'That's extremely interesting.' I remembered the pretext for my call. 'I think that'll set the scene for a chapter on Crowther and his suicide very well.' I thanked Firth and rang off. I waited for a few minutes, staring at the phone as I considered the implications of what the DJ had told me. Then I went through to the study to tell Eve and Charlie what I'd learned, but it turned out they had news for me. Big news, at that.

'Adam, we've got something to show you. Charlie found it, and we both agreed you might think it important.'

Eve signalled to Charlie, who turned over an early photo of Northern Lights taken when they were onstage.

'That's Carl Long behind the drum kit,' Charlie told me.

I read the names of the line-up under the image. The photo had obviously been taken soon after Crowther joined the group, because both Carl Long and Robbie Roberts were present.

'What strikes you about that photo?' Eve asked.

'Only the time it was taken; before the line-up changed.'

'Nothing else?'

I examined the photo once more, but was unable to see

what Eve was driving at. 'Tell me.'

'Look closely at Carl Long, and then look at Gerry Crowther.'

I peered at the two men. 'They do look a bit alike. Is that what you mean?'

'Alike? They could be taken for brothers. Their hair colour, build, shape of the face and features. Unfortunately, you can't judge their respective heights with Long being seated, but apart from that it would be dead easy to mistake one for the other.'

On close inspection, I had to agree with Eve's assessment. 'What happened to Carl Long?' I asked.

'That's something we haven't been able to find out. There's only background information in Lew's notes. He seems to have disappeared as completely as Crowther.'

I looked from Eve to her nephew. 'Are you thinking what I think you're thinking?'

Charlie grinned. 'I think so.'

'The body recovered from the Tyne might have been that of Carl Long, not Gerry Crowther?'

'That's it,' Eve agreed. 'Which means that Crowther might have killed Carl Long and dressed him in his own jacket so he could disappear. Nobody would bother looking for a dead man. But it still doesn't explain his motive.'

'It might have been fear,' I told them, and went on to relate what Pete Firth had told me.

'This is getting weirder and weirder,' Eve said. 'How do we sort it out?'

'We ought to check with Pattison. He might know something about what happened to Long. The fact that it isn't mentioned in those files doesn't mean he isn't still alive and kicking. You ring him, Eve, but don't mention we've found Crowther's address.'

The call lasted only minutes. Eve skirted the question of Crowther by saying we might be making progress.

When she put the phone down, she told us, 'Lew has no idea what happened to Carl Long. He neither saw nor heard of him after he left Northern Lights. His royalties are still sitting in the bank. So, what do we do next?'

'I think we ought to go see Mr Charles Hardin tomorrow, and find out if he really is Gerry Crowther.'

'Oh, good!' Charlie exclaimed.

'Not you, Charlie,' Eve told him. Her tone was one that brooked no argument. 'We don't know what the state of this man's mind is. He could be dangerous.'

Charlie looked mutinous, but for once I had to agree with Eve's assessment. 'Sorry, Charlie, Aunt Evie's right. We'd never be able to face your mum and dad if you got hurt.'

Charlie begged and pleaded, and eventually won a small concession. We would allow him to tag along, but only if he promised to remain in the car – and this time to actually stay there.

Later, as we were eating dinner, Eve came up with a bright idea. 'Before we go dashing off to Allerscar, wouldn't it be sensible to find out what we can about Hardin?'

'I'm not with you. Find out from whom?'

'If anyone can tell us about him, it'll be Johnny Pickersgill. I think it would at least be worth a phone call.'

Eve was right, of course. Pickersgill liked to know about everyone on his patch. 'Good idea, Evie. I'll phone him after dinner.'

The call was unsuccessful. 'Would you believe it, he's gone to watch a cricket match at Headingley and won't be back until late. His wife promised to get him to phone or call in the morning.'

'You'd better buy extra milk when you go for the paper. Johnny won't pass up the chance to call, and that usually means a gallon of tea.'

Sure enough, we'd not long finished breakfast when

Pickersgill arrived. Eve provided him with a mug of tea and asked, 'How was the cricket?'

Pickersgill frowned. 'A waste of time, the way Yorkshire batted. Anyway, what did you want to ask me? Is it to do with that Leeds case?'

'Sort of,' Eve told him, 'all we wanted was a little information.'

He passed her his empty mug. 'Information comes at a price.'

When she'd replenished his drink, I asked, 'What do you know about a man called Hardin, who lives at Allerscar?'

'Why do you ask?'

I explained our theory about Hardin's true identity.

'Hardin's a strange character. Recluse hardly fits him. More like a hermit, I'd say. He's definitely anti-social. As far as I'm aware he rarely leaves his property, and only then to go shopping. Even that is kept to a minimum. He grows a lot of his own fruit and vegetables, keeps hens and all he buys in the village shop is milk and butter, plus meat and fish; things he can't produce on his land.'

'Do you know anything about him?'

'It seems he wants to leave his past behind. The only two things I know for certain are that Hardin isn't his real name, and that he has no criminal record, or convictions of any kind. More than that, I can't say.'

The conversation with Pickersgill deepened the unease I was already feeling. After he'd left, I expressed my doubts to Eve and Charlie. 'I'm seriously concerned about the wisdom of making this visit. I read the report of the suicide again last night. Although the coroner ruled it as an open verdict, there was a question mark over how the victim came about those head injuries. If Crowther is alive, by visiting him and raking up the past, we could risk antagonizing someone with homicidal tendencies. Perhaps the real reason he's locked himself away all this time is because he can't be trusted near other people.'

'On the other hand,' Charlie pointed out, 'he might be as much a victim as the man who died. I was thinking about all those lucky escapes.'

'I suppose there's only one way to find out,' Eve told us. 'Let's go see what he has to say for himself.'

I parked the car at the end of the short drive leading to Lovely Cottage and looked at the building with a tinge of trepidation. The windows facing the road were all shuttered, which seemed curious, given that the day was sunny and warm. I commented on this.

'Perhaps he's gone away,' Eve responded.

Part of me hoped she was right, and I noticed her voice seemed to echo that feeling. 'There's only one way to find out,' I told my passengers. 'I'm going to take a look around.'

'Shall I come with you?' Eve asked.

'No, both of you stay here.'

I got out of the car and closed the door behind me. The steel five-barred gate was of the type much used by farmers. No fancy wrought ironwork here. The gate closed behind me with a resounding clang that did little to calm my overstretched nerves. I walked slowly along the drive, looking to the left; then to the right, and then straight ahead, conscious all the time that I might be under observation.

I reached the corner of the building and looked back towards the car. Eve and Charlie had got out of the vehicle and were standing by the gate, watching me. Their anxiety was plain.

There was a garage alongside the house, with a narrow concrete path between the buildings. As I walked slowly along it, conscious that I was in an extremely vulnerable position, my attention was distracted by a couple of panels leaning against the garage wall. I recognized the name on them. It was that of a manufacturer of soundproof cladding. Had this been used to construct a recording studio, I wondered?

I emerged at the rear of the building and stood for a second, taking in the magnificent view. Beyond the property the fields stretched into the distance, to where the Pennines provided a suitably dramatic backdrop. Closer, the small area of lawn behind the house gave way to a huge vegetable garden on one side, with an equally large orchard on the other. Beyond these were two greenhouses, of the type more usually associated with a market garden than a private house. Alongside these was another large building, instantly recognizable. It was a windmill, and next to it another structure, that from its dimensions I guessed to be a hen house.

'What are you doing on my property?'

I turned towards the speaker. His question was straightforward enough, and would be easy to answer, given chance. The shotgun pointed at my chest didn't encourage conversation.

Chapter Seven

'I asked what you're doing on my property.'

'I … er … Mr Hardin?'

'Get out!' The expression on the man's face was menacing, but I caught a fleeting impression of something else in his eyes, although at the time I didn't recognize it. I was far more concerned with the twin barrels, which were pointed directly at the bacon and eggs I'd had for breakfast.

'I only want to talk to you,' I said, holding both my hands up.

'I said, get out. You're trespassing.' The gun moved, indicating I should return along the path.

I stood rooted to the spot, uncertain what I should do, when I heard another voice.

'Please don't shoot him. He's my favourite uncle. Besides which, Aunt Evie would be very upset.'

The man turned to look at Charlie, who was standing by the garage, with Eve a couple of paces behind him.

The gunman lowered his weapon and stared at Charlie in surprise – a feeling I shared. The youngster, seemingly unaware that he had said anything out of the ordinary, stayed for a second, motionless, one hand raised, then, as he walked forward, I said, 'My name is Adam Bailey. The lady over there is my fiancée Eve, and that's her nephew Charlie.'

'Bailey? I've heard your name recently.'

'From Neville Wade, perhaps? I'm afraid we weren't exactly truthful with Mr Wade. I'm not writing a book about 1960s pop groups. If you're Charles Hardin, we've been asked to find you by Lew Pattison.' As I spoke, I stepped sideways, intending to shield both Charlie and Eve should the gun come back into line. 'Pattison asked us to locate you because of the song you wrote for Trudi Bell. He needs clearance on the copyright. He recognized your keyboard style, Mr Hardin. Or should I say, Mr Crowther? Mr Gerry Crowther?'

For a second, I thought that Crowther was going to raise the weapon again, but then, as if bowing to the inevitable, he pushed the lever and broke it, removing the cartridges. 'You'd better come in and explain,' he told us grudgingly.

Eve, her face depicting the relief she obviously felt, walked forward and grabbed my arm. I felt her shudder with relief. Charlie followed behind.

Once inside, we passed through the mud room, where Crowther paused to remove his wellingtons, and entered a beautifully fitted kitchen. He placed a kettle on the hob of the Aga cooker. 'I'll make a drink in a few minutes,' he told us, 'and while we're waiting, you can tell me why Pattison is so desperate to contact me. And how you found out where I live.' He was very cautious, looking at us with suspicion.

Eve explained about the music shop. 'The rest was easy. Adam recognized your alias. He's also a Buddy Holly fan.'

'Funny, that. I worried for years that the name I'd chosen might be a giveaway, but as I'd got away with it for so long, I assumed people would have forgotten. What did you mean about Pattison and copyright?'

'He needed to locate the composer of the song before he'll allow Trudi Bell to record it. He's aware that the composer could lodge a claim for royalties unless he has a proper contract. He was a bit shaken up, because he recognized your keyboard style, and along with everyone else he believed you had committed suicide in '65.'

'That was what everyone was intended to believe. It was all planned. The escape from the theatre, having an eyewitness who would conveniently see me walking towards the river, and the anonymous phone call to say someone had jumped off the bridge. But it all went wrong on the night.'

'Why did you choose to disappear?' I asked. 'Was it to do with Carl Long?

'What's he got to do with this?' I could see Crowther was becoming suspicious and knew I'd have to tread carefully.

'We believe that the body pulled from the Tyne was Carl Long. Very convenient for you,' I added.

'I didn't know he was dead until long afterwards. His death was simply ... unfortunate.'

I tried again. 'I think you're going to have to provide more than that by way of an explanation.'

'I appreciate that, but it isn't easy, even after all this time. I had nothing to do with Carl's death. It was only much later that I realized what must have happened to him.'

'Which was?'

'That he'd either fallen or jumped to his death. The state poor Carl was in, either of those was more than a distinct possibility.'

'I don't understand,' Eve said, 'How come Carl Long was wearing your jacket? The Buddy Holly one.'

There was a long pause as Crowther pondered Eve's question. Eventually, he began to tell us what he knew about events on that cold winter's night so long ago.

'I had it all planned. I wanted to do this one final gig in Newcastle, then walk off the stage at the end of the set and vanish into the night. People would put two and two together, and with the arrangements I'd made, they would assume I'd taken my own life by jumping from the Tyne

Bridge. That was the scheme. It had to be concocted in secret. The only other person who knew, the only person I could trust with something so extreme, was Neville Wade. He knew the reason I had to do what I did, and he helped me prepare and carry out my plan.'

Crowther paused for a second, before describing what had actually gone on. 'I wanted to make my final performance something really special. Call it vanity if you like, but I wanted to leave a legacy for all the people who liked my music. If I was going to bow out, it had to be with a memorable exit, one they would talk about long after they thought I was dead. With that in mind I went to the theatre at lunchtime, long before the other members of the group got there. My idea was to get in an extra rehearsal whilst I could do it in peace and quiet.'

He stopped speaking again, so I prompted him. 'Did something happen at the rehearsal?'

'Actually, the rehearsal didn't take place. When I arrived at the theatre, Carl Long turned up out of the blue. He was waiting outside the stage door. Carl left the group after I joined them. It wasn't an easy decision. I quite liked Carl, but his style of playing simply didn't fit with the sound I had in mind for the band. I hadn't seen him for over two years, and I barely recognized him. He was in a mess, to put it mildly. How much of a mess I didn't appreciate until he told me what he'd been through. When I saw him, he was dirty, unshaven, and he smelled awful. That rank smell of body odour which suggested he hadn't washed for days. He was only wearing a filthy sweater and thin cotton trousers, despite the bitterly cold weather. If you've ever spent time in Newcastle you'll understand that when the wind blows there it's almost Arctic. Anyway, Carl was shivering and he looked as if he hadn't eaten for days.

'I took him inside and made him drink a couple of mugs of tea, and fed him a sandwich I'd scrounged from the theatre manager. That perked him up a bit; enough to explain what had happened to him. Basically, it was every performer's worst nightmare. Carl had got hooked on drink, then on drugs, a downward spiral culminating in his becoming a heroin addict. That had taken all his money, including the severance fee he'd got on leaving Northern Lights. Carl told me he was clean, and had been off the drugs for three months. The problem was that his addiction had left him penniless, and homeless. He'd been sleeping rough, which explained his appearance. However, he reckoned he had a chance to put everything right. Not in this country of course, because word had got out.'

'I don't understand,' Eve said. 'What do you mean about word having got out?'

'The music industry was a real gossip shop back then. I guess it might still be, but I meant that Carl was unable to get work here because of rumours about his addiction, and that he was unreliable. People were reluctant to hire him, even though he was a good musician.'

'So he was in effect begging?' I asked.

'I suppose so. He had come to ask for money, he referred to it as a loan, but I think we both knew different. Carl told me he'd been offered work as a session musician in the States, but that he needed money for the air fare.'

'Did you believe him, or did you think the money was for drugs?'

'It could have been, I suppose, but the story made sense. Motown and the Wall of Sound were becoming big news, together with the Surf Sound, bands like the Beach Boys. Whatever Carl's motive in coming to me was, I knew I'd give it to him, even though I was fairly sure I'd not see my money again.'

'An air fare to America would have been a tidy sum,' Eve suggested. 'Did you always carry a lot of cash on you?'

'No, I didn't, so I arranged with Carl to meet him after

the gig. I explained that I'd have to go to the local branch of my bank and get them to cash a cheque.'

'Whose idea was it to meet on the Tyne Bridge?' To this day I'm not sure what prompted my question. Nor did any of us realize the significance of Crowther's reply at the time.

'It was Carl's idea, and at the time it spooked me, because it was almost as if he'd read my mind. He said, "Why don't I meet you on the Tyne Bridge at midnight, and the next time you'll hear from me is when I've made it big in the States." We had a chuckle about that. I agreed to the meeting and later arranged with Neville Wade for him to make the anonymous phone call at 12.15 a.m. reporting the man jumping off the bridge. Before Carl left, because it was so cold, I lent him my Buddy Holly coat. He promised to return it when we met later, but of course I never saw him again.'

'What happened after the gig?' Eve asked.

'I was later than intended, which meant I didn't get to the bridge on time. I had to lie low for ages, much longer than I'd anticipated, waiting for the fans to disperse. That ruined part of my plan, which involved being seen by someone who knew me en route to the bridge. I arrived there a few minutes after midnight, but there was no sign of Carl. I waited as long as I dared, but then I had to leave, because I knew Nev would be placing that phone call, and I couldn't risk the police turning up and finding me on the bridge, alive and well.'

'What did you do when Carl didn't make the meeting?'

'I continued with my plan. Next morning I caught a train for York. I'd already bought this place, so I headed straight here and took up my new life. I thought Carl must have changed his mind about the money. I remember being mildly peeved about the coat, but I didn't really begrudge him it. It was only months later after Nev told me about the body being recovered that I knew what had actually happened to Carl. It was really rather sad.'

'This eyewitness who was supposed to have seen you heading for the river, I assume that was Julie Solanki.'

'Yes, it was. How did you know that?'

'I'll explain later. When we read the inquest report, which mistook Carl for you, there was some speculation by the coroner as to whether his injuries had been sustained in the fall, or whether someone had struck him. Have you any reason to believe his death was other than accidental?'

Crowther's expression changed, became guarded, tense. 'I don't know. I suppose it's possible.'

That answer was more puzzling than revealing. Rather than press him on it then, I opted to change tack. I was about to ask him a further question when Eve forestalled me by asking the same thing.

'Why don't you tell us what made you decide to leave Northern Lights in such a dramatic fashion? And why you've chosen to emerge from the shadows after all this time.'

As Eve spoke I saw once again the flicker of emotion in Crowther's eyes, and this time, without the distraction of a shotgun pointed at me, I recognized it. The emotion was fear. But what had Crowther to be afraid of, living out here in a hermit-like existence? It looked as if he wouldn't respond, so I provided a little more impetus.

'I think I can guess the answer to Eve's last question. I believe that once you'd written that song you didn't want just anyone to perform it. You wanted it to be your daughter.'

Chapter Eight

'How did you find out that Trudi is my daughter?'

'It wasn't difficult,' Eve told him. She explained about our visit to Mytholmroyd and the interview with his former teacher. 'Once we had your mother's Christian name, putting that together with Sheila's surname, it was the obvious conclusion.'

'I could hardly believe my eyes when I saw Trudi on TV. I knew at once who she was, even before they announced her name. She looks so much like Sheila did at that age. I was thrilled when I heard her name, because I knew Sheila had called her Trudi after my mum. It meant that Sheila didn't hate me for what I'd done.'

Crowther's expression turned gloomy, as he continued, 'I don't think she'd be anywhere near as understanding if she ever got to find out that I didn't kill myself. I dread to think what her reaction would be if she learned that I'd deserted them.'

Eve stared at him for a moment, and when she spoke, her voice reflected incredulity, tinged with anger and contempt. 'You chose to disappear, knowing that Sheila was expecting your child? Why did you do that? Was it something to do with the drink and drugs?'

Crowther stared at her, his astonishment obvious. 'What do you mean? I've never touched drugs. I detested them for the effect they had on performers and the example it set for young impressionable fans. I still do, for that matter. As for boozing, that wasn't my thing either. In fact I rarely took a drink, and on the few occasions I did, I had nothing more than a half of lager.'

'That wasn't what we were told. Lew said he'd heard rumours that you were hooked on drugs and often legless, and that it had been going on for months before your disappearance.'

'I don't know who told him that, but it certainly isn't true.'

'If it wasn't drink or drugs, why did you leave like that? Were you afraid of the responsibility of parenthood?' Is that why you ran away?'

Crowther winced, recognizing the judgemental tone in Eve's voice, but his reply took the wind out of her sails, and shocked all of us to silence. 'No, I wasn't afraid of becoming a father. In fact I'd been looking forward to it from the minute Sheila told me she was pregnant. I left because I was afraid for my life, but even more so for the lives of Sheila and the child she was carrying.'

His statement left us dumbfounded. After a few seconds, I looked at Eve, and then at Charlie. Both of them were staring at Crowther, open-mouthed. It made me wonder what my own expression was like. Eventually, I managed to ask, 'Can you explain?'

For a long moment I thought Crowther would not respond. As I waited, I thought of the precautions he took to maintain his privacy. Adding together the secluded position of the house, the shotgun, the fear in his eyes, and suddenly, Pete Firth's story made sense. 'Are you referring to those accidents you had?'

Crowther's expression became even grimmer, if that was possible. 'They weren't accidents. They were deliberate attempts on my life. Someone tried to kill me. Five times, to be exact. It was only sheer luck that they didn't succeed.' He paused and frowned. 'How did you find out about them? Who told you?'

'Pete Firth,' I replied, 'he thought it would make an interesting chapter in the book I'm supposed to be writing.

He only mentioned four incidents, though. The keyboard that almost electrocuted you, the girder that nearly brained you, the time you were mugged, and the car crash. I make that four times.'

'There were a couple of other things that happened, ones that no one else knew about. One of them was seemingly trivial, and had little to do with an attempt on my life, or so I thought at the time. The group had been playing a gig in Chester, and Lew had booked us into a hotel near there overnight.' Crowther smiled. 'It was in the days before pop groups gained a reputation for bad behaviour. I'd booked another room for Sheila. I didn't want her exposed to the sort of publicity some musicians' girlfriends were getting in the press. Naturally, I spent the night with her. When I went back to my own room next morning it had been broken into, and the briefcase that I kept all my sheet music in had been stolen. A lot of it was stuff I was working on, and much of it was unpublished; there was a lot of good material in there. It was an annoyance rather than anything else, because the originals were back at my flat in Leeds.'

'Why do you think it might be connected to the other events?' Eve asked.

'I didn't to begin with, but the person who broke in left a message for me. On the bed was a turnip with a kitchen knife driven through it. The turnip was on the pillow, just where my head would have been had I been occupying that room. I thought it was nothing more than the thief's sick sense of humour, until the other stuff started happening. Apart from that, there was another, far scarier incident that nobody else knew about. Like the break-in, I dismissed it, and for a long time I thought it was no more than someone's careless driving. I was almost knocked down crossing the road by a van that failed to stop.'

'That's an unfortunate chain of events,' Eve interrupted, 'but there's no reason to believe they were anything other than accidents, surely?'

'No, I agree, but then the person responsible wrote to me to tell me they weren't accidents,' Crowther replied. 'They also warned me that they weren't going to give up until I was dead, which was no more than I deserved. They accompanied their warning with a string of abuse, calling me all the names under the sun and blaming me for unspecified crimes. To begin with, I dismissed the letters as the work of a crank. There are a load of nutters out there and when you're in the spotlight they're like moths to a flame. But when they referred to the things that had happened to me; things that only someone responsible would know, I began to take them much more seriously.'

'Why didn't you go to the police, or get protection?'

'I didn't reckon the police would be too interested, not to begin with, anyway. By the time I thought of doing that, they'd moved on to threaten Sheila, and I knew I couldn't take the risk. I might have done if it had been only me, but I couldn't endanger Sheila. They said they knew she was a slut and a whore because only a woman such as that would consort with the likes of me. Therefore, they'd decided that she should die too. They told me they would do her first so I could suffer the loss, and then deal with me. That was the last straw. Because they knew so much about me, I dare not talk to anyone else about the attacks, or what I planned to do.'

'Except Neville Wade,' I suggested.

'Yes, except for Neville.'

'How did you know you could trust him?'

'Because Neville saved my life. Not once, but twice. He pulled the plug on the keyboard just in time to prevent me dying from the electric shock, and he saw the girder come loose from the crane and pushed me out of the way.'

'Have you any idea who might have been behind the threats? Who hated you enough to want to kill you and those closest to you?'

'Not a clue. Don't think I haven't asked myself that question over and over again. Every single day, to be precise.'

'When you said they called you a load of names, was there a hint in them of what might have sparked their vendetta?'

'Not really, as I recall, the terms were "a thieving, murdering bastard" or something similar.'

'And you've no idea what that might refer to?'

'That's another question I ask on a regular basis. And come up with the same answer. I have absolutely no idea.'

From out of nowhere, a vision came into my mind. It was of a young girl, standing by the river in Newcastle late one winter's night, and of what she thought she'd seen there. 'We spoke to Julie Solanki. She's Julie Firth now, married Pete. The night you vanished, she was collecting a packet of drugs for Pete from a dealer.'

Crowther smiled faintly. 'I remember that. I'd just been to the bank to get Carl's money when the guy stopped me and gave me the message for Pete. What about it?'

'When we spoke to Julie, she said she'd seen you after the gig, whilst she was waiting for the dealer to arrive. She said you were heading for the Tyne Bridge, and that you saw her, but didn't acknowledge her. She also said you were being followed by two people she reckoned were acting furtively, sticking to the shadows, taking care not to get too close to you.'

'I don't recall seeing Julie that night. There was nobody by the river where she was supposed to meet that dealer when I went past.'

'Of course you don't, because it wasn't you that Julie saw, it was Carl Long. Julie said that she recognized you by your Buddy Holly jacket. But if you gave that to Long before the concert, her identification of you is totally wrong.'

'I get that, but what's your point?'

'I believe the reason that Carl Long didn't keep his meeting with you is because he was already dead. I think the two men Julie saw made the same mistake as she did. I believe they saw the jacket and assumed the wearer had to be you. There was a strong likeness between you and Long. I think they followed him to the bridge and either knocked him unconscious or killed him outright, then threw him into the river. They wouldn't bother to check for identification. It might have been late at night, but at any moment someone might have come along and disturbed them.'

I thought for a moment. 'How did they fix the car crash? That can't have been easy. I assume they claimed the credit for it, if credit's the right word.'

'I paid for an engineer's report after the car was recovered. Both the brakes and the steering had been tampered with. I lived in Leeds at the time, and my flat didn't come with a garage, just a parking space round the back, so when I was away playing a gig or on tour, the car was parked outside. It would have been easy. According to the engineer, what had been done would have taken no more than a quarter of an hour for someone with sufficient knowledge and the right tools.'

'I don't suppose you kept a copy of that report, did you?' Eve asked.

'I did. I kept all the evidence I could collect. I can't show you it, though. All the paperwork is in my safe deposit box at the bank.'

'What was the idea of that?'

'I wasn't prepared to keep anything here. I was worried in case someone managed to find me – like you did. The whole point was to make the disappearance complete. Leaving anything referring to Gerry Crowther would have been a dead giveaway.'

Crowther went to the Aga and brewed us a drink, which gave us chance to mull over what we'd been told. I looked out of the window at the scene outside the house. 'I wasn't aware there was a windmill here,' I said. 'I live at Laithbrigg and know the area reasonably well, but I've never heard of the mill. Is it working?'

'It is, and the reason you won't have heard of it is that it's only been there a couple of years. It's taken me a long time to build it, working alone.'

'You built it?' Eve was astonished. 'That must have taken some doing. Have you had previous experience in building?'

'Not until I bought this place. It was pretty near derelict when I moved here. I learned all sorts of skills' – Crowther smiled slightly – 'such as how to electrocute yourself, how to fall off a ladder, hit your fingernail with a hammer; those and many more.'

'And did you make all these units?' Eve asked, glancing round the kitchen.

Crowther nodded.

'Doing this place up must have taken years, and cost a fortune,' Eve observed.

'Time and money were things I wasn't short of,' he said as he passed Charlie a glass of home-made lemonade, which he said was delicious.

As I thanked him for the tea, one thought at the back of my mind was that, given the obvious strength of Crowther's feelings for the girl he'd deserted, it seemed out of character to have left her penniless. 'It must have been a struggle for Sheila over the years, bringing up a child on her own,' I suggested. Tact has always been one of my stronger points.

Crowther winced. 'That has been a constant worry for me. Until I saw Trudi on TV I had no idea if Sheila was all right, or if the baby had survived. I didn't even know if it was a boy or a girl. I did make provision for Sheila, so that she didn't suffer too much financially, but that's of very little comfort.'

'How did you manage to do that, without revealing that you were still alive?'

'My bank manager arranged it. He has also been very helpful, and knowing that everything I told him was confidential made it easier.' Crowther smiled again. 'I think he enjoyed doing it. He seemed to revel in the conspiracy. Apart from that, I am a valued customer. Luckily, I'd never spent much of the money I'd earned, either as a performer or a songwriter, and that meant I was pretty well-off. He wrote to Sheila telling her that before my "death" I'd set up a trust fund for her and the child. He advanced her a lump sum, plus a regular monthly income he said came from the interest on investments and royalties. He also instructed her to contact him if she needed extra funds in case of emergencies.'

Crowther smiled wryly. 'Sheila's never taken him up on that offer, neither has she married.'

'One good thing,' Eve suggested, 'after all this time – if you did decide to reappear, it would all be totally different. There surely can't be any danger now.'

Crowther frowned. 'I'm not sure about that. Perhaps you're right, and the danger has long since passed. I do know that I'd like to see Sheila again, if only to apologize, and I'd love to meet Trudi. But I'm not sure if could cope with show business and the limelight again.'

'If we were able to set up a meeting with Sheila and Trudi, how would you feel about that?'

Crowther looked at Eve, considering her question for some time before responding. 'In a word, terrified. And excited too, I suppose.'

I was still dwelling on what had happened to cause Crowther to disappear. 'I don't suppose you kept those anonymous letters, did you?'

'I destroyed the first one, but I kept all the others. They're in the bank.' He looked at each of us in turn. 'Does that sound paranoid?'

'I don't think so. It isn't paranoia if someone actually is threatening you. I'd like to take a look at them sometime. I also think you should show them to Sheila if and when you meet up with her. That way she can grasp the potency of the threat, and the sacrifice you made for her and Trudi. I think she would appreciate what a terrible decision you had to make.'

I had been reluctant to raise the subject of Mitchell's death, but as our talk with Crowther progressed I was increasingly puzzled that he had failed to mention it. I felt sure Wade must have told him. The vet had been shocked by the news, and I couldn't believe he would have omitted to pass it on.

In the end, I decided to take the bull by the horns. 'Did Neville Wade tell you what happened to Jimmy Mitchell?'

'He mentioned that Jimmy had died, no more than that.'

I was a bit flummoxed, and saw Eve staring at me, her expression one of doubt. Either I had to tell him outright or hide the truth. I felt it unfair that he should be denied the full facts when he was making his decision. 'Mitchell was murdered. We found his body when we went to talk to him.'

Crowther's face registered a range of emotions: shock, fear, and finally perplexed acceptance. In response to his demand, I told him what had happened, deciding as I did not to pull any punches. Although he was clearly disturbed by the thought that Mitchell's death might be related to the threats against his life, I sensed that it had not weakened his resolve. Although he was wary about committing to a decision then and there, I felt confident that when he did make his mind up, it would be to proceed with Eve's idea. I was unsure whether this was down to maturity or paternal desire to meet up with his daughter. Then again, it could be that his feelings for Sheila were still too strong to be resisted any longer.

When we left, it was with the understanding that we would return again in a few days' time, by which time he would have had chance to mull over our suggestion about meeting up with Sheila. In the meantime we'd elicited a promise from him that he would sign a copyright release form once Lew Pattison had drawn one up. In return, we had given Crowther our word that we would not reveal his whereabouts, even to the impresario.

As soon as we got back to Eden House I told Eve and Charlie there was something I needed to do, and asked them not to disturb me. I went into the study, and in the quiet of the sun-filled room, tried to concentrate on an errant memory. It had been prompted by something Crowther had said that didn't sound right. I wasn't sure what was niggling me, but I felt certain he'd contradicted the facts I'd heard, or read. I walked to and fro, glancing occasionally at the stack of folders on my desk. The information was in there, I was certain of that, but I wasn't about to wade through them again. It was only when I'd ceased trying to remember the facts that I made the connection, but even then the full significance didn't occur to me.

It's often said that chance plays an important part in our lives, and this was no exception. Had it not been for a chance intervention, Gerry Crowther would have died that night in Newcastle.

Chapter Nine

Eve and Charlie spent some of their time prior to our return to Allerscar trying to work out how best to find Sheila Bell and inveigle her to the meeting with her erstwhile lover without giving the game away. During that time I mulled over what Crowther had told us, trying to square it with our store of knowledge. I felt sure something wasn't right, but couldn't be sure what. Eve noticed my preoccupation and asked what I was thinking about.

'I was trying to make sense of those attacks on Crowther and the threatening letters he received.'

'What about them?'

'He seemed to have accepted them at face value, convinced that it was someone with a grudge, but I don't believe it's as clear-cut as that.'

'What other motive could there be?'

'I don't know, but it seems too obvious, too blatant. Admittedly Crowther made enemies through his reshaping of Northern Lights, and that must have caused huge resentment, but think about it, Evie. The group weren't that successful before he joined them. It's not as if Crowther had suggested replacing someone like Paul McCartney or Mick Jagger.'

'Maybe it was a crazed psychopath after all?'

'That doesn't fit either.'

'Why not?'

'Consider the careful planning behind several of those incidents. And if we're right about Mitchell, that doesn't tally with the insanity theory. It's more like someone silenced him to prevent him telling us what he knew. Add to what the police said about his house being ransacked, and perhaps Mitchell had evidence of who was behind the campaign against Crowther.'

'I still can't see what the motive might have been.'

The problem was, neither could I, and it would only be pure chance that led to us discovering the solution.

After a few days, I suggested one of us ought to phone Pattison and tell him the news. Eve agreed, but told me that she wanted to speak to Pattison's wife Alice first.

'Why?' I asked her, 'what are you up to?'

'We thought it would be better to wait until we know what Gerry Crowther had decided before talking to Lew,' Eve told me.

Her air of innocence didn't impress me. 'And the reason for that is …?'

'It was Charlie's idea really. He thought if Crowther is willing to meet up with Sheila, we should tell Lew to say that the songwriter would only agree to sign the copyright release once he'd talked with the singer. We could stress to Pattison that the man's name has to be withheld, or the deal is off.'

'And Charlie thought that up all on his own?'

'He did, but it gave me another idea. If I speak to Lew's wife on the quiet, I can find out when Lew is likely to be unavailable. We could arrange the meeting for when he's not about. That way Sheila is more likely to accompany Trudi rather than asking Lew to bring her. What do you think?'

'I think is it's very difficult to decide which of the two of you is the more devious. I'd accuse you of corrupting Charlie, Eve, except that it seems to be a clear case of hereditary evil.'

I looked at Charlie, who was grinning broadly. 'I don't know what you're smirking about. I once told your mother you'd go a long way – probably to prison. I can see now that I was dead right.'

Eve's call to Alice Pattison gave us the necessary impetus to go ahead with the scheme. 'Lew caught a flight to America yesterday evening. He's gone there to arrange recording sessions for a couple of his artists. Alice reckons he could be away for a week, maybe even a fortnight.'

'With Pattison away it might be difficult getting Trudi and her mother to come to Yorkshire,' I pointed out. The disappointment on Charlie's face was comical.

'Alice reckons not.' Charlie's frown vanished at his aunt's words. 'She said if we tell her what we need to do with contracts, she can pass the message to Lew when he phones her. The company has an office in Detroit, so he'll be able to send a telex to London, giving detailed instructions to Trudi.'

'In that case I suggest we head for Allerscar this morning and see if Crowther has made his mind up.'

'I bet he says yes,' Charlie piped up. 'He'd be daft not to. Besides, I reckon he'll be mad keen to meet his daughter.'

I couldn't resist the opportunity to tease Charlie. 'You're only saying that because it will give you chance to meet Trudi. You can't wait to see if she looks as good in real life as she does on that poster on your bedroom wall.'

Charlie blushed slightly, but denied the allegation. I didn't believe him, and nor, to judge by her expression, did Eve.

We arrived outside Crowther's house shortly after 11 a.m., just as a van I recognized as belonging to our local greengrocer was pulling away from the end of the drive. Crowther, who was in the process of closing the five-barred gate, recognized us and gave a small wave.

I gestured to a potato sack that was leaning against the gatepost. 'I wouldn't have thought you'd need to buy fresh produce when you've got that huge vegetable plot at the back of the house. It's bigger than most allotments I've seen.'

'I wasn't buying, I was selling. That,' Crowther gestured to the sack, 'is by way of part-exchange. It's some fertiliser for the stuff in the greenhouses.'

'It sounds as if you've got the makings of a thriving business,' Eve suggested, 'a sort of miniature cottage industry.'

'Not so miniature,' Crowther smiled, 'and you're right. I'm hoping to expand it. The farmer who's my neighbour is hoping to retire, and I've been negotiating to buy several fields from him. I plan to use one of them for larger greenhouses. With luck I'll be able to generate sufficient power from the mill to service them.'

'What will you use the rest of the land for?'

'I'm hoping to grow sufficient wheat on it to grind my own flour, which means the windmill should prove a worthwhile investment. In a couple of years, I should be bagging and selling home-produced flour. I've already got a couple of village shops keen to try it out.'

Once we were seated round the kitchen table, Eve asked the question we'd come to have answered.

Crowther thought for a moment before responding. 'I've decided to take the chance,' he told us. 'I'm fed up of living in the shadows; of being afraid to leave the house, even to walk to the village. You've no idea what it's been like all these years, never knowing when someone might be lurking, waiting to harm me. Even though the world thought I was dead, that was mere chance, and it's only been recently that I've come to realize that I'll never be at peace until I face my demons once and for all.'

He paused for a moment, his face sad and reflective. 'I've missed my daughter's childhood because of that fear. I only hope that Sheila can see her way to forgive me. I dread the idea that she might think of me as a coward. That wasn't why I planned my disappearance. Yes, of course I was worried for myself, but I could have put up with that, hired bodyguards or something. But I could never have forgiven myself if whoever was responsible had taken out their hatred on Sheila and the child she was carrying. So the answer to your question is yes, go ahead and tell Lew, but I'd rather that nobody else but Sheila and Trudi know where I live. Do you think that can be arranged?'

'I think that's perfectly understandable, and I believe the plan that Eve and Charlie have concocted between them will set your mind at rest on that score.'

I sat back and watched Crowther as Eve explained their scheme. For the first time since we met him, I noticed an air of calm and optimism in his face. The thought of emerging from the shadows, of casting off, albeit only gradually, the half-life he had been living for so long had obviously cheered him immensely.

Not being part of the conversation gave me the opportunity to shift the focus of my attention to another topic. I was still in the process of mulling this over when I realized I was being spoken to, or more accurately, spoken about.

'Don't worry about Adam, he often goes into a trance-like state. It might seem as if there's nothing going on in there, but I do believe there's a certain level of activity, even though it may not resemble life as we know it. If he lives up to expectations, any moment now he'll surface and claim that he was thinking, you'll see.'

I'd hate to disappoint an expectant audience. 'Sorry, did I miss something? I thought I heard someone speaking, but I couldn't make any sense of it, so I assume it couldn't have been anything important.'

Crowther looked from me to Eve and then back again. 'Are you sure you two aren't married?'

'No, and nor are we likely to be unless Eve minds that wicked tongue of hers.'

Eve stuck the offending article out at me. I ignored her.

'I was thinking,' I began.

'What did I tell you?' Eve gave me an unrepentant grin.

'As I was saying before being so rudely interrupted, I've been thinking about the copyright release form that Pattison's office will have to draw up for you to sign. Given what Lew told us regarding what happened back in the sixties, I think it might be wise to take one or two simple precautions.'

'Sorry, I'm not with you.' Crowther frowned. 'What was it that Lew told you about the sixties?'

'When they were trying to find you, before Carl Long's body was fished out of the Tyne and everyone assumed it was you, Pattison employed a firm of private detectives to search for you. Before long, news of what was going on was leaked to the press, who had a field day over it. Lew still isn't certain if the leak emanated from the enquiry agents, or within his own organization.'

'I can understand that, but I don't see where it ties in to the contract that's going to be drawn up now.'

'Look at it this way. Your reappearance from the dead would be certain to make sensational news headlines, don't you think?'

'I suppose there's some truth in that, although I'm by no means the sort of household name I was back then.'

'Still, rather than run the risk, don't you think it would be sensible if the composer's name on that contract wasn't Gerry Crowther?'

'That makes sense, I suppose, but whose name would you suggest putting on the form?'

'That seems obvious to me. What's wrong with the name you're known by locally? Charles Hardin?'

'Of course, and only real fans would know that it's an alias.'

'Even if they did happen to work out the Buddy Holly connection, nobody would automatically link that to Gerry

Crowther and go rushing off to the papers.'

'That's brilliant,' Crowther said, 'but is it legal?'

'Is what legal?'

'Would it invalidate the form if we entered a name that wasn't real?'

'I don't think so. I believe you're allowed to call yourself what you like, as long as it's not with fraudulent intent.'

Crowther turned to Eve. 'I think you got it wrong. I reckon there was a lot going on in Adam's head, and very productive it was too.'

Eve smiled but failed to respond. She was staring at me in an uncomfortably meaningful way. I knew that she had gone at least some way towards working out the additional agenda concealed within my suggestion. Rather than provoke her into making an untimely remark that might reveal my true motive, I carefully avoided her gaze.

Once we were inside the car on the return journey to Laithbrigg, Eve came straight to the point. 'OK, Adam, out with it. What were you playing at in there? Don't try and fob us off like you did Crowther, with all that publicity stuff. What were you really after with that Charles Hardin bit? I'm sure there's far more to it in that devious mind of yours than simply avoiding an embarrassing leak to the press.'

'I wondered about that as well,' Charlie added.

'OK, let's think about it this way. Crowther had been the target of several attempts on his life prior to his disappearance. We also believe that Carl Long might have been murdered by someone who mistook him for Crowther. That caused the vendetta to cease. News that he's alive and kicking might be all that's needed to start it all off again. Especially if we believe Mitchell's death was linked to our search for Crowther. And this time the targets might well be Sheila and Trudi Bell.'

Eve nodded. 'I can see why you didn't want to say that

in front of Crowther. It would have set his paranoia working overtime.'

'I'm not saying we keep Gerry's identity hidden forever, that might not be practical or possible anyway, but I think it would be wise to do so until such time as we're in a stronger position.'

'I'm not sure what you mean by "a stronger position", and I've certainly no idea how we get there.'

'The only way that comes to mind at the moment would be by trying to discover who was responsible for the attempts to kill him back in the sixties. And unless the people responsible are out-and-out psychopaths, the best way to do that would be by finding out what their motive was.'

'You said "people" and "they",' Charlie butted in. 'How do you know it wasn't just the work of one person?'

'Do you remember what Julie Firth told us about the night Crowther disappeared? When she thought she'd seen him by the river? Well, that was obviously Carl Long, but Julie also said she'd seen two people she thought might have been following him. That makes it far less likely to have been the work of a lone psychopath, don't you think?'

That night, following a lengthy conversation with Pattison's wife, Eve reported that Alice would keep us up to date with developments.

'I told her we'd located the composer, and that for the time being he wished to be known simply as Charles Hardin. I also explained that he'd requested a meeting with Trudi Bell, as he had certain ideas about the arrangement of the two songs, and he wanted to make sure she performed them to the best possible advantage.'

Twenty-four hours or so later, Alice Pattison phoned us back to give us an update. I listened in on the extension as Eve spoke to her friend. 'Lew's absolutely thrilled,' Alice reported. 'He's happy to keep the composer's true identity secret, and he's sending a telex to his deputy giving instructions about drafting the release form, which will be sent to you. He's also going to ask him to contact Trudi or her mother regarding the meeting, and will them give your phone number as a contact point.'

After that, events moved forward at speed. First of all, we received a phone call from Lew's deputy at the London office of Pattison Music and Management. 'My name's Harvey Jackson. I've received instructions from Lew and I need to make sure I have everything correct before I go ahead.'

'Fire away,' I told him.

He went through the items one by one, even to the extent of spelling out Hardin's name and mine, together with my address. He also asked me to confirm that it was in order to pass my phone number to Trudi or Sheila Bell. I agreed that I had no objection to this.

'OK, I'll pass the message, and I'll ensure those forms are sent to you via tonight's post.'

It was my turn to cook dinner that evening, so when the phone rang, Eve took the call. Several minutes later, she and Charlie joined me in the kitchen, where Eve imparted the exciting news. 'That was Sheila Bell on the phone. It seems that Trudi has a singing engagement in Sheffield on Friday evening. Sheila suggested they could travel to York on Saturday, and make their way here, but I told her we'd meet them from the train if she lets us know the time. I hope you don't mind, but I suggested if they want to they could stay here on Saturday night.'

I was the recipient of a fixed glare from Charlie, as if daring me to refuse. 'Do you think we ought to expose Trudi to one of her most ardent fans?'

'I'm sure Charlie will behave himself like the gentleman he's been brought up to be,' Eve told me severely.

Next morning, I had just made coffee when Charlie walked into the kitchen. He was carrying a bunch of folders in his hand, which he set down on the kitchen table. 'What have you got there?' Eve asked, punctuating her question with a yawn. 'Don't tell me it's homework?'

Charlie grinned. 'Hardly, this is some research I did last night.'

'Research? Into what?' I asked.

'I was trying to find someone with a motive to kill Mr Crowther.'

'And did you succeed?' Eve gave another huge yawn.

'Actually, there are several candidates, but one thing I did come across that I think you might be interested in.' Charlie paused and opened one of the files. 'This folder contains all the press cuttings about Northern Lights. The ones that interested me were the reviews. Those of one reviewer in particular: Diane Little. She wrote some very damning reviews of Northern Lights, mostly directed at Crowther more than any of the other band members. She criticized his singing, his keyboard playing, and his songwriting.'

Eve and I examined the paperwork Charlie had produced.

'I have to say, Charlie, that whether you're right or wrong, this is an impressive piece of research. What do you think, Evie?'

'I was wondering whether Diane Little was acting on orders, and if not, what she had against Crowther.'

I looked through the cuttings again. Most of them were gig reports, plus press releases, but towards the bottom of the pile was the collection of reviews. Many of the music critics were highly complimentary about the group's performance, and in particular about Crowther's skill both as a musician and as a songwriter.

The glaring exceptions were the half-dozen written by Diane Little. Charlie certainly hadn't exaggerated when he'd described the reviews as damning, or that the journalist had reserved her most savage criticism for Gerry Crowther. What, I wondered, had sparked such vitriolic attacks? Of one thing I felt certain; there was far more to Diane Little's criticism than mere differences in musical taste. This was personal, but I couldn't begin to think of a possible motive behind the scathing assault.

I went back to other reviews covering the same events and the contrast between these and Diane Little's was stark. Reading any two versions alongside one another, you almost felt they were describing different groups playing separate venues.

'I think we should make a point of asking Lew Pattison about that journalist when we get the chance. If she is still involved in the music industry, Pattison will be far more likely to be able to tell us about her than if we tried to discover her background for ourselves, and he's sure to know if she is in the habit of slating other artists in a similar fashion.' Eve looked at me. 'What do you think, Adam?'

'I can't believe that journalist would be interested in pursuing a long term vendetta against Gerry Crowther just out of spite. There has to be a stronger motive.'

Chapter Ten

It was mid-morning on Friday when Sheila Bell rang back and confirmed the time she and Trudi would be arriving in York the next day. She also took up Eve's offer to stay with us on the Saturday night. I was intrigued to see how Charlie would approach the impending meeting with his pin-up girl. Would he be tongue-tied with embarrassment, or worse still say something trite or inappropriate? I guess most boys of his age would be socially inept when they came face to face with the object of their wildest dreams. I certainly would have been.

When Saturday arrived, fortunately for Charlie's peace of mind their train was only a couple of minutes overdue. When the doors to the first-class carriage opened, the second passenger to alight was a woman whose striking good looks could have enabled her to pass herself off as the singer's elder sister rather than her mother.

She turned to take a suitcase from inside, and as we moved forward to greet her and introduce ourselves, Trudi emerged from the compartment, hauling a second, larger case. She seemed oblivious of the curious stares from a number of other passengers, who had obviously recognized the young singing sensation.

'Sheila Bell? I'm Adam Bailey, and this is my fiancée, Eve Samuels, and Eve's nephew Charles Rowe.'

There was a moment's handshaking, before I offered to carry their cases, only to find that Charlie had already taken possession of Trudi's, which earned him a smile of gratitude. 'Thank you, Charles,' Trudi told him, her voice soft and pleasantly musical.

As we walked across the concourse towards the car park, I covertly checked out the girl's appearance. Although the likeness to her mother was obvious, I thought I could also detect a strong similarity to Crowther in the line of her jaw, the slightly slanted eyebrows and of course that distinguishing mole on the left of her chin. It had been that mole I had seen fleetingly on the television shot of Trudi, which had convinced me that my theory about her parentage was correct.

Eve walked alongside the visitors, with Charlie and me in close attendance. As they walked, Eve asked about the train journey, and enquired about the previous night's concert, which it seemed had been a sell-out success.

Once we reached the car, Eve elected to sit in the rear with Sheila and Trudi, much to Charlie's disappointment. As we drove through York's Saturday morning traffic, however, the topic of conversation shifted towards the impending visit to the composer, and speculation as to his reason for the requested meeting.

'What is he like, this Mr Hardin?' Sheila began, 'It seems rather an odd request. The man from Pattison Music and Management was a bit vague. All he said was that Mr Hardin had insisted on seeing Trudi before signing the contract. Can you tell us any more about what his reasons are?'

In the rear-view mirror I could see Eve staring fixedly at me, a touch of panic and a plea for help in her expression. 'I feel sure you'll like him,' I told Sheila, 'and I would ask you to listen very carefully to what he has to say.'

'I don't understand,' Sheila responded.

'I think you will when you see him. It is a very sad story. Mr Hardin was a very talented musician, with the world at his feet, but suddenly that world collapsed. He has had to sacrifice a great deal during his life, at a time when he ought to have hoped things would be good for him, and I believe the reason he insisted on the meeting is that he wants to ensure that Trudi doesn't suffer as he has done. I'm sorry if all that sounds very cryptic, but it's his story, not mine, and I would prefer you to hear it from him, but once again, I would implore you to hear him out.'

My remarks brought that topic of conversation to an abrupt close, which was hardly surprising. For the rest of the journey, apart from some admiring comments about the scenery and enquiries about how long we'd lived in the area, little was said, and I left Eve to field those less taxing questions.

We reached Allerscar at lunchtime, and pulled up outside Crowther's house. As I looked towards the building I noticed an immediate change. The shutters that had been covering the windows to the front of the property on our previous visits had been opened, giving a far more welcoming effect.

'Is this it?' Trudi asked. 'What a super house!'

As we reached the back of the house, Sheila and Trudi paused to admire the view. They were still gazing at the splendid landscape when Crowther emerged from the house. I'd wondered how he would greet them. Would it be something dramatic, or mundane? If his words weren't dramatic, the effect certainly was.

'Hello, Sheila.'

His tone was matter-of-fact, as if they'd parted only recently, rather than sixteen years ago. Sheila Bell turned her head, and I saw her face go white with shock as she stared at the man in front of her. Recognition was instantaneous; her reaction extreme. She screamed once, then swayed, like a boxer who has sustained a heavy punch, and if Eve had not been alongside her to support her, I think she would have collapsed.

She continued to stare at Crowther, her expression one of shock and disbelief mingled. Her mouth moved, but following that one piercing scream, no sound came forth.

'It isn't a trick, Sheila, I promise you. It really is me,' Crowther told her.

Sheila recovered, and freed herself from Eve's steadying hand. I saw her mouth close into a tight, thin, angry line. She stepped forward and swung her fist. Crowther must have seen the blow coming, but he made no attempt to block or evade it. Sheila's fist made contact somewhere around the cheekbone. The thud of the punch landing was followed by Crowther staggering backwards.

Crowther spoke again, one eye on Sheila's fist, which was still clenched. 'I'm sorry, Sheila. I know I earned that, and a lot more besides, but I had my reasons. Please believe me. I didn't want to leave you, or the child.' He glanced towards Trudi as he spoke, and smiled slightly. For her part, Trudi looked completely bewildered.

'I had to make everyone believe I was dead. It was the only way to save my life, and possibly yours. I could have put up with the danger if it had only been me that was being threatened, but I couldn't risk any harm coming to you – or Trudi.'

'I don't know what the devil you're on about,' Sheila spat the words out. 'You didn't even know Trudi existed. You simply vanished, and we thought you were dead. We all did. You were dead. Your body was fished out of the river. I don't understand. Why did you desert us? Why aren't you dead? If that wasn't your body, then whose was it, wearing your clothes?'

I cleared my throat to attract attention. It didn't work first time so I repeated the action. 'Why don't we go inside and Gerry can explain everything. If you remember, Sheila, I did suggest that it was a rather sad story, and that you should hear it out to the end before making a judgement.'

'Will someone please explain?' Trudi spoke for the first time. 'Will someone please tell me what's going on?

Mum, who is this man? Is this Mr Hardin? Why didn't you tell me you knew him?'

'Because I didn't know him. Not by the name Hardin, at least. That isn't his real name. His real name is Crowther, Gerry Crowther. He's your father.'

Trudi clutched her mother's arm. 'But my father's dead, he died before I was born.' She shook her head in confusion. 'Mum, please, tell me, what is all this?'

Sheila put her arm round Trudi's shoulders and held her close. 'I've no idea. But I'm going to find out!'

As we filed through the mud room into the kitchen, I managed a whispered aside with Crowther. 'Did you get to the bank and retrieve those anonymous letters?'

He nodded. 'I went through to Harrogate and picked them up yesterday.'

Once we were inside the house, Crowther indicated everyone should sit down. I remained standing by his side.

Sheila cast a glance round the kitchen. The luxurious fittings and expensive-looking units seemed to rekindle her anger. 'Well?' she demanded, 'What have you to say for yourself? What is it you think made it worthwhile for us to travel all this way to see a man we thought was dead? A man who would have been better off remaining dead, as far as I'm concerned.'

Crowther winced, almost as he had when Sheila had punched him. I wondered fleetingly which of the two was the hardest blow to take. He didn't speak for several seconds, obviously gathering his thoughts before he committed himself. Eventually, he gripped the back of a chair, and speaking directly to her, asked, 'Do you remember that car crash? Or the time I was mugged? Or when I was nearly electrocuted by that faulty keyboard, or brained by the falling girder? Do you remember those accidents?'

'Of course I remember them, but what has that to do with anything?'

Again he fixed his gaze on her. 'Do you recall joking with me, and saying how accident-prone I was becoming, and that it was getting to be dangerous just being with me, or standing too close to me?'

Sheila's expression had softened slightly, from open hostility to a kind of wary suspicion. Acceptance was still a long way off, though. 'What of it?'

'Those weren't accidents. I thought so, to begin with. But then I found out they were deliberate attempts to kill me. They damned near succeeded too, on more than one occasion.'

If Sheila's initial reaction to Crowther's existence was one of shock, this statement caused only astonished disbelief.

He continued, with a speech I guessed he'd rehearsed over and over during the preceding days. 'I know it sounds incredible, and you probably think it's the ramblings of a lunatic, but I promise you it's true. I didn't believe it myself to begin with. Like you, I thought it was no more than a chain of bad luck and then the letters started to come. That was when I began to get really scared. Those letters quoted details that only someone who had arranged the incidents could have known. For long enough I believed I could cope, but then something worse happened. It was the car crash that made me decide to pack it all in and disappear. Because then, for the first time, I realized that I wasn't the only one in danger. My very presence was putting the lives of you and our unborn child at risk. I could never have lived with myself if anything had happened to you.'

Incredibly, given the situation, Crowther smiled before continuing. 'So rather than risk that, I decided to kill myself, or at least make it appear as if I had committed suicide. What happened in Newcastle was planned down to the most minute detail. I had help, from Neville Wade, who knew the score and has been a true friend. He smuggled me out of the building when he was seeing to his drum kit. He made an anonymous phone call reporting that he'd seen and heard someone jump off the Tyne Bridge.'

Sheila was still trying to come to terms with this. It was obvious by her expression that she still only half-believed what Crowther was saying. 'I don't understand. What about the body? If it wasn't you, who was it? They were wearing your jacket, weren't they?'

'That's another matter – it's not connected.' Crowther looked at me. He shook his head and sank to the chair. 'Adam, please, will you explain?'

'We believe that what happened that night was a tragic case of mistaken identity. Although for Gerry it was an incredible piece of luck, it helped him with his plan to disappear and in turn, to protect you. Eve and I are friends of Lew Pattison, we only became involved after Gerry sent the demo tape of the song for Trudi. Lew recognized Gerry's style of playing and asked us to find him. In the process, I interviewed the girl who thought she'd seen Gerry near the river that night. She thought he was being followed by two men acting suspiciously. However, it turns out Gerry had lent his jacket to Carl Long, who had fallen on hard times and wanted a loan. Gerry had arranged to meet him on the bridge to hand over some cash. Given that Long and Gerry were very similar in build and appearance, we think that those men saw the jacket and in the dark, just like the girl, believed they had caught up with Gerry, hit him over the head, and threw him into the river. When a body was eventually recovered, nobody bothered to check properly whether it was Gerry. That jacket was sufficient for everyone to believe that it was Gerry who had died that night. I have to say, I'm not sure without that body being recovered that the faked suicide would have been convincing enough.'

Sheila looked from me to Crowther, her face reflecting confusion, another stage towards acceptance, perhaps.

Trudi looked sickened by the implication of cold-blooded murder.

'You said you had proof,' Sheila said after a while.

Crowther didn't move. After a moment, Eve said, 'Show her the letters, Gerry.'

Crowther picked up a folder from the dresser and placed it on the table. Slowly, almost unwillingly, Sheila opened it up and began to read the letters within. Trudi peered over her mother's shoulder, and their likeness was even more apparent. Eve and I watched them read. I knew that she was as keen as I was to see what they contained, but we realized we would have to wait our turn. I saw Sheila and Trudi's expressions change, mirror images of horror, and knew what they were reading must contain something truly evil.

Slowly, and with silence in the room broken only by the ticking of the antique clock in the alcove, Sheila and her daughter read each of the menacing letters, disgust growing on their faces. Eventually, Sheila looked up at her former lover.

'Why didn't you tell me? Why didn't *Nev* tell me? Why didn't you share the trouble you were in with me? Did you think I'd desert you because there was danger?'

'I daren't take the risk. These weren't the only communications I got from them. They also rang me. Not once but several times. They told me other stuff, things that proved they were watching me closely. They said if I told anyone, you would be dead within days. They even told me what they would do to you.' Crowther shuddered at the memory; a memory obviously too painful to repeat.

'It was clear that without me on the scene, the threat against you would be lifted. Once I was out of the way, and they believed they'd achieved what they set out to do, which was to kill me, there would be no reason for them to try and harm you. That was why I planned my fake suicide. I worked on the idea for weeks. I even made sure you were provided for, with enough money to raise the child on your own. Once that was in place, I carried out the plan. I admit I was puzzled when Carl didn't show up to collect his money that night, but even when I'd heard that his body had been found, I didn't regard it as suspicious. Not until Adam and Eve told me what that Julie had seen.'

Sheila bent her head and began to study the anonymous letters once more. I looked at Eve, who nodded slightly, as if in answer to something I'd said. She walked over to Trudi's mother and placed one hand gently on her arm. 'Sheila, I can understand how upsetting this must be, and it will probably be some time before you can take it all in, but can't you see that everything Gerry did was solely to protect you and your unborn child. That was his only concern. Not for his own welfare. Remember, he'd lived with the threat for months. It was only when they turned their attention on you that he decided to act. We've read and heard a lot about Gerry and Northern Lights since Lew asked us to get involved, and it's obvious he could have become an international star had he continued his career. We spoke to a former neighbour and teacher who has known Gerry since you were both at school. He told us that music was the most important thing in Gerry's life. I can't even begin to guess at the level of sacrifice involved in passing up the chance for immense fame and fortune. He gave all that away – to ensure no harm came to you and Trudi.'

Sheila looked up from the letters. She stared across at Crowther, and I thought I could see the glint of tears in her eyes as she spoke, her voice as soft and gentle as a caress. 'She's right. There was nothing more important than your music. I always knew that.' She turned to Eve, 'I used to tease Gerry about it. I said I meant more to him than anything else, except his music, and if it came to the crunch, I wondered which he'd choose.' She smiled slightly. 'Well, now I know, don't I?'

After a second or two, Sheila asked Eve, 'How did you know Trudi was Gerry's daughter? Did he tell you? I realized he must have worked it out from the name, and the fact that she looks a bit like I did at her age.'

'No, Adam guessed the truth.' Eve explained how we'd worked it out.

'What I don't understand is why all this happened.' Sheila looked at Crowther. 'Who hated you so much?' She gestured to the letters. 'What they accuse you of in there, is any of that true? If so, how come I didn't get to know about it?'

'I have no more idea now than I did then, Sheila. Don't think I haven't asked myself that question. Over and over again, every day, year in, year out. And time after time, I come up with the same answer. I can't think of anything I've done, or anyone I've offended, to make them hate me that way.'

There was a long, uncomfortable silence. Trudi stared at Crowther and then her mother, her expression complete confusion. Sheila slid her arm round the girl's shoulders again and held her close. Eventually, she spoke, clearly addressing her former lover. 'Is there somewhere I could talk to Trudi alone?'

The request took us all by surprise. After a moment, Crowther said, 'Of course there is. I'll show you.' He opened the door leading to what I guessed had been intended as a dining room, but which, from the brief view I got, appeared to be empty of furniture. Seconds later, he returned alone.

He closed the door and looked first at me, then at Eve. 'What do you think? How did it go, I mean? I'm not used to talking that much. It's a habit I've rather got out of.'

'I think it went OK,' Eve reassured him.

'You told the truth, and you said you'd done it to protect her and Trudi,' I added, 'that's sure to have made a good impression. Especially after Eve reminded Sheila of how much you'd forfeited in order to keep her from harm.'

'Adam's right,' Charlie told Crowther. 'If you're honest with them, girls like that sort of thing. And they love it when you tell them it's for their benefit.'

I'd forgotten Charlie was there. We all turned in his direction.

'And what makes you such an expert?' Crowther asked, his tone good-humoured.

'I've two older sisters to put up with, plus Aunt Evie, and my mother. If that isn't enough of a challenge, I'd like to know what is.'

His wry comment broke the tension, and we all laughed, even his aunt, who was still smiling as she attempted to strangle him.

'Should I offer them something to drink?' Crowther asked, 'I'm not up on entertaining folks. Apart from Neville, you're the only visitors I've had since I moved in here.'

It was a bleak and sobering reminder of the lonely nature of his years in hiding. 'Wait and see what they have to say when they come back,' Eve advised. 'I have the feeling your future might be under discussion in that room, as well as your past.'

'It feels a bit like being a prisoner in the dock, awaiting the deliberations of the jury.'

Eve's prophecy was proved strikingly accurate, when, after a few minutes, Trudi returned, alone, her face tearstained. She looked at the man she now knew to be her father, her expression unfathomable. 'Mum wants to talk to you,' she told him.

Once Crowther had left, Trudi looked round the kitchen, then walked over to where Charlie was standing. They began talking, in a low murmur, little more than a whisper. Although Eve and I could hear that a conversation was taking place, their voices were too quiet to make out the gist of it. I couldn't see the girl's face, but from Charlie's expression and body language I guessed that she had asked him something, and Charlie was responding, providing reassurance.

I realized something we'd all overlooked. Behind the fame and public persona that came with being a singing star, Trudi was simply another teenager, less than twelve months older than Eve's nephew. Trudi turned and smiled a little uncertainly at us. 'I think Mum might want to stay here tonight with Mr ... er ... my father. Would it be all right if I come to your place on my own? I know Mum said you'd offered, but I just wanted to make sure.' She looked anxiously from one to the other.

'I told her it would be OK,' Charlie added, glaring at each of us in turn, as if defying us to contradict him.

'Charlie's right,' Eve reassured her, 'we'll be happy to have you to stay.'

Moments later, Crowther and Sheila returned. Although neither of them was smiling, it was clear that some form of agreement had been reached. 'Sheila and I have a lot to talk about,' Crowther said. 'Things we can only discuss on our own.' His voice reflected a level of confidence I hadn't seen before, which augured well. 'We wondered if you could look after Trudi tonight and tomorrow?'

'Trudi's already asked us,' Eve told them. 'And Charlie would never have forgiven us if we'd said no to the girl he idolizes.'

I have to say that if Eve had tried her hardest, she couldn't have come up with a more effective revenge on Charlie for his earlier comment than by embarrassing him in front of Trudi. He went bright scarlet, and his colour was enhanced even more when Trudi turned and smiled at him.

We left a few minutes later, and whilst I took Sheila's suitcase from the car, we waited for Trudi and Sheila to say their farewells. Charlie nudged me, he was smiling, and knowing how keen an observer of people he was, I thought I could guess what was coming. 'Adam, do you remember when Mr Crowther was talking about the work he'd done to renovate the house, didn't he say he'd only bought one bed? Maybe I got that wrong.'

'No, Charlie, you didn't get it wrong, as you know very well. However, we do have several beds at Eden House, and all our bedroom doors have locks on them, so don't let what's happening here influence you.'

'I wouldn't dream of it,' he protested. 'And I have to say I think you've got a very dirty mind.'

Chapter Eleven

As I drove, I listened to the conversation in the back seat. Eve was asking Trudi about her childhood. 'It must have been difficult for your mother, bringing you up on her own, but I must say she's done a terrific job.'

'I did miss having a father, but now I know why he wasn't there I can understand. Mum has been great. I never gave it any thought before, but she must have been heartbroken when I insisted that I wanted to make singing my career. She never told me what had happened, just that my father was dead. I realize now that she must have been afraid of history repeating itself, but she never showed it. As for the rest, the trust Gerry ... er ... my father arranged ensured we had all we needed, and then there was Mum's salary. She's a teacher,' Trudi explained, 'and a very good one. Even without her pay, we were never short of money.'

Trudi's words acted as a catalyst, and as I mulled her phrase, "we were never short of money" the elusive memory that had haunted me since our first talk with Crowther hit home. So sudden and surprising was the revelation that I slammed the brakes on, bringing the car to a juddering halt. 'Adam, what is the matter?' Eve asked. 'Are you all right?'

I smiled into the rear-view mirror. 'I'm fine. Sorry about the emergency stop, but what Trudi said sparked off a memory. Something about having enough money set me thinking.'

'It must have been some thought,' Charlie remarked,

'because it nearly sent me through the windscreen.'

'Sorry about that, Charlie. Think back to the first time we saw Gerry and he told us about meeting Carl Long. He said that Long told him he was penniless, living rough and needed money for a flight to America so he could get work.'

'Yes, what of it?'

'That's rubbish. Why did he go to Crowther for help? Why was he sleeping rough, as he claimed?'

'I'm still not with you,' Eve told me. 'Neither am I,' Charlie agreed. Trudi simply looked baffled.

'According to the biographical notes Lew Pattison gave us, Carl Long came from a very wealthy and privileged background. Not only had his grandmother left him a very large bequest in her will, but his father had a highly paid job in the City, and his mother was an American heiress. As for sleeping rough, the family owned several houses both here and in the States.'

'Perhaps they disapproved of his lifestyle and disowned him.'

'If that's the case, why did his parents spend a small fortune on private detectives they employed to search for him? By then it was a year or so too late, but it doesn't sound to me as if they'd washed their hands of him.'

'Why would Carl Long tell Mr Crowther a load of lies?' Charlie asked.

'My guess is that he was the decoy needed to get Crowther to the Tyne Bridge. We all know pretty much what happened after that. The plot failed because Long overdid it. They were very similar in appearance, and in the darkness, anyone seeing that jacket would have been fooled into thinking they were looking at Crowther.'

I'd opted for the scenic route, and to let Trudi see the dale at its best, I drove at a leisurely pace through Rowandale Forest and over the high moor beyond. As we began our descent towards Laithbrigg, I saw flashing lights in the distance ahead of us. After rounding a couple of hairpin bends, I had to brake. A police car was parked across the narrow road, blocking access to the lower slopes. The driver walked back to us.

'Sorry, sir, you can't go any further. You'll have to divert.' He gestured towards a narrow lane to our right.

'What's the problem?'

'A car's gone over the edge and down into the beck. That's all I know. That road takes you through Gillside and you can rejoin this one on the outskirts of Laithbrigg.'

'It's OK, we live in Laithbrigg, that's not a problem. Let's hope nobody's seriously hurt.'

'I wouldn't like to say, sir.' He didn't sound too hopeful. 'It's quite a drop – and it ended up on its roof.'

The final leg of our journey was completed in thoughtful silence, broken only by my comment that the road over Rowandale High Moor was a treacherous one, especially in winter, but I was surprised such an accident had happened on a clear bright summer afternoon.

We'd not been long in the house, and Eve had just shown Trudi round, when I suggested we treat the youngsters to a meal out that evening.

'You're just trying to get out of doing the cooking.'

'Don't judge everyone by your standards! I just thought Trudi might feel a bit lonely and upset by what's happened, and by being left with virtual strangers. She can't have expected her mother to desert her when they came here this morning.'

'Sheila hasn't deserted her.'

'No, but it might seem that way to Trudi. If we got to the Admiral Nelson there will be lots of people about and that in itself will be a distraction.'

Eve smiled. 'That's a really kind thought, Adam. You can be nice when you put your mind to it. It may not happen often, but it's good when it does.'

Sometimes, when you're talking to Eve, it's like being

near a scorpion. You've got to beware of the sting in the tail.

A few minutes before we were due to set off for the Admiral Nelson, the phone rang. Eve answered it, her greeting of, 'Hi, sis,' informing me that it was Charlie's mother calling from America. She had rung a couple of times already to check on Charlie's condition. 'Yes, he's fine,' Eve reassured her. 'Hang on, I'll get him, if I can drag him away from the TV and his other distraction. No, I'll let him tell you.'

As Charlie was assuring his mother that he was fully recovered and being well looked after, Eve told me, 'Apparently they're off to some pop concert soon. Harriet didn't get chance to tell me what it was, but apparently the twins are really excited and want to tell Charlie all about it. Tony wangled the tickets somehow.'

I heard Charlie's voice change, as he greeted one of his sisters. 'Hi, Sammy, how's the Big Apple. 'Really? Queen, did you say? Where are they playing? Madison Square Gardens. Well, lucky you! No, Sammy, I'm not a bit jealous. Hang on a second, you'll find out why.' He shouted through to the lounge and Trudi appeared. 'Sammy, I've someone here who wants to say hello.' He handed the receiver to Trudi. 'Here, Trudi, please say hello to my sister Sammy, will you?'

Trudi laughed as she did as he asked. 'Hi, Sammy, my name's Trudi, Trudi Bell. I think Charlie is really nice, and I think you're very lucky to have a brother like him. Hope you're enjoying your holiday in the States. I heard Charlie say you're going to Madison Square Gardens, is that right? To see Queen, yes? I played there a few months ago as a support act. It's awesome. I'm sure you'll enjoy it. If you get chance to meet the boys, say hello to Brian May for me. He's a really nice guy. Bye, now, I'll put Charlie back on.'

It seemed that Sammy was having difficulty believing

what she'd heard, because she demanded to speak to Eve or me. Charlie handed me the receiver with a grin of pure evil. 'She wants someone to tell her who that really was.'

'Hi, Sammy.' Charlie hovered close to the phone, with Trudi alongside him. Both of them were afflicted with a severe attack of giggles. 'Yes, Sammy, that was Trudi Bell. Yes, the Trudi Bell, the famous pop singer. No, we're not winding you up. She's staying with us for a few days. It's too long a story, but I'm sure Charlie will tell you everything when you get back. Say hi to Becky for me.' I passed my regards to her parents and hung up.

'That'll teach her to try and rub my nose in it,' Charlie said. He turned to Trudi and gave her a warm smile. 'Thanks for doing that. Older sisters can be a real pain sometimes. When they're not being a pain, it's because they're asleep.'

Although it might have caused questions had we taken a couple of youngsters into a pub in a town or city centre, out in the wilds of the Yorkshire Dales much of the social activity centred around places such as the Admiral Nelson. We had been there a while without so much as a raised eyebrow until one of the regulars recognised Trudi. That did our standing in the community no harm, and any chance that the young singer would feel out of place or neglected vanished in the warmth of the greeting she received from many of the drinkers.

My reasons for suggesting the Nelson were not only because of the excellence of the beer, but also because the landlady was a superb chef. I was watching Trudi handling her new admirers, admiring her skill and tact, when a voice close by said, 'Did'st tha see it?'

I turned, to find Ezekiel Calvert standing alongside me. I wasn't surprised to see him, or to find that his glass was empty. 'See what, Zeke?' As I asked, I automatically reached out and took his glass, handing it to the barmaid with a nod.

As she was refilling it and attending to the rest of my order, Calvert said, 'T' accident on t' High Moor, o' course. Or supposed accident.' He sniffed.

'No, it had already happened when we got there. What do you mean by "supposed accident", Zeke? Did you see what happened?'

'Aye, I saw some of it. I were up on t' moor. We've a couple of hen harriers after t' young grouse.'

As head keeper for the Rowandale estate, and with the grouse shooting season little more than a month away, much of Calvert's time would be spent up on the moors. 'Some of it? What does that mean?'

I was treated to a withering glance. I wondered if Eve had been giving Zeke lessons in them. 'It means I didn't see it end. I saw what were going on before, though – and I heard t' rest.'

'Would you care to explain?' It was easier to ask than trying to solve Zeke's puzzles.

'I heard t' noise of engines first.' Calvert made it sound more like 'injuns'. 'It were plain somebody were going too quick on that road. I looked over t' valley and then I saw them.'

'Them?'

'Aye, two cars. First off I thought they were racing each other, but then I saw t' one behind shoving t' other wi' them cow-catcher things.'

'You saw two cars, and one of them was fitted with bull bars?'

'That's right, only it weren't a car. It were one of them pick-me-ups.'

I bit my lip at Zeke's description of a pick-up truck. 'What make was it?' I couldn't for the moment think of too many vehicles in the UK that would have been fitted with bull bars, but perhaps they had been added as extras.

'No idea, it were too far away, and going too fast.'

'What happened next?'

'I saw it ram t' other car. Not once, but three times. Then they went round a bend out of sight. Tha knows, where t' moor top is.'

I pictured the area. A large shoulder of land obscured the road from where Zeke must have been standing. 'Was that the last you saw of them?'

'Aye, but I heard them. There were another loud bang, then nowt but t' sound of t' engines, then a hell of a crash. I reckon that were t' car going off t' edge. Then, nowt. A few minutes after, I heard one of 'em drive off.'

'And you reckon the pick-up driver was deliberately forcing the car off the road?'

'Aye, that's what I told Johnny Pickersgill.'

At that moment, the landlord interrupted to inform us that our meal was ready. We collected Charlie and Trudi, who were attempting, without much success, to play darts, and headed for the dining room. Word of our celebrity guest must have gone round the bar like wildfire, because not only did the young waitress request Trudi's autograph, but when we emerged back into the bar, I noticed that almost all the locals seemed to be staring at us. Trudi seemed to take it all in her stride, a fact that Eve commented on as we walked back up the hill to Eden House.

'It can get a bit tiresome,' Trudi admitted, 'not like in there, but if I'm out shopping with Mum and people come up to us in the street. It used to worry me at first, but now I'm used to it.'

'I have to admit I never had that problem. People rarely recognized me in the street.'

Trudi looked at me. 'Were you famous? Sorry, that sounds awful.'

I laughed. 'I used to be a foreign correspondent, but when I appeared on TV it was usually from somewhere remote in Africa, so people didn't connect that image with a man walking down the high street here.'

'Was that why Mr Pattison asked you to find my father?'

'No, it was because Adam and my Aunt Evie specialize in murders and mysteries,' Charlie told her.

When we entered the house, he was in the middle of telling her about the events from eighteen months earlier, when Eve and I had met – and nearly been killed. Halfway through his account, Trudi interrupted.

'Sorry, Charlie, but did you say you live in a *castle*?'

'Er ... yes.' Charlie seemed hesitant to admit it.

'You mean a real castle, with suits of armour and dungeons and things?'

Charlie nodded. 'Yes, but Dad got someone in to seal off the dungeon where the skeletons were found.'

'Skeletons? What skeletons?'

'Enough, Charlie,' Eve interrupted. 'You can tell Trudi the rest in the morning. The poor girl won't get a wink of sleep if you fill her mind with horrors just before bedtime.'

It was difficult to tell which of them was more disappointed by the ban, and I heard Trudi extracting a promise from Charlie that he would finish his story first thing next day.

Chapter Twelve

We returned to Allerscar the following afternoon, by which time Trudi had heard all about our adventures at Mulgrave Castle, and discovered Charlie's aristocratic background. I guess a lot of people his age would have been anxious to impress by telling a pretty girl such as Trudi chapter and verse, but Charlie seemed more embarrassed about his heritage than proud. Watching Trudi's awed expression, though, I could tell she was impressed. We were glad of the distraction hoping it would keep Trudi's mind away from the events of the past twenty-four hours.

When we arrived at Lovely Cottage, there was no sign of life. We knocked on the front door, but to no avail. As we marched in single file up the path alongside the house, I could see no sign of either Crowther or Sheila. We tried the back door, which proved to be open, but when we called out, we got no response. I was beginning to get concerned, and so, judging by her expression, was Eve.

'Perhaps they're down in the garden,' Charlie suggested.

We walked slowly down the path beside the lawn, past the long, neat rows of young plants until we reached the greenhouses. There was no sign of life in them, and it was only after we rounded the hen huts and reached the windmill that we saw the couple in the distance. They were standing at the end of the orchard, close to the wall that marked the end of Crowther's property. Their arms were around each other's waists, and it was clear they were oblivious to everything but each other.

I glanced sideways, and saw Charlie and Trudi exchange knowing smiles. Eve coughed, loudly enough to attract the couple's attention. They turned, and Crowther greeted us. 'Hi there. We were just discussing my plans to expand the market garden and produce my own brand of flour.'

I'll bet you were, I thought. Judging by the way they'd been looking at one another, the last things on their minds had been either flour or vegetables. Later, as we were seated around the kitchen table over a cup of tea, Sheila asked Trudi the question that signalled her decision.

'How would you feel about living here? With your father and me,' she added.

Trudi hesitated before answering. 'I don't know. But I think I'd like it, Mum, if that's what *you* want.'

'We do, Trudi, but it has to be the right thing for all of us.' It was Crowther who said this, not Sheila, and up to that point I'd wondered how much Trudi's fame had set her apart from other teenagers. Her reply, however, proved that despite her stardom and all that went with it, despite the adulation of countless fans, she was as normal as a teenager could be.

Trudi thought for a moment before adding, 'I could only agree if I had a recording studio, or at least a music room of my own, together with my own personal accompanist.' Into the silence that followed, she added, 'When he can spare the time from planting potatoes or parsnips, or cropping cucumbers or carrots, that is.'

Crowther burst out laughing, something I don't remember having heard before. 'I think I might be able to spare a few minutes in my crowded work schedule for you.' He reached out and took his daughter's hand. For a moment she tensed, then visibly relaxed as he said, 'Come along, and I'll show you my purpose-built, state-of-the-art recording studio. Or, as it's more commonly known round here, the garage.'

The outer shell of the building was where the resemblance to a garage started – and finished. Inside, there would have been insufficient room to fit anything bigger than a bicycle. Much of the space was taken up with the acoustic blocks, which, as Crowther explained, not only kept extraneous sound out, but reflected back almost every decibel of sound produced inside the room.

As I looked round, I realised that although my knowledge of the music industry and the various devices used was sketchy; either the shop owner had not told us the full story, or Crowther had bought a lot of equipment elsewhere. I asked him about this.

'I bought what he had, but his stock was limited, so I had to go elsewhere for much of this stuff. With it, I can replicate almost every musical instrument, and provide the effect anything from a full concert orchestra to a brass band if I need to.'

He walked across the room, pausing to flick several switches before beckoning Trudi forward. 'How do you fancy trying out that song I wrote for you?'

Trudi hesitated.

'Go on, Trudi, we'd love to hear it.'

I saw Sheila look sharply at Charlie as he spoke, then exchange glances with Eve. Better be on your best behaviour, young man, I thought. Now you've got her mother to contend with as well as your aunt.

'OK.' As she spoke, and as she looked at the sheet music he placed before her, I realised how alike father and daughter were. At first sight you only saw the strong resemblance between Trudi and her mother, but closer inspection showed her similarity to Crowther.

What followed had a hint of magic about it, as Trudi performed the song for the first time. Her clear, sweet voice was echoed and emphasised by Crowther's consummate artistry on the keyboard. When the song ended we all applauded. Sheila was clapping loudest and smiling broadly, but I could see the tears in her eyes.

After a moment, Crowther suggested she look at the other sheet music he'd placed on the stand. 'It's brand new, so I'll give you a minute or two to read it through.' As he waited, Crowther played a few notes. At one point, I thought I recognized a snatch of a familiar melody, but then Trudi looked up and said, 'OK, I'm ready.'

The second piece was even more enchanting, a haunting ballad about lost love regained. As he played, Crowther's eyes went from Trudi to Sheila and back, and I realized that this song was for them – was all about them.

'I wrote that earlier today,' Crowther told us when it ended. 'What do you think?'

Eve spoke for all of us. 'If that doesn't make number one then there's no justice in this world.'

Some of the practical matters regarding Sheila and Trudi's move north had to be left for later consideration. 'We must think about Trudi's change of school, and I'll have to give my notice in. That will mean going back to London, and I think you should come with us, Gerry.'

'That's a good idea.' Crowther held up the draft contracts Pattison's assistant had sent me and announced, 'I'll go to London with Sheila and Trudi. Together, we'll sort out Sheila's flat and make arrangements for them to move here. I will also sign and deliver these to Lew Pattison, so that Trudi can record the songs I wrote for her.'

Crowther looked at his daughter, and I think even he was surprised by her response. 'I will only record them on one condition. And that is that you play the accompaniment. These are your compositions, and nobody could do them justice like you.'

I remembered Crowther saying that he didn't much fancy the idea of a return to showbusiness. It seemed as if Trudi wasn't giving him much say in the matter.

Nevertheless, I was surprised with how easily he capitulated. 'It that's what you want, Trudi, I'd be proud to play for you.'

I was surprised by his statement, as I noticed the others were. 'Does that mean you're officially declaring yourself alive again?'

Crowther nodded. 'Yes, and what's more if possible I'd prefer to do so in my own name, rather than hiding behind an alias. That belongs to the time when I was afraid for myself, for Sheila, and for Trudi. Whatever problems being me again might cause, we face them together.'

'That might not be wise,' I said. 'Let's see what we can do.'

Sheila smiled encouragingly at him, and I guessed Crowther's new resolve owed a lot to her. She looked around the sparsely furnished lounge. 'Let's face it, Gerry, this house does need considerably more work to do the building justice. If everyone's lifestyle was as meagre as yours has been, furniture stores all over the land would have gone out of business. When we pack up my flat we can decide what furniture we want to bring here.'

Crowther smiled. 'It was all I needed at the time, but I agree, we will have to get a lot more to make this a nice home.'

'In the meantime, Trudi can continue to stay with us, can't she, Adam?' Eve asked.

'Of course she can, she's very welcome.' I wouldn't have dreamed of refusing, even without Charlie's threatening glare.

We returned to Laithbrigg early that evening. As she got into the car I noticed Trudi was clutching the sheet music Crowther had given her. 'I need to memorise the words and the melody,' she explained. 'I think Mr … er … my father rather likes the idea of me recording this while we're in London, with him providing the backing.'

When we reached the top of the hill overlooking the village, I noticed two cars parked outside Eden House. One of them I didn't recognize. The other, I knew well. It was Johnny Pickersgill's patrol car. Why, I wondered, was our amiable village bobby visiting us on Sunday evening? And who had he brought along with him?

My second question was answered when the man got out of his car and walked down the drive. 'Who is that?' Charlie asked. 'I feel I ought to know him.'

'The last time you saw him was at home when you were badly injured and drugged with painkillers,' Eve told him. 'That's Detective Inspector Hardy. But what he's doing here, I've no idea.'

Neither had I, but one thing for sure, I knew it wasn't a social call. I introduced our guests, and saw Hardy's eyes widen with surprise at Trudi's name. 'I'd like a word with you and Miss Samuels, Adam, in private I think.'

We took him through to the study along with Pickersgill, leaving Charlie to entertain Trudi. I waited until Eve had supplied both officers with a mug of tea before asking, 'OK, what's the problem?'

'We were asked to investigate a road accident that happened yesterday,' Pickersgill began the explanation. 'I don't know if you heard about it, but a car went off the road on Rowandale High Moor?'

'Yes, we were in the pub last night and Zeke Calvert mentioned it. He saw some of what happened and didn't seem to think it was an accident, though.'

'Neither do we,' Hardy picked up the tale, 'for several reasons. First of all, the car was stolen. That doesn't in itself mean that what happened wasn't a tragic accident, but when we heard Calvert's story and got the results of the post-mortem, we realised we were dealing with something far more sinister. The pathologist said that the driver's injuries weren't all consistent with those he might have suffered from the car going off the road. He believes the man was hit repeatedly with a blunt, heavy object, such as a hammer, probably after the vehicle crashed. Putting those facts with the gamekeeper's account of what he saw and heard, I believe we have a killer on the loose in this area.'

'That sounds very disturbing, but I can't see how we can help you. I know Eve has some dodgy friends, but I don't think any of them are car thieves.'

Hardy smiled briefly, but I couldn't see much evidence of humour in his eyes. 'Perhaps it would help if you told us why the dead man was carrying your business card in his pocket? And why he had a road atlas in the car with the village of Laithbrigg circled in red? By the look of things, he was either on his way to visit you, or had already been. However, as the car was heading towards Laithbrigg before the incident, I'd suggest he was on his way here.'

Eve and I looked at one another, perplexed and troubled by this news. We had handed several business cards out during the interviews we conducted in our search for Crowther. But we couldn't work out who might have been coming to see us, or why. 'Have you identified the dead man?'

'No, he had nothing in his pockets save some cash and your card. We rather hoped you might be able to put a name to him. If it had been his own car rather than a stolen one, that would have been different, of course.'

I had an idea of how to narrow down the identity. 'Where was the car stolen from?'

'Outside a house close to Leeds city centre. Why do you want to know?'

'We handed a few cards out recently, but only two in Leeds.' I felt a heavy sickness in the pit of my stomach. The dead man had to be Pete Firth. Admittedly Pete was a bit of a Jack-the-lad, but I'd rather liked him. I could tell Eve shared my fear, and was equally upset at the thought that Firth had been murdered. Despite my concern, one thought struck me. Why had Firth been on that road? If he had been coming to Laithbrigg, there was no way he'd have taken such a circuitous route, one that was twenty or so miles longer than the direct way. He might have been lost, of course, but even that I doubted. Had he been coming from the north, rather than the south-east, that would have been a different matter.

I explained my suspicion to Hardy and Pickersgill, adding that I supposed there was an outside chance that Firth had given my business card to someone else. Even to me, it sounded as if I was clutching at straws.

'There's an easy way to settle it,' Eve suggested. 'All we have to do is phone Firth's home and see if he's there.'

Having put forward the idea, Eve was given the unenviable task of making the call. The conversation went on for some time, and I could tell Eve wouldn't have good news to report. The agitated squawking I could hear at the other end of the line told me that Eve was speaking to Julie and she was extremely upset. After a few minutes, two questions from Eve more or less convinced me that the dead man had to be Firth. 'And he didn't tell you where he was going? Did he mention the possibility that he might be coming here to see Adam?'

More squawking followed, with Eve attempting to reassure Julie. It didn't seem that she'd been blessed with success when she eventually put the phone down. She looked at me, then at Hardy. 'Julie says that she hasn't seen Pete since the day before yesterday. He told her he'd had a visitor but wouldn't say who. Whatever happened really upset Pete. Julie says she's never seen him in such a state. Then he packed a small bag and left. He told Julie that he'd be back in a few days. She's ever so worried, because it's so out of character.'

'It sounds to me as if the body must be this man Firth,' Hardy said when Eve had finished. 'Now, would you mind telling me exactly what is going on? Johnny here says you've got involved in another investigation. I'd have thought you'd fight shy of them, after your previous experiences.'

'We didn't set out to investigate anything,' I protested. 'And as far as I'm concerned, we still aren't investigating. All we agreed to was a request from a friend of Eve's, who wanted to find someone.'

'What sort of someone?'

'We were asked to try and find a dead man.'

'By the sound of it, I'd say you've been remarkably successful, wouldn't you? I assume you mean this man Crowther?'

'How did you know that?'

Johnny smiled. 'Shotgun certificate! I wasn't at liberty to say,' he added by way of explanation.

Between us, Eve and I took Hardy through the whole story, stressing our concerns regarding the findings becoming public knowledge.

Before they left, Hardy said he was going to look into the original findings to try and determine how the body in the Tyne had been identified as Gerry Crowther. He also got me to promise to visit the mortuary the following morning, to try to help identify Firth's body.

Although Charlie later tried to pump us for information, Eve and I resisted his pleas.

Next morning I set off for Thorsby Hospital mortuary to meet a constable and view the corpse.

'I shouldn't be away that long,' I told Eve, 'I feel sure it will only be a formality, sadly.'

I was getting to be really good at making rash statements I couldn't justify. Contrary to my prediction, it was early afternoon when I returned to Eden House. My mind was filled with questions. Unfortunately, it was empty of answers. Before I could attempt to search for solutions, I had to answer Eve's queries, and settle her concerns.

'Where on earth have you been? I've been ever so worried.'

'Sorry, darling, it took longer than I anticipated.'

'Why was that? I thought it would be a formality. I even rang the mortuary, and they said you left ages ago.'

'I had to go see Hardy afterwards. That wasn't planned.'

'But why? Was it Firth's body? Was he the victim?'

I hesitated before replying, knowing there was no easy way to answer. 'No, it wasn't. It was Steve Thompson.'

Eve looked astounded, much as I imagined I must have looked earlier when I saw the corpse. 'That doesn't make sense. Hardy told us the car was stolen in Leeds, and Thompson lives in Newcastle.'

'Lived,' I corrected her.

'Don't be so bloody pedantic. What on earth was Thompson doing stealing a car in Leeds?'

'I have absolutely no idea.'

'And where is Pete Firth?'

I could think of no better answer than my previous one.

Having got the identification, and with the information we'd supplied, the police were able to piece together most of Thompson's movements from the time he left home until his death. We learned about it the following day, when we received a visit from Johnny Pickersgill, who provided explanations – in return for copious amounts of tea.

'It seems that Thompson told his wife he had to go to Leeds on business, as he put it. He went by train, we think, and returned the following day in a car he told her he'd hired. She said she mooched around the house all that day, and eventually, after a sleepless night, announced that he was going to see "that author bloke".' Pickersgill grinned. 'I suppose that means you. That was the last she saw of him.'

'We still don't know why he went to Leeds, unless it was to see Firth,' Eve suggested.

Pickersgill shook his head. 'We're still not sure. However, DS Middleton informed us that during the house-to-house enquiries after the Jimmy Mitchell murder, one of Mitchell's neighbours reported talking to a man answering Thompson's description a couple of days ago. When she told him what had happened to Mitchell, she said he went as white as a sheet.'

'So you think Thompson learned what had happened to Mitchell then went to see Pete Firth and nicked the car to get back home? Then after he thought over what he'd been told he decided to come and see us, is that it?' Eve asked.

'That's our belief, yes.'

Despite this, I was left with some big unanswered queries. Why had Thompson gone to visit Mitchell? And what had been said between Thompson and Firth that had them both spooked? Above all, where had Firth disappeared to and why? All valid questions, none of them answerable.

We debated long and hard whether or not to tell Gerry and Sheila about Thompson's murder. By 'we', I meant Eve and I. The discussion took place when we were alone, with Charlie and Trudi watching an American cop show on TV. 'We have to tell him. We must make sure he knows the danger,' I told her.

'What if it sends him back into his shell? What if he runs away again? I don't think we should put Sheila through that a second time.'

'Having met her, I don't believe she'd let that happen. As I remember, she didn't have any choice in the matter before.'

'I still think it's wrong.'

'Look at it this way, Eve, there's been no threat against Crowther. The violence has occurred because people were about to talk to us. That sounds to me as if someone is trying to cover up past crimes rather than attack Gerry.'

'If people were killed to stop them talking to us, how come Neville Wade is unharmed?'

I looked at Eve, and saw the same thought had occurred to her even as she spoke. I glanced at the clock. 'It's too late to call him now. The surgery will be closed. I'll phone him in the morning.'

'If Wade has been left alone, I guess that means he doesn't know anything incriminating,' she suggested.

'That sounds logical, and I'll go further. I believe Mitchell and Thompson might have been the men Julie saw that night on the bridge. They might have been the ones who mistook Carl Long for Crowther, knocked him on the head, and dumped him in the Tyne.'

'But why? They wouldn't do that, surely? They must have known it would be the end for Northern Lights.'

'True, but if they were paid enough, or coerced into doing it, that might have taken precedence over their music career. Let's face it, the industry is a very uncertain one.'

'Coerced, in what way?'

'I'm not sure, but I remember something Julie Firth said about Mitchell. Julie would have been what, seventeen or eighteen at the time?'

'No more than that,' Eve agreed.

'She told us she went out with Mitchell once, but that she was too old for him. Thinking back to that era, many of the fans would be under the age of consent. If someone had proof that Mitchell and Thompson had been with underage girls, they would have been ripe for blackmail.'

'That's disgusting, but having met Thompson, I wouldn't have put it past him, and Mitchell's reputation was less than savoury, as I recall, without what Julie said. You may be right about their sexual habits, but they weren't who Julie saw on the riverbank.'

I eyed her smug expression suspiciously. 'And what

makes you so sure of that?'

'They were in the dressing room when Gerry disappeared. Everyone said so.'

'OK, so I forgot that point – I can't be expected to remember everything.'

'Poor thing, getting forgetful are we?' Eve patted me gently on the head, only to find herself in an armlock. 'I surrender,' she cried. 'So why do you reckon the killer hasn't had another go at Gerry, if he was the prime target all along?'

'Just because we know Gerry's alive and well, it doesn't mean the killer does. I think the killer might have been told we were asking about Northern Lights, and gathering a lot of information, which is why they were afraid of either Mitchell or Thompson spilling the beans on something they knew, could even be drugs.' I shrugged. 'They might still believe that the body pulled from the Tyne was Crowther's. And even if they suspect Crowther is alive, they can't have any idea where to look for him. He could be anywhere from Land's End to John O'Groats. He might not even be in this country, as far as they know.'

'OK, you've convinced me. I suppose I was assuming the killer had knowledge simply because we did.'

We told Gerry and Sheila next morning, along with Charlie and Trudi. I was surprised by how well they took the news. 'It isn't going to affect our plans,' Sheila told everyone. 'Last night, Gerry asked me to marry him and I accepted.'

There was a break, as Trudi hugged her mother and after a slight hesitation, her new-found father and we congratulated the couple. 'Let me make it plain,' Sheila told us, 'I want to be known as Sheila Crowther, not Sheila Hardin or Sheila anything else. If someone has a problem with that, or intends to harm my husband or my daughter, they'll have me to contend with. Some evil people have already cost me almost twenty years of happiness. I am not prepared to forfeit another day.'

'Why don't I phone Alice Pattison and find out when Lew will be back from America?' Eve suggested. 'We could come along with you to London, if that makes you feel any easier.'

'There's only one problem,' Crowther told us. 'I need to find someone to tend my plants. I've a lot of vegetables will need picking soon, and there's watering to do. Added to that, the hens have to be fed and the eggs collected.'

'Leave that with me,' Eve told him. 'I think I know someone who might be prepared to help.'

Next morning I rang Neville Wade, and was relieved to hear the vet was in the best of health. Before I ended the call, I asked him a question that sprang to mind following my discussion with Eve the previous day. When I replaced the receiver, I wandered through to the kitchen and told her. 'Wade said the most exciting thing that's happened since we saw him was a German Shepherd bitch giving birth to a litter of nine puppies.'

'You were on a long time just for that news.'

'I took the opportunity to ask him about Thompson and Mitchell. It seems I was right, sadly. Their taste was for very young girls, but he's no idea if anyone might have been blackmailing them. I told him about Gerry and Sheila getting back together.'

'Was he pleased?'

'I'm not sure. He sounded happy enough, but I sensed that he had reservations. Although I did suggest Sheila might want a word with him!'

'I don't envy him. Anyway, while you were on the phone I managed to arrange a babysitter for Gerry's hens and plants.'

'Who? How?'

'Henry Price, the milkman. I remembered he has a big garden and grows a lot of produce, so when he delivered our milk a few minutes ago I popped outside to talk to him. I asked him if he could fit in tending Gerry's stuff. He'd be happy to. He finishes his deliveries by late morning and then has nothing to do for the rest of the day. He's also keen to talk to Gerry about offering eggs for sale on his milk round.'

Chapter Thirteen

Eve's conversation with Alice Pattison was frustrating, as she was unsure when her husband would be back from the States. 'He'd hoped to be able to fly back this weekend,' Eve reported, 'but it looks as if it will be later this week. Alice has promised to phone as soon as she knows anything. She's aware how important it is.'

In the end, we set off on Friday. The previous afternoon had been spent introducing Crowther to Henry Price, who was to take care of the produce during his absence. Eve, Charlie, and I would be staying with the Pattisons. We drove there after seeing Crowther, Sheila, and Trudi safely installed in Sheila's flat. That evening, we brought Lew and Alice up to date with everything that had happened. When we explained how we'd tracked Crowther down I could see Pattison was impressed.

'We were lucky,' Eve told him, 'because Adam recognised Crowther's alias. He made the connection between the name Charles Hardin and Crowther's idol, Buddy Holly.'

'Of course! A lot of musicians idolise their predecessors and contemporaries. Billy Quinn was a huge fan of Duane Eddy, and Wayne Barnett, who left the group, was a great admirer of Dion.'

When it came to describing current events, both Lew and Alice were shocked and appalled by the violent deaths of the two former members of Northern Lights, stunned by the events that had caused Crowther to disappear, and the implications of our theory about Carl Long's death.

'That isn't the worst,' I told Lew. 'We believe the only way the killer could have learned about us going to talk to band members was via a mole in your organisation, as you suggested previously, and we believe it must be someone who has been with you a long time. Have you any idea who it might be?'

Pattison shook his head. 'I've no idea. Most of my staff have been there since I started the business. I can't believe anyone would be that disloyal.'

When we told him of Trudi's plans to record the songs Crowther had written for her, with her father playing the accompaniment, I could see Pattison the businessman take over. 'This could make Trudi an even bigger star,' he told us. 'That song is a class above all the other material she's had to work with so far.'

'Wait until you hear the other one,' Eve told him. 'We think that's better still.'

'Then we'll need a second contract,' Lew said.

'There is one minor problem, but I think Alice could answer it. Is it in order for Crowther to sign the contracts in the name of Charles Hardin? Although he wants to come out of hiding, we're keen to protect his identity as long as we can.'

'I'm no expert on contracts,' Alice replied, 'it isn't my field of law, but I can't see a snag. Many actors and actresses do it, and authors too.'

'Plus a lot of performers,' Pattison added. 'A large percentage of them have almost forgotten the name they were born with. How are we going to protect Gerry's anonymity when they cut the record, though?'

'We had an idea about that as well,' Eve told him. 'Are you busy on Sunday?'

On Sunday morning Lew and Alice ferried all of us to the offices of Pattison Music and Management to sort out the contracts. The offices were not exactly what I'd envisaged. The mental image I'd conjured up was of a far newer building, one that was heavy on plate glass with plenty of stainless steel to hold it in place.

In fact, the red brick exterior housed a far more traditional suite of offices and meeting rooms, with the accent on comfort rather than an outward display of luxury. Lew told me that the idea was to create an atmosphere of solid, reliable reassurance to their clients, who were involved in what was a very chancy industry, with a high failure rate. The walls of the reception area were decorated with large photographs. The subjects were all groups or solo artists in concert. Although I cannot claim to be a music aficionado, even I was able to put a name to most of them.

We headed straight for Lew's secretary's office and as I was the only one with sufficient skill on a typewriter, I was given the job of typing the second contract, a rather wordy document.

'Better leave the desk just as you found it,' Lew warned me, 'Melissa's obsessive about tidiness.'

'Yes, and it wouldn't do to upset her,' Alice added, 'She'll sulk for days, and Lew's life won't be worth living.'

When that was done, we got back in the cars and drove out to the suburbs, to the recording studio, where we witnessed a little showbusiness magic. Lew proved his experience in the industry had a practical grounding as he acted as session manager, watching over the recording in a professional manner.

We all returned to the Pattisons' house, where Lew and Alice had organised a party to celebrate Gerry's return. At one point Lew said, 'I owe you and Eve more than I can hope to repay, and I feel sure Gerry is of the same mind. I must settle up with you for all your hard work.'

'Don't even think of it, Lew,' Eve told him, 'Adam and I wouldn't hear of it. If you feel desperately anxious to lighten your wallet, send a donation to a worthy charity.'

I saw that Pattison was about to object, but I nipped it in the bud. 'Apart from anything else, Lew, our work isn't done yet.'

Pattison's gaze strayed to Crowther, who was talking to Alice and Sheila. He looked relaxed, smiling, content. 'I don't follow you.'

'There are two murders that remain unsolved, and I for one don't believe the danger to Crowther and his family is by any means over. Luckily, we don't believe those responsible know that Gerry is still alive. We're sure they think he perished that night in Newcastle. However, that could change at any moment, and we want to be one jump ahead of them should that happen.'

'How do you plan to do that?'

Eve and I had been discussing that very issue. 'I think we ought to revisit your offices tomorrow, when all the staff are present. I think we should go around asking questions of anyone who was involved around the time Northern Lights was performing. If we're right, and there is a mole within your business, our presence might just panic them. Or at the very least alarm them sufficiently for them to make a mistake and give themselves away.'

'That's fine by me, except that I won't be there. I'll speak to Harvey, my number two, and he'll take care of you.'

Next morning, having arranged matters with Sheila, we dropped Charlie off at her flat. She and Gerry were going to take Charlie and Trudi on a sightseeing tour. Eve and I went from there to Lew's offices.

Having announced our arrival to the receptionist, we waited for a few moments in the large foyer before a door to our left opened. The man who entered was about the same age as Pattison. He was small, fair-haired, slight of build, and good-looking with slightly effeminate features. He walked over to us with a quick, short stride which could uncharitably be described as mincing. His voice was gentle and pleasantly welcoming.

'Mr Bailey? Miss Samuels?'

He shook hands with each of us in turn. 'My name's Harvey Jackson; Lew's assistant, we've spoken on the phone. Lew phoned to tell me you were coming, and that you needed to look round and talk to everyone. He was hoping to have got back in time to meet up with you here, but by the sound of it, things aren't going too well at the recording studios, so he doesn't think he'll make it in time. I've a little job to do, so if you wouldn't mind waiting in Lew's office, I'll get you a drink.'

As we walked along the corridor leading to Pattison's office, we had the chance to inspect yet more photos. The artists were much more recognizable, and I was able to identify several icons of the British music industry. The statement those images made about the stature and achievements of Pattison Music and Management was hardly subtle, but any aspiring performer could hardly fail to be impressed, even overawed, on seeing them – which was probably exactly what Pattison intended. Minutes later we were seated in his office, unseen the previous day, revelling in the opulence of the furnishings. All pretensions to modesty had ended at the threshold. If the rest of the building made a statement about the reliability of the company, Lew's own suite shouted their success. As I sank into the soft, embracing cushions of the sofa, I had a momentary fear that I might never free myself from their clutches. Jackson held open the door for a pretty, blonde woman, who I guessed was in her late thirties. She advanced towards us carrying a tray containing a coffee pot and a plate, on which was a young mountain of biscuits. Jackson introduced her as Pattison's secretary, Melissa Norton. 'Melissa will be in the outer office should you need anything.' He coughed politely, as he addressed Eve, 'If you need to freshen up, the facilities are through that door to the left. Please excuse me; I have to interview a comedian.' He smiled slightly. 'At least, he says he's a comedian, but he hasn't convinced me yet.'

He raised his hand in salutation and departed in the wake of the secretary. Eve said something, but my attention was distracted, and I had to ask her to repeat it.

'I said that he seems very nice. Don't you agree?'

'Er … yes, I suppose so.' I was still pondering what I'd seen.

Eve misinterpreted my hesitation. 'You didn't like him? I never thought of you as someone who would take an instant dislike to a man having only met him minutes before.'

'That's not it at all,' I protested. I was about to say more, to explain, but before I could speak, the office door opened and Melissa Norton re-entered the room, accompanied by another woman, who could have been her twin, so alike were they in looks and attire. Melissa introduced her as Judith Lane, who she told us was Harvey Jackson's assistant and the company's personnel manager.

'Mr Pattison asked us to dig out the personnel files for anyone who has worked for the company for fifteen years or longer,' Judith explained. She set down a sizeable mound of files on the coffee table.

'Those are the ones for anyone still with the company,' Melissa told us. 'Do you need the ones for people who are no longer with us? Sorry, I mean the ones who don't work here now, not those who've died. Mr Pattison said to ask you, as he wasn't sure.'

'I think these will do just fine,' Eve looked at me for confirmation. 'What do you think, Adam? Will these give you all you need for your research?'

'I'm sure they will.' As I spoke, I saw a look of relief pass between the two women.

'I'm awfully glad about that,' Melissa told us, 'the others are stored in the basement and not easily accessible.'

Our examination of the files was long, boring, and ultimately fruitless. We had barely finished when Jackson rejoined us, with more apologies, which we dismissed as unnecessary. 'Lew asked me to show you round and introduce you to members of our team. Would you care to start in the boardroom? Two of our most senior executives are waiting in there.'

The boardroom reminded me of a banqueting suite in a stately home, and as I looked at the huge oblong table that almost filled the space, I wondered if they had to use microphones when they held a board meeting. The two men seated at the far end of the table were all but dwarfed by it.

'Allow me to introduce you,' Jackson was clearly enjoying his role as tour guide. Having explained who we were, he introduced the men.

I admired Jackson's style. Apart from Lew, he was the only one who knew the book story was a cover, but I could tell he had convinced both men by the look of weary tolerance on their faces.

'Graham Stead,' Jackson indicated the middle-aged man seated on the left, 'is our contracts and royalties manager. He also has overall responsibility for the admin side of the business, which frees Barry, Lew, and myself to look after existing clients and headhunt new ones. Barry Walker here is our talent scout, one of the best in the business. Barry has signed some of the biggest names in show business to this company, long before they were famous. He specialises in vocalists and bands, while Lew covers all aspects of the industry, and I concentrate on speciality acts, plus new ventures. These days, that includes sport as well as entertainment. Lew is very keen to develop that aspect of the operation. Acting as agents for top sportsmen is becoming big business with the amounts they earn nowadays.'

We chatted to the two men before moving on to meet

the rest of the staff. I was impressed by how well everyone slotted together to perform a multitude of tasks, and I could tell Eve was too, by some of the questions she asked on our tour round the building.

'We could have twice as many people working here,' Jackson told her in answer to a question about staffing levels, 'but they would spend a lot of the time twiddling their thumbs. Yes, it can get a bit manic at times, but it's never boring, and seems to work efficiently.'

'One thing that does surprise me is how many secretaries you have.' I told him. In addition to Melissa Norton and Judith Lane we had met three others. One worked for Barry Walker, another for Graham Stead, while the third acted as liaison and filled in for any of the other four when needed.

'Ours is a business that relies heavily on swift and accurate communication, whether by phone, telex, by cable, or in letter form. Added to which, Melissa and Judith spend a lot of their time acting as mother hens for the clients,' said Jackson. 'That entails everything from ordering their new stage clothes to arranging accommodation, flights, and even concert dates and venues, which is Judith's speciality. It frees us up to devote our time and energy to developing the business.'

At the end of the tour, we thanked Jackson for his help, and as we shook hands I suggested he join us. 'We're going across the road for a coffee,' I told him, 'and we'd like to have a chat with you in private.'

Jackson looked at me for a moment, clearly speculating on my motive, before agreeing. 'Give me a few minutes while I make a phone call and then I'll join you,' he told us.

We crossed the road and entered the small coffee bar I'd noticed earlier. 'Would you mind explaining what we're doing here, and what that was all about?' Eve demanded.

'It'll become clear soon,' I told her. 'I'm only surprised you haven't guessed already.'

We had ordered coffee and were contemplating the cream cakes in the Perspex display cabinet when I spotted Jackson. I pointed, and Eve looked round in time to see Pattison's deputy enter the café.

'I'm sorry, I got tied up,' Jackson explained. 'How can I help? Is it something you prefer not to discuss in our office?'

'Actually, it's the other way round. I felt you'd be happier talking in private.'

He frowned. 'I don't understand.'

'I wanted to ask you about Billy Quinn.' I waited, conscious that Eve was staring at me in bewilderment.

Not so Jackson, who knew exactly what I was referring to. 'I'm sorry; I still don't see the need for secrecy.'

I smiled, understanding his desperate attempt to maintain the pretence of ignorance. 'I'm talking about your relationship with Billy Quinn. I am right; you and he were lovers, weren't you?'

The colour drained from Jackson's face. He stared at me, plainly horror-struck by the allegation. His reaction confirmed my guess even before he spoke. When he did, there was alarm in his expression, but far more potent was the distress. 'How did you know? How did you find out? Did someone tell you?'

'You told me, although not in so many words.' I pointed to his left hand. 'That ring must be unique. I saw a photo in Pete Firth's house, among the memorabilia he and Julie had of Northern Lights. I could see someone's hand resting on Billy's shoulder, in what was clearly a gesture of affection. The person was wearing that ring.'

Although the extent of my knowledge had shocked him, the knowledge of how I'd come by my deduction seemed to ease his fears. 'I was worried that someone had talked. I know I shouldn't be concerned after all this time, and things are different nowadays, but I would still prefer this didn't become public knowledge. The other members of the group knew about Billy, but not about me. The photo was Billy's idea. He thought it was a great joke that even though the photo would be used for publicity, he and I would be the only ones who knew the story behind it.'

'We have no interest in revealing your secret. However, in the light of certain things we've been told as we talked to members of the group, we would like you to answer some questions about what happened back then.'

Eve saw the wary expression on Jackson's face and spoke for the first time. 'You can trust Adam, Harvey. He means it, and so do I. If he even thought about revealing anything you tell us, he'd have me to answer to.'

I changed the subject slightly. 'Was Billy very upset when Crowther committed suicide?'

Jackson nodded, the distress returning to his face and his voice. 'Billy really liked Gerry. Liked and admired him, both as a musician and a person. He was very excited about something he and Gerry were about to start work on, but of course, it never happened. He told me once that Gerry and Neville were the only decent ones in the band, and if Nev could keep it in his pants a bit more, he'd be even nicer. I won't repeat what he said about the others, not with a lady present. Ladies,' he added with a self-mocking smile.

'I can guess what he said by what Neville Wade told us. Did Billy have any idea why Crowther might have killed himself?'

Again there was a long hesitation before Jackson replied. 'Yes, he did, but I don't know what it was. All he said was, "there's something really wicked going on. I wish I could tell you, but it isn't safe". That was it.'

'And you've no idea what Billy was referring to?'

'No, all I knew is that he was extremely worried for Crowther's safety after he vanished.' Jackson grimaced.

'With very good reason as things turned out.' By the sound of that, Jackson was unaware that there might be a chance of Crowther being alive.

'Has anyone attempted to use your relationship with Billy to extract information from you, or coerce you in any other way?' Eve asked. Damned good question, I thought.

'Blackmail, you mean?' Jackson shook his head, his anger instantly apparent. 'No they have not. Nor would I let them. I would not allow anyone to sully his memory in such a sordid way.'

The vehemence of his feelings for Billy Quinn and his protective attitude to his dead lover convinced me that if there was a mole in Pattison Music and Management, it certainly wasn't Harvey Jackson. I hesitated before asking the next question, mindful that the memory could still be painful. 'Can you tell us what happened the night Billy died? We've heard one or two stories, but it would be nice to get the record straight.'

'You mean you've heard those wicked slanders about Billy going on the pull and getting raped?' There were tears in Jackson's eyes, but they were of anger, not sorrow. 'That's all they were, rumours without foundation. The worst of it was, I couldn't contradict them, not without exposing our relationship,' he hesitated, collecting his thoughts. 'This is what actually happened. We went out to a nightclub. I suggested it, because I knew Billy was down in the dumps and thought it would cheer him up. I'll never forgive myself for mentioning the idea. The place we chose was one of our favourites. They were more tolerant to people like us than most pubs and clubs. You have to remember that things were very different in those days.'

Jackson sipped his coffee. 'Unfortunately, I'd eaten something that gave me an upset stomach. We'd only been in the club a few minutes when I needed the toilet urgently. I can't recall how long I was gone, maybe a quarter of an hour or so, but when I went back into the bar,

Billy was nowhere to be seen.'

The stress in Jackson's face was plain, but Eve, rested her hand on his and speaking ever so gently, persuaded him to continue with the unacceptable part of his tale. 'What happened next?'

'I couldn't believe that he'd walked out and left me, knowing I was poorly. I mean, it wasn't as if we'd quarrelled or anything.' He smiled; a sad, reminiscent expression. 'We rarely quarrelled, to be fair. I waited and waited, and when he didn't return, I asked the barman if he'd seen Billy leave.'

He stopped again, as each memory outdid the pain level of the previous one. 'He told me Billy had got into conversation with a man who walked in soon after I went to the toilet, and that Billy left with him a few minutes before I came back to the bar. He told me the man had his arm around Billy's shoulder, affectionately, and I've never been able to forgive myself for what I thought then. I was insanely jealous, because I thought Billy had met someone else,' Jackson gulped for breath, but tears ran down his cheeks unheeded. 'I thought he'd gone off, left me for someone new. I was angry, so angry, and hurt.

'That was it. That was the last I saw of Billy. It wasn't until late the next day that Lew got a phone call from the police. It was Lew who told me that Billy's body had been found in an alleyway near the club. He'd been stabbed and left there amongst all the empty bottles and dustbins.'

'Did you tell the police all this?' Eve had taken over the questioning.

'How could I? It wouldn't have served any useful purpose. It wouldn't have changed anything, certainly nothing that mattered to me. Billy was gone, and that was an end to it. I thought of killing myself, but unlike Gerry Crowther, I didn't have the guts to go ahead with it. Telling people about Billy and me would have only caused them to snigger and say awful things. And of course I would probably have ended up in prison.'

'Do you think the man Billy left with was the one who killed him?'

'I suppose he must have been, but I've no proof.'

'Did that barman give you a description?'

'Yes, but it wasn't worth anything. He told me he was white, mid-twenties, medium height and build. That description could have fitted millions of men.'

We left soon after that, having assured him again of our absolute discretion. He remained seated, his half-drunk coffee unnoticed in front of him. The expression of sadness and heartbreak in Harvey Jackson's face will remain with me for a long, long time.

Chapter Fourteen

Following our largely unproductive visit to Pattison's offices, we felt it was time to pool our meagre store of knowledge. We had learned nothing important there, certainly nothing pertinent to our enquiry. And although we were no nearer a solution, advertising our presence might have set alarm bells ringing. We had achieved nothing – little did we know we still had to reap the whirlwind of our actions.

That evening, Lew and Alice hosted another dinner party, but this time the social atmosphere ended with the dessert. From then on, it was strictly business. We decided to hold what Eve jokingly referred to as a council of war. I pointed out that it would be tricky trying to plan a battle strategy when we'd no idea who the enemy was. The humour in my remark seemed to go right over her head.

'I'll leave you to explain what we're trying to achieve,' I told her.

Eve eyed me suspiciously. She's good at that. 'Why me, when you're supposed to be the expert? I thought you used to talk for a living?'

'That was only because my producers hadn't met you.'

Eve also does a very good line in hostile glares. The one I received was of medium calibre.

She opened the discussion, to which even Trudi and Charlie were included. As chance would have it, this was a good decision.

'We're convinced the violent incidents that preceded Gerry's disappearance stem from someone in, or closely connected to, Northern Lights. If that seems like stating the obvious, what we're trying to establish is who wanted Gerry dead, and is now desperately trying to cover their tracks by eliminating people who know too much. We think the murders of Mitchell and Thompson were an attempt to prevent them talking to us.'

'A highly successful attempt, I'd say,' Alice commented.

'We thought it would help if Gerry and Lew told us all they can about the people involved in the group. I know we have the notes Lew sent us, but we need more than the factual information. We need the in-depth personal knowledge. Their characters, likes, dislikes, addictions, even seemingly trivial things that might be without apparent relevance.'

'And we're talking about the victims as well as the survivors,' I added. 'Their personal traits could be equally important, by holding a clue we could have missed elsewhere.'

'Let's begin with the line-up as it was when you left, Gerry,' Eve said. 'If we take them one by one, what can you tell us about each of them?'

'Start with Neville Wade,' I prompted Crowther.

'Nev was a competent drummer. Not world class, but certainly above average, and definitely good enough for us. Off-stage he was and is a staunch friend, who knew the trouble I was in and did everything he could to help me, then and now. He's dependable, discreet, and loyal. If he had a fault it was one shared by a lot of pop musicians, in that his favourite form of exercise was chasing girls.'

I looked across at Pattison. 'Anything to add, Lew?'

'No, I'd say Gerry summed Nev Wade up pretty well.'

'OK, what about Billy Quinn?'

'There is only one word to describe Billy's playing, and that word is genius,' Crowther said. 'Billy could stand comparison with the very best. Had he lived, whatever happened to Northern Lights, I believe Billy Quinn would have gone on to become a legend. Off-stage, Billy loved a joke. He was a happy, well-adjusted, rounded personality.'

Crowther looked across at Pattison.

Lew asked, 'Do they know about Billy?'

'Of course they do. You can't hide much from these two.'

Lew continued, 'Billy never made a secret of the fact that he was a homosexual, but he didn't flaunt it either. Whether his orientation had anything to do with why he was murdered, I wouldn't like to say.'

'Well we would,' I said, cutting in just before Eve. 'We know for a fact that it had nothing to do with why he was killed. Our theory is that he saw or heard something, possibly to do with one of the attempts on Gerry's life, and started asking questions. His knowledge represented a danger, so he was eliminated.' It sounded bleak the way I said it. But then it was bleak.

Taking advantage of the silence, I asked Crowther, 'Was there anything you could think of that Billy might have witnessed that would give a clue as to why he was killed?'

Gerry thought about this for a while, and when I saw his expression change, I knew he had recalled something. What followed was worth the price of admission on its own. 'All I can think of is that on the night of the Newcastle gig, Billy was the only other member of the group in the theatre when Carl appeared. Like me, Billy wanted to give the best possible show, so he'd come early to rehearse. I know for a fact that he saw me talking to Carl.' Crowther shrugged, 'I don't suppose it means anything, but it's all I can think of.'

'I think it could mean an awful lot. If Billy saw you talking to Carl Long, and then you disappeared, he might have put two and two together. If he mentioned what he'd seen to the wrong people; that could have sealed his fate.

What I would like to know is if that body was recovered from the Tyne before Quinn's murder, or later.'

'Is that important?' Pattison asked.

'It might be. If Quinn suspected that there had been foul play that night in Newcastle, the discovery of Gerry's jacket would have come as a huge shock to him, and he might have started asking questions – questions that led to someone deciding he had to be silenced.'

'I said there was nothing you could hide from these two,' Crowther told Pattison.

Eve smiled at the backhanded compliment. 'What about Pete Firth?'

'Pete was a good guitarist. Nowhere near Billy's class but more than competent for the sound I wanted to achieve. As for his personality, I'm afraid Pete is a bit on the weak side. He's likeable, but couldn't resist a pretty face, or a drink or drugs.'

'That's true,' Pattison agreed, 'I had to deal with a couple of near scandals because of Pete's behaviour following a close encounter with LSD.'

Eve hesitated before prompting their memories further. 'The next bit could be tricky, but what can you tell us about Steve Thompson?'

'Professionally, I had nothing but admiration for Steve's ability,' Crowther told us. 'He was a highly talented saxophonist with a superb feel for the emotion in any piece of music, plus a better than average singing voice.' He paused, obviously reluctant to say more.

'Go on, Gerry, you'll have to tell them. Either you will, or I shall.'

Crowther grimaced at Pattison's comment. 'We had a great deal of trouble with both Steve and Jimmy Mitchell,' Crowther said eventually. 'I think it would be better if Lew explained this bit, because he was more closely involved than me. I only got the outline. Lew can tell you the unexpurgated version.'

'Not all of it, Gerry,' Pattison told him, with a meaningful glance towards the end of the table, where Trudi and Charlie were listening intently. 'What I have to say isn't very pleasant, I'm afraid. One night, following a gig in the Midlands, Steve and Jimmy took a couple of girls back to their hotel room and apparently wouldn't take no for an answer. Of course, we only had the word of the fans for what actually happened, but rather than risk the scandal and the police involvement, I paid out a considerable sum of money. I'm not defending my actions in any way, but both Mitchell and Thompson maintained throughout that the girls were both up for it, and actually initiated the intimacy.'

'There were other instances,' Crowther added, 'even worse, if you understand me,' he said, pointedly.

'We had heard something to that effect,' I agreed. 'All that might seem damaging, but to be fair, I don't think we've heard anything so far that would suggest a reason for anyone wanting to pursue a vendetta against Gerry.'

'It would have been lunacy,' Pattison said. 'They must surely have known that if any harm had come to Gerry, Northern Lights would have been finished. Without him, they would have folded, or returned to obscurity. And that would mean all the money, the glamour, the high life, the girls, the booze, the drugs, all of it would be over.'

'In that case, perhaps we'd be better looking at those for whom it had already ended,' Eve suggested. 'I mean the members of the original line up who were replaced when Gerry joined.'

'I think you'd be better talking to Lew about them, rather than me,' Crowther pointed out. 'Apart from their musical abilities, I know much less about them than I think Lew does.'

'You knew Carl Long,' I suggested, 'tell us about him.' Even though Eve and I had formed our own opinion of him I wanted to hear their version of events.

'Carl had ambitions to be a great drummer, but to be honest he was barely average. I'm not saying Nev was the greatest, but he was streets ahead of Carl. The problem was, Carl couldn't accept that his talent was limited. Off-stage, from what little I knew of him, I'd say he was likeable, but weak and easily led, with a liking for money and a rooted objection to working for it.'

'If he was all that bad a drummer,' Eve objected, 'doesn't that cast doubt on his story about being offered session work in America?'

Crowther looked stunned by Eve's suggestion. 'I suppose it does,' he agreed. 'Do you know, I've never even thought about that, but now you've said it, there's no way he would have got that sort of work. There were far too many better drummers around.'

'Did you know anything about his background, his family, that sort of thing?'

Crowther shook his head. 'We were never that close.'

'Lew's notes suggested he came from a wealthy family, yet on the night he came to see you, he claimed to be penniless and having to resort to sleeping rough,' Eve told him.

'That's rubbish,' Pattison interjected. 'Sorry, but there's no way that can be right. Carl's mother and father pestered the life out of me for news of him, using my contacts in the music industry. I happen to know they spent a small fortune trying to trace him. They didn't give up until his father died a few years later.'

'Our theory is that Long was used to entice Gerry to the Tyne Bridge, which would result in him being dumped in the river. However, Carl overdid the acting, and when he accepted the loan of Gerry's jacket, that was enough to signal to the attackers that the wearer was Gerry. A classic case of hoist with your own petard,' Eve explained.

Everyone seemed to agree with her on that point so I asked, 'What can you tell us about the others who left the group? Tony Kendall, Robbie Roberts, and Wayne Barnett.'

Crowther gestured to Pattison to take over. 'You tell them about Barnett,' he growled.

'Wayne Barnett played keyboard, guitar, and sang. He was competent both as a musician and a singer, but nothing special. Nobody could tell him that though. He thought he was an all-round maestro, but his was a minority opinion – a minority of one, I'd say. When I told him Gerry wanted him out of Northern Lights, Wayne went ballistic. He damned near wrecked my office, then tried to sue everyone. Finally, he went on the rampage at one of the group's gigs. He's working as a session musician, picking up jobs where he can. He's even worked on some tracks for me. I've seen him at the recording studio regularly. I would say though, if anyone had a serious grudge against Gerry, it was Barnett.'

'Robbie Roberts, by contrast, seems to have done all right for himself, by what we read,' Eve said.

Pattison nodded. 'Robbie once told me the best thing that happened to him was when Gerry sacked him. Once he'd left Northern Lights he started *Music Magic*, a magazine devoted to pop and rock. As you probably know it's still highly successful, a publication no serious pop fan would be without. Robbie also moved into property and made a huge amount of money. He now lives overseas and only visits the UK occasionally.'

'That would seem to rule him out,' I agreed. 'Which leaves us with Tony Kendall. We went to the address you gave us in Newcastle, but the house had been demolished. All there was were some fields.'

Pattison shrugged. 'I have no idea what happened to him. Tony was always a wheeler-dealer with an eye to making a profit, no matter how small. I once had words with him because I caught him selling off complimentary tickets for a charity concert and pocketing the money. I wouldn't have minded so much had the money not been intended for the charity.'

'Lew's right,' Crowther added, 'Kendall was a fairly good musician, but his heart wasn't in it. He was only in it to earn a bit of extra cash – and for the girls.'

'We've got a bit more in the way of information, but I'm still not convinced we've heard anything that might suggest a motive for harming Gerry.'

Pattison disagreed with me. 'Apart from Barnett,' he said. 'You haven't had to deal with him; I have. Wayne Barnett is a good session man but he has a mean, vindictive streak, and I don't think you should look beyond him. I reckon you should go to this detective, Hardy, did you say his name was?' I nodded. 'Go to him and lay the facts in front of him and let him take it from there.'

'I agree with you,' Eve said, 'but I know Adam has his doubts.'

Looking around the table I could see the others were of a similar mind to Eve and Lew. 'Don't get me wrong, I'm not discounting Barnett. It might well be him behind it, but I have this feeling that there's something we're still unaware of. Something that would give a far stronger motive than just revenge.'

'I think you ought to spend some time in the public gallery of the criminal courts,' Alice said. 'You'd soon realize that violent crimes can be committed for the most trivial of reasons.'

It was obvious that I was outnumbered, and for a moment thought I was alone in my thinking. Help came from a most unexpected source.

'May I say something?' Charlie asked, his tone diffident. He went bright red as everyone turned to stare at him. It must have taken considerable courage for a youngster to intrude in such a deep discussion. 'I don't know if I'm being silly, or if I've missed the point, but I agree with Adam.'

'And why might that be? Have you anything to back up that statement?' Lew's tone, if not patronising, was certainly far from encouraging.

'I read the papers you sent, Mr Pattison, especially the notes about this man Wayne Barnett. And if remember right, he tried to sue everyone, yes?'

Pattison nodded, and Charlie continued, 'That would have meant a lot of publicity, wouldn't it?' Pattison nodded again, and I could see he was both baffled and intrigued by where Charlie's reasoning was leading. 'Then Barnett took a sledgehammer to the group's bus, broke a roadie's jaw and tried to strangle Mr Crowther. Have I got that right?'

'You have, absolutely right, and that proves my case entirely.' Pattison turned away, dismissing Charlie.

He'd reckoned without Charlie's determination.

'Actually, you're wrong, totally wrong. What I've just said completely disproves your theory.'

Pattison glared at Charlie, and I could sense he was about to make some cutting comment about young whippersnappers contradicting their elders.

'Why do you say that, Charlie?' I intervened hastily.

Charlie took a leaf from his aunt's book, by enumerating his points on his fingers. 'He tried to sue six individual members of Northern Lights, plus the group as a whole. That's seven legal actions, in full glare of publicity, involving famous people. An assault, GBH, and criminal damage, all conducted in the open, with no attempt to disguise who did it. All those were hot-blooded, open actions. Nothing in the least bit secretive. That's totally different to the attempts on Mr Crowther and the murders recently. They were furtive, with no trace of who was behind the campaign.'

Charlie stopped there, still red in the face with embarrassment at being thrust under such close scrutiny.

The long silence was broken eventually by Alice Pattison, who turned to her husband and told him, 'You owe this young man a big apology, Lew. Charlie is absolutely correct, and the rest of us couldn't see it.' She turned to Charlie and smiled. 'That was an exceptionally well-thought through and reasoned summary, Charlie. If you wish to consider a career in law, I would be happy to stand sponsor for you.'

Charlie's scarlet complexion deepened even further. Whether that was due to Alice's praise, or Trudi's admiring glance, I wasn't sure. Pattison, to give him his due, reached across and shook Charlie's hand. 'I'm sorry, Charlie, that should teach me a lesson. I ought never to pre-judge an issue without taking on board everyone's opinion.' He looked round the table. 'I suppose that rules Barnett out as a suspect, does it?'

'Not necessarily,' I told him, 'but what it does is to rule others in. Which I suppose means we're little further forward than when we began. In fact,' I added, hoping to end on a cheerful note, 'we ought also to bear in mind that the perpetrator could be someone totally unconnected with Northern Lights, someone we haven't even considered yet.'

The glum faces around the table told me I hadn't lost my innate skill for cheering people up.

'Where do we go from here?' Eve asked later. The Crowther family, as I had begun to think of them, had departed by taxi, and we were having a nightcap.

'Do you mean physically, or with the investigation?'

'Both, I suppose.'

'I don't think we can do much more to find out who tried to harm Gerry. I suggest we leave the rest to the police.' I shrugged in defeat.

'I think Adam's right,' Alice said. As she was speaking I saw Eve staring at me, a curious expression on her face. 'You've done everything Lew asked of you, and more besides. Let the professionals handle the murder enquiries. Besides which, if young Charlie's right,' Alice smiled at him, 'there's nothing you can do without first discovering the motive.'

'Hah!' Eve invested the single word with as much sarcasm as possible. 'It's easy to tell you don't know Adam Bailey like I do. I don't believe that rubbish he spouted about leaving it to the police. It simply isn't in his nature. He used to be paid to lift stones and see what crawled out. That leopard hasn't changed its spots.'

'Either way, I think we would be better off back at Eden House,' I suggested. 'I think we should return home tomorrow.'

The only one who seemed disappointed by my proposal was Charlie, and we all knew the reason for that. 'Look on the bright side;' I told him, 'she'll soon be a neighbour, more or less.'

If that cheered him, it wasn't immediately obvious.

Before leaving the capital, I phoned Harvey Jackson. 'Are you alone?' I asked.

'Yes, why?' His tone was cautious, apprehensive. In view of what we'd discussed the previous day that was hardly surprising.

'I need you to cast your mind back. You mentioned that Billy was concerned about something. Can you remember whether he knew about Crowther's body being recovered from the Tyne?'

'Yes, he did, and it really upset him.'

'Did he say anything about it?'

'Not very much. He kept saying "something isn't right", but what he was referring to, I've no idea.'

'Thank you, Harvey, you've been a great help.'

I could tell by his puzzled tone of voice that he couldn't understand how he'd helped. I put the phone down and told Eve what I'd just learned. She thought for a moment,

'That means Quinn knew or suspected that it wasn't Gerry's body. And if he started asking questions of the wrong people ...'

Chapter Fifteen

I'd only been to London a dozen or so times since I retired from TV journalism, and each visit left me less and less bothered if I never had to go there again. Nevertheless, I was surprised to hear Eve echo my sentiments after we had retrieved the car from the long-stay car park at York railway station. As we headed back towards the Dales, Eve stared at the countryside. 'Gosh, it's good to be back,' she exclaimed.

She saw my surprised expression and chuckled. 'How can you compare those crowded, noisy, grimy streets with the peace and quiet, and the glorious scenery we're treated to every day?' She gestured to her left. 'Where can you find something in London to match that?'

It was easy to see her point. The dale glistened in the warm sunshine, the crops in the fields on the lower slopes gradually turning from green to gold, while on the higher reaches, the heather was beginning to come into bloom, giving a purple tinge to the dark, peaty majesty of the moorland.

'I take your point, but I was a little surprised that you feel as strongly as that.'

'I think you have to love where you live, or move,' she said, 'but it isn't hard to love this landscape.'

'What you mean, Aunt Evie, is that this is now your home, and you're more content here than anywhere else,' Charlie commented.

'That's very true. You're getting to be extremely perceptive, Charlie.'

'Perceptive and deceptive,' I muttered, but fortunately, Eve didn't hear me, or so I thought. I'd seen Charlie and Trudi exchanging pieces of paper the previous day. When I quizzed him about it, Charlie admitted that they contained phone numbers. 'I gave her yours and the one at Mulgrave Castle,' he told me, 'and Trudi gave me the number of the London flat.' Charlie gave me a grin that was a mixture of triumph and apprehension.

'She won't be living there much longer,' I pointed out, a trifle cruelly, perhaps.

'No, but she's promised to let me have the Allerscar number as soon as they have the line connected at Lovely Cottage.' He paused and looked at me, a worried frown on his face. 'You won't tell Aunt Evie, will you? She might not approve. You know what she's like.'

I tried not to smile. 'OK, as long as you promise to behave yourself.'

'Adam!' His shocked expression reassured me more than his subsequent denial.

I didn't sigh with relief when we reached Eden House, although it was tempting. Perhaps it's as well I didn't, but then counting chickens before they're hatched has never been one of my favourite occupations. From the outside, everything appeared normal, exactly as we had left it. Normality ended once I opened the front door. I stood aside to allow Eve and Charlie to precede me indoors, but Eve stopped dead on the threshold, an expression of shock mingled with horror on her face.

'Adam, look! We've been burgled. Someone has broken in and ... oh, no!'

I looked at where she was pointing. The photos that had hung in the hallway and the corridor leading to the rooms at the back of the house were no longer on the walls. They were strewn about the carpet, the glass smashed into fragments, the frames broken, the images torn to shreds. It was wilful, wanton vandalism.

The story was much the same in the lounge, the dining room, and the study. The latter had been locked, but that had seemingly not presented much of a deterrent to the intruder, who it appeared had not bothered with finesse. The door frame was splintered, and the marks of a jemmy or crowbar were clearly visible in the chipped paintwork. The trail of damage inside covered the carpet. The notes Pattison had sent us seemed to have borne the brunt of the attack; their only use now being as confetti.

'Try not to touch anything. I'm going to phone Johnny Pickersgill.'

I went along the corridor, but almost immediately retraced my steps to where Eve and Charlie were standing in moody silence. 'I'm not going to phone Johnny,' I explained. 'The bastard has cut the phone line.'

'What should we do?' Charlie asked.

'The only thing we can do is get in the car and drive across to the police house.'

For our second return to Eden House we were accompanied by our friend and village bobby. A measure of Johnny's devotion to duty was that he abandoned a mug of tea he had barely touched in order to visit the crime scene. He prowled round the house, careful to avoid touching anything that might possibly be construed as evidence, as we waited for the fingerprint officers he had summoned from Dinsdale HQ, plus Inspector Hardy.

'It looks as if someone doesn't like you very much,' he murmured as he examined the worst of the damage. I wondered if he was considering entering that sentence for the understatement of the year competition. 'What's more,' he continued, 'this wasn't a five minute, in and out job. Whoever did this took their time over it, and was determined to cause you as much inconvenience and distress as possible, safe in the knowledge that they would not be interrupted. Which means –'

'That they knew we were away.' I finished his sentence

for him.

'Exactly, and that leads to another interesting question. Who knew about your trip to London? Either before you went, or while you were away?'

'Around here, apart from Gerry Crowther, his fiancée and daughter, the only person we told was Henry Price.'

'I can't somehow picture Henry doing this because you've failed to pay his milk bill, can you?'

Despite our distress, Pickersgill's suggestion made Eve smile. 'At a guess, I'd say it might have something to do with what you've been up to recently,' Pickersgill continued.

'He's right,' Charlie appeared from the study. 'Come and look at this.'

We followed him into the room, treading carefully on the few patches of carpet that were free from debris. The large gilt-framed mirror on the side was remained in place, undamaged. The reason for that was plain. A message was scrawled across it, using Eve's lipstick, I guessed. It read, 'MIND YOUR OWN BUSINESS YOU NOSEY BASTARDS'.

'That's my best lippie,' Eve muttered, seemingly more upset by that than the message itself.

I turned and stared at the desk. The intruder had taken a heavy object, possibly a large hammer, to it, and to my electric typewriter. The splintered remains of a couple of the drawers were of little use except as kindling, and I knew that I had made my last typo on the faithful machine. I said as much, and as I glanced down at the carpet, added, 'I hope the typist in Lew's office kept a carbon copy of those notes, because if not, and if we need them again, someone is going to have a lot of work to do.'

My comment was light-hearted, but I saw Eve's expression. I stared at her, but she refrained from commenting. This was unusual for Eve, and I wondered what she was thinking, but seeing me look at her, she shook her head. Whatever her thought was, she wasn't prepared to share it at that time.

'Let's check the lounge,' she suggested instead.

'It isn't a pretty sight,' Pickersgill warned.

'Where is?' Eve muttered.

'Is this upsetting for you?' he asked.

'Not half as upsetting as it will be for whoever did this if I get them within arm's reach,' Eve said, savagely. 'I'd throttle the life out of them, given the chance.'

'That's odd, I thought a knife was your weapon of choice.'

'Oi! Any more remarks like that and I won't put the kettle on.'

As Pickersgill had warned us, the lounge was a mess. At first glance, it looked as if there had been a blizzard raging in the room. The carpet was barely visible beneath what appeared to be a heavy fall of snow. The source was the lounge suite. All the cushions that formed the seats and backs of the sofa and easy chairs had been gutted, the filling scattered around to give an effect many a Hollywood set designer would have been proud of. The small nest of tables had been smashed almost beyond recognition. More kindling, I thought. In the corner of the room, the television set had been given similar treatment to my desk and typewriter, the screen little more than a few jagged edges of glass framing a gaping hole.

'There is hatred in all this,' Eve murmured, 'cold-blooded, implacable hatred.'

I thought of the message scrawled on the mirror. 'Perhaps not, maybe it's only designed to look that way. Perhaps this is merely a device designed to distract us or warn us off.'

'If that's so, it hasn't worked,' Eve growled.

Seeing the look of grim determination on her face, I pitied whoever was responsible if she ever got near them.

The kitchen had escaped the attention of the intruder. It

was difficult to judge whether Eve or Pickersgill was more relieved, especially on discovering that the kettle appeared undamaged. 'This appears to be the point of entry,' he gestured to the back door, and was about to approach it when Eve stopped him.

'Let me get a dustpan and brush first.' She pointed to the broken glass from the door, which was scattered across the quarry tiles. 'I don't want those tiles getting scratched.'

The intruder had shown as little finesse to gain entry to the house as he had once inside. The pane of glass next to the lock had been smashed, enabling him to put his hand in, turn the key and walk in. As I looked at it, I wondered what the insurance company would have to say on the matter. It didn't take long for my worst fears to be realized.

It was with considerable trepidation that we followed Pickersgill upstairs, leaving Charlie to keep a lookout for the arrival of the fingerprint men. Luckily, whether the assault on the ground floor had exhausted the intruder's rage, or they had feared a further attack would entail too much risk, all the rooms on the upper floor were untouched. 'At least we'll have somewhere to sleep,' I said. I was determined to stay upbeat.

'I'm not sure how much sleep I'll get, knowing what's downstairs,' Eve replied.

We returned to the ground floor, where Eve suggested it was time to brew a pot of tea. Pickersgill gave her a broad smile of approval. 'You're a lucky man, Adam. I wish my wife could read my mind the way Eve can.' He paused for a moment and reconsidered, 'No, perhaps it's as well she can't.'

As we waited for the kettle, he told us, 'I do have a bit of good news, regarding that hit-and-run accident. We found the vehicle that was involved, or rather a couple of birdwatchers did. They were in a disused quarry the other side of Rowandale looking for a Lesser-spotted something-

or-other, and came across an abandoned pick-up that someone had tried to torch. Luckily the arson attempt failed, because we were able to match paint scrapings from the car that Thompson was driving to scratches on the bull bar. Also, we got some fingerprints from the steering wheel, so if we can identify a suspect, we might be able to charge them with murder. I've also sent them through to Leeds to see if DS Middleton can match them with anything they got from Mitchell's house or garage.'

The fingerprint officers were still busy creating dust for us to clean up, when Inspector Hardy arrived. He had news for us. 'I checked back into the body in the Tyne. The investigation was sloppy. After all that time in the water, there wasn't much to identify. Conclusion: they'd found a body, a man was thought to be missing in the river, they confirmed the jacket on the deceased belonged to the missing man, case closed. Were it not for the incidents of the past few weeks, for which Gerry Crowther has alibis, I might have been tempted to consider him as a suspect in killing the man they found in the river. However, as all these incidents are quite obviously linked, I think it safe to discount him now. So, what happened here?'

We briefed him on what we knew, supported by Pickersgill. His assessment was similar to mine, and at some point during our discussion, Hardy enquired about our trip to London. We explained what we knew, which wasn't much. 'We're still no nearer discovering who was behind the attempts on Gerry Crowther's life. Even a motive would be a massive step forward.'

'That's often the way of it. Sometimes it isn't down to detective's inspiration or routine police work. In many instances, pure chance gives us the clues we need to solve a case. Perhaps luck will be on our side this time.'

I was to remember Hardy's comment later. Chance provided us with the name of the mole in Pattison's organisation, and chance most definitely led to our discovery of a motive – chance, plus the villains themselves.

By common consent, we opted to dine at the village pub that evening, although by the time we reached the Admiral Nelson, we were almost too late to order. As we left the house, I closed the door behind me and prepared to walk down the drive. 'Haven't you forgotten something?' Eve asked.

'Such as?'

'Locking the door might be a good idea, don't you think? It may seem an old-fashioned notion, but it's quite popular, I believe.' Have I mentioned that Eve has a sarcastic turn of phrase at times?

I shrugged. 'It didn't seem worth the effort. Pretty much everything of value is broken. Besides which, locked doors didn't prevent the previous intrusion. I don't see what more they can do, except perhaps burn the house down.'

Eve shuddered. 'Don't say that, Adam, even in jest. Please, for my peace of mind, lock the door.'

I found it impossible to resist her coaxing tone and the appeal in those big eyes. Besides which, it *was* the sensible thing to do.

The bar at the pub was all but empty. 'Are we too late to order?' I asked the landlord.

'I'll ask the missus.' He disappeared into the kitchen and returned a few minutes later. 'You're OK, seeing it's you, she'll cook you a meal. What brings you here midweek, anyway?'

I explained about the burglary. 'By the look of things, they didn't steal anything. We don't think that was their intention. The house is a hell of a mess, though.'

'If you'd said that, my wife would have cooked you something even if it had been near closing time, Adam.' He poured our drinks, before uttering the Yorkshireman's favourite saying. 'These are on the house.'

When the meal was ready, we ambled through to the dining room. This prevented me from suffering a humiliating defeat at darts by a fifteen-year-old. Charlie showed great skill for someone who did not frequent pubs. As we dined, we discussed what to do about the carnage at Eden House. 'First thing, I'll have to get in touch with the insurance company in the morning. Quite how I do that is another matter. Maybe we should buy some carrier pigeons. Then I'll have to see how quickly the GPO can fix our phone line.'

'British Telecom,' Charlie interrupted. 'That's who it is now.'

I nodded in appreciation of his help and continued, 'It's going to be a damned nuisance being unable to communicate with anyone. I don't fancy trying to negotiate with insurers or phone suppliers while having to feed a public call box with coins.'

'Isn't there someone whose phone we could use? If we recompense them, I mean. It isn't simply the outgoing calls. The fact that no one can phone you back is going to make it intolerable.'

We sat there in depressed silence for a few minutes, until Charlie said, 'Aunt Evie, what was it you were going to tell Adam?'

I realized later that it was Charlie's way of trying to lift our spirits, by distracting us from all that had gone wrong. His question had Eve baffled momentarily. 'What are you on about, Charlie?'

'When we were in the study, wasn't there something you were going to tell Adam, but not while Mr Pickersgill was there.'

'Oh yes, I'd quite forgotten about that. You remember what you said when you saw what they'd done to your typewriter, Adam? Something about not being able to type, wasn't it?'

I nodded. 'What about it?'

'That, plus what you said about the paperwork Lew sent us made me wonder. I suddenly realised that the person who was in the best position to act as the mole might be the person who typed those notes up in the first place. Unless they're completely dense they must have had some idea as to why Lew suddenly wanted that job doing, referring to people who had been out of the limelight for so long. Maybe they didn't get the full implication, but if they are involved, the fact that it was all about Northern Lights must have triggered alarm bells.'

Eve paused, possibly for breath, but more likely for dramatic effect, before continuing, 'Then a few minutes later Johnny Pickersgill said that whoever had done this must have known we were in London and there was no chance of them being disturbed, and that made me think the person most likely to know that was a member of Lew's workforce. I want to find out who that is and confront them about the damage to my home – our home.'

I could see tears of anger in her eyes and put my hand on hers. 'I love it when you refer to it as our home. It reminds me what a lucky man I am.'

The magic of the moment was broken by Charlie. 'If you two are going to go all soppy and sentimental on me, I'm off back into the bar to see if there's anyone to play darts with.'

'You're only jealous because Trudi isn't here for you to stare adoringly at,' I teased him.

'What's even worse,' Eve added with a wicked smile, 'with our phone out of action, you can't even call her.'

Charlie stared at his aunt, assessing how much she knew, and how much was guesswork. Eve chuckled. 'Come off it, Charlie, you didn't imagine your little note-passing episode had gone unnoticed by me or Trudi's mother, did you?'

Chapter Sixteen

The week following the burglary was marked by a seemingly endless round of frustration, fuelled by our inability to communicate with the outside world with any degree of ease, and the implacable determination of those at the end of such calls as we could make to throw as many obstacles in our way as they could think of.

After countless attempts to conduct sensible conversations with either British Telecom or our insurance company, I resorted to underhand means. The very real threat of refusing to pay had not worked. My plans to present a consumer programme on national television exposing the shortfalls in their customer relations commanded instant attention. However, with an insurance company, attention and action have only their initial letter in common.

Having been told that in order to process the claim, they would need to send an assessor out, I asked when this would happen. I was informed by the helpful but dim clerical person that they would pass my details to the assessors. They then asked for a telephone number where the assessor could contact me to arrange an appointment.

As I had been feeding coins into the hungry public phone box for the past fifteen minutes, that remark caused a severe sense of humour failure on my part. Without descending into the use of choice Anglo-Saxon vocabulary, I nevertheless succeeded in putting across my low opinion of the shortcomings of the insurance industry, the company, and the individual I was speaking to. My response was the sound of the dialling tone.

My relief at seeing the arrival of the British Telecom engineer to fix the phone was exceeded by the delight of Eve and especially Charlie, who had been walking around me for the previous few days with all the caution of an explorer circling a lake he believed to be infested with man-eating crocodiles.

Not that our problems ended there, far from it. Resuming negotiations with the insurers, I soon came to the conclusion that my card had been marked, 'difficult customer, be as obstructive as possible'. They informed me, with a trace of glee, that their assessor was on holiday.

'Well, lucky for him,' I replied. 'What am I supposed to do in the meantime?'

There was no answer, so I ploughed on. 'Should I go ahead and replaced the damaged items?'

I was told that they could not be responsible for the claim should I do that. 'Very well,' I told them cheerfully – I can do glee as well as the next man – 'as the house cannot be secured without your authority, I'm putting you on notice that you will be responsible should another incursion happen.'

They grudgingly agreed to allow the repairs to the back door, but no more than that.

Without television to distract us, and being unable to restore our living areas to habitable status, there was little to encourage us to stay home in the evenings. The takings at the Admiral Nelson benefited by our frequent forays to dine there, and those of the locals who had the patience to listen were treated to a diatribe regarding the evils of the insurance industry as a whole, and one company in particular.

On those evenings when we did stay at Eden House, the lack of a television proved more frustrating for Eve and Charlie than for me. They resolved this by using the transistor radio which had escaped the attention of the invader. It was on one of these evenings, when they had left the radio on while they went outside to admire the sun, setting over Rowandale High Moor, that my attention was caught by a tune being played by the resident presenter. I was in the process of preparing dinner, a chicken and rice dish I had grown to like during my time in Africa. As I listened, the hauntingly familiar refrain was accompanied by a superb guitar solo. When the melody ended, I stood for a moment, thankful that I hadn't diced my finger along with the chicken breasts.

My mind was in a whirl, and it was only much later that evening that I got my thoughts in order. 'I need to go to Thorsby tomorrow,' I told Eve and Charlie.

'Any particular reason?' Eve asked. 'I thought we had all the shopping we need – apart from something to sit on, which we can't get until some bloke returns from Benidorm.'

I explained the reason for my trip, before adding, 'If I'm right, we need Crowther here. He's the only person who can tell whether I'm on to something, or whether I've got the wrong end of the stick.'

As it transpired, having the phone back in working order was the least of our difficulties. Discounting the intransigent attitude of the insurance company, when we tried to contact those we needed to speak to, we met with further frustration. This time, fortunately for domestic harmony, Eve had to put up with the barriers to progress. Her first call, to Lew Pattison, ended swiftly. As she put the phone down, she told us, 'Lew has gone to Italy, and from there to Canada, and won't be back in England for another ten days. I'll try Sheila next.'

Although the Crowther family had not left the country, Sheila told Eve they would not be returning to Yorkshire as quickly as they had hoped.

'They have to wait for the landlord to inspect the flat,' Eve explained. 'Until he's satisfied Sheila hasn't wrecked the place or allowed squatters to take over, he won't release the bond she paid to secure the place. Unfortunately, he's on holiday in Spain.'

'Probably supping San Miguel in a bar in Benidorm with that bloody insurance assessor.'

'One good thing,' – for some reason I couldn't understand, Eve seemed anxious to change the subject – 'is that I spoke to Harvey Jackson, and he's agreed to get all Lew's notes photocopied and sent up to us.'

Two days later, the postman, who must have been considering the advisability of investing in a surgical truss with the heavy parcels he had to deliver, brought us the replacement notes. We all went through them, and with the light of what we had learned, Eve came up with an interesting theory. 'Have you taken on board what Lew said about Robbie Roberts?'

'Only that he started a pop magazine and became really successful.'

'That's right, *Music Magic*. My question is, how did he do it?'

Charlie and I exchanged puzzled glances. 'Sorry, you've lost me,' I admitted.

'OK, imagine you decide to start a magazine. Don't worry what the subject is, concentrate on the mechanics. Where do you begin?'

I guessed that the lack of enlightenment on Charlie's face mirrored my own. 'Sorry to appear dim, but we still haven't caught on.'

'OK, let's look at what you would need.' Eve enumerated the points, using the fingers of her right hand. 'First, you need business premises, whether bought or rented. You need an office, with furniture, telephone, and at least one typewriter. There would be stationery and so forth to buy. In addition, you would require access to printing facilities, plus paper and ink. To run the operation, you would need staff. Not only in the office, but news-gathering – and most important of all, sales and marketing.'

'I get all that, but what's your point, Evie?'

'Where would the money come from? If you didn't have it stored in an old sock under the bed you'd need an investor or a very understanding bank manager.'

The penny dropped. It had taken some time to fall, but at last I got the message. 'What you're saying is, where did Roberts get the money to fund the magazine until it was established enough to pay its own way?'

'Exactly. And that is a question we really need to address.'

Although the delay to proceed with replacing our demolished possessions was extremely frustrating, it enabled us to help Gerry and Sheila with the removal from Sheila's London flat.

Eve got a phone call from Sheila, and although I only heard one half of the conversation, I was aware that I was in the process of being volunteered. 'I can understand that,' Eve told Sheila, 'and I'll ask Adam if he'll do it for you. I feel sure I can persuade him to say yes.'

After she rang off, I walked out of the study. Eve smiled sweetly at me. This is often a danger signal, but on this occasion it was clear she was going to ask a favour. 'That was Sheila on the phone. They've decided a lot of her furniture isn't worth bringing up here. They're going to send what they don't want to a saleroom. The thing is, Sheila says it isn't worth getting a removals firm with a huge pantechnicon for what they want to carry. The alternative is to hire a van, but as it's almost twenty years since Gerry drove, he doesn't feel confident of driving a strange vehicle, especially with the amount of traffic on the roads these days. They want to come back as soon as possible. Sheila said Gerry's getting twitchy about his tomatoes and broody about his hens.'

'I can understand that. Have you come up with a solution?'

'Well, I did wonder if we could help. Perhaps if we hire a van and collect their stuff we could bring them back here lock, stock, and barrel. You could drive the van and I'll take your car.'

'That's a lot of time, trouble, and expense,' I pointed out.

'Sheila said they'll pay all the costs. What do you think?'

'What's it worth?' I glanced towards the stairs as I spoke, the implication obvious.

Eve smiled seductively and sidled up to me, her body pressed against mine. 'If you agree, big boy, I'll do your favourite thing, specially for you. I'll bake you a chocolate cake.'

That wasn't quite what I had in mind. Still, the cake was delicious.

The journey to London and back was long, tiring, and would have been extremely boring had I not been accompanied by Charlie. The trip went smoothly, the only tricky moment coming when I had to thread the vehicle between two lines of parked cars on the street where Sheila's flat was. As it transpired there was ample space; nevertheless, it was a little nerve-wracking in a van I was unused to, and I could see why Crowther was so reluctant to undertake the drive.

We'd been on the road since dawn, and returned to Yorkshire in the early evening. Having parked the van outside Crowther's house, and waited until Crowther satisfied himself that Henry had taken good care of things horticultural, we set off for Laithbrigg and the Admiral Nelson, where Eve had booked a table. Next morning the operation was complete. Having offloaded the contents of the van, I left Eve and Charlie at Allerscar to help shift furniture while I returned the hire vehicle to Leeds. Early that afternoon I caught a train back to Thorsby, where Eve met me at the station.

'Our celebrity guest will be staying with us again soon,' she told me. 'There's been a mix-up over the new bed they ordered for Trudi, and it won't be delivered for another couple of weeks. Sheila's upset, thinking they've already imposed enough on us, but I told her not to worry. Charlie, on the other hand, is delighted.'

Two days later we received a phone call from Alice Pattison, with some dreadful news. 'The papers here are full of the story,' she told me. 'A fire has destroyed a block of flats in North London. Police and fire officers believe it was arson. Luckily, nobody was hurt. They reckon the fire originated in an empty ground floor flat. Adam, the flat was where Sheila and Trudi Bell lived.'

That evening, Sheila had invited us to an unofficial house-warming dinner. The news of the fire came as a terrible shock to all three of them. Sheila's face was a mask of distress as Eve repeated what Alice had told me. I was especially concerned by Crowther's reaction. The bleak stare with which he received the news, plus his opening words, revealed his state of mind.

'This would never have happened but for me. It's starting all over again, isn't it?'

I could see where his thoughts were headed, and was determined to stop him going there. So, by her response, was Sheila. 'I don't understand why this is happening. Who could hope to gain by doing such things? And why? What is it they want? Harming Gerry, or me, or Trudi won't achieve anything.'

It was time to produce my theory, if only as a distraction. Sheila's words provided the perfect opportunity. 'I can't tell you who is doing this – not yet. However, as to the why, I think I can answer that. I think the motive behind everything that happened in the 1960s was money. Vast amounts of money, probably millions of pounds. The current violence is a desperate attempt by those responsible to avoid exposure for the crimes they committed. In order to prove whether I'm right, I need you to come to Laithbrigg tomorrow. I need Gerry to confirm if my idea is correct, or way off target.'

I paused to allow them to take on board what I'd said, before adding, 'This time around, though, there is one huge difference. This time, Gerry, apart from knowing why this is happening, you won't be fighting the evil on your own. The people responsible are desperate, and desperate men make mistakes. With all of us in a tight circle we can protect each other until it's all over.'

I was quite proud of my stirring speech. Parts of it touched on being inspirational. Some of it I actually believed.

Next morning, we collected Gerry and Sheila from Allerscar. Charlie and Trudi had suggested waiting at Eden House to give them more room in the car. 'No way,' I told them. 'Until this is over, we stick together wherever and whenever possible. No going off on your own. Safety in numbers, right?'

They agreed, sobered by the reminder of the danger we faced. My words prompted another thought, which in turn caused a little delay in collecting Trudi's parents. 'I think we should persuade Gerry and Sheila to stay with us for the time being,' I told Eve. They took some persuading, and I had to promise to drive Gerry back to Allerscar each day to look after the garden and hens before he would agree.

In addition to waiting for them to pack some clothing, we had to take delivery of a tray of eggs plus a sizeable amount of fruit and vegetables Crowther had picked for us that morning. 'It isn't much by way of a thank-you,' he told us, 'but it's the best I can do for the time being.'

When we returned to Eden House, it was time to test my theory out. Gerry and Sheila were clearly shocked by the amount of damage, and I could see Crowther was about to put on the hair shirt of repentance, knowing that the attack had been the result of our efforts on his behalf. 'Luckily,' I told them, 'almost all the stuff they damaged had been earmarked for replacement. Now, we can get the insurance company to pay out instead of us having to bear the cost.'

One of the greatest assets a reporter can acquire is the ability to lip-read. As I finished my little speech of reassurance I glanced beyond Sheila, in time to see Eve mouth the word, 'bullshit'.

I led them into the study, where I gestured to one item that had already been purchased by way of a replacement. 'I bought this in Thorsby the other day, so you'll have to bear with me, because I'm not familiar with the controls yet.'

'Would you like me to do it, Adam?' Charlie suggested. 'I have one like this in my bedroom at the castle.'

I thanked him and handed him the record I'd taken from a carrier bag. 'I also bought this in Thorsby, and I'd like you to listen to it very carefully.'

As Charlie placed the stylus on the edge of the black vinyl, I watched Crowther's face carefully. This was the moment of truth. We would know soon whether I'd identified the motive for the crimes correctly, or if it was a red herring. The instrumental was familiar enough to Eve, to me, and I guess to Sheila. Even Charlie knew it vaguely, but I was fairly certain Crowther had never heard it before. Within a couple of bars, his expression changed from mild interest to a puzzled frown and then to rapt attention. He stared at the turntable, then looked at me, then back to the record player, his mouth open in astonishment. He signalled to Charlie. 'Stop playing. Take it off.'

I was already sure my idea was accurate, but confirmation came swiftly. 'Where did you say you got that?' Crowther pointed to the record.

'In the music shop in Thorsby. I take it you recognize the melody?'

'Recognize it? I should do. I wrote that bloody tune. What I want to know is, who recorded it without my permission?'

Crowther looked round, at Sheila, then Eve, saw they were both staring at him. 'What's wrong? Have I missed something?' he asked.

I explained as gently as I could. 'That track was recorded in 1968. Three years after you supposedly died.'

There was a long silence, before I told Crowther, 'The same instrumentalist recorded three more singles between 1968 and 1970. They're also on that album. Would you like to hear them?'

Crowther nodded, and Charlie replaced the stylus on the record. Within the first few bars of each tune, it was clear by Crowther's expression of outraged horror that he recognized them only too well. When the last notes of the final one died away he looked at me, confirming what we all had realized minutes earlier. 'They're my compositions – all of them. I wrote every single note of those four tunes. Who is the thieving bastard?'

I think we were all shocked, because none of us had heard Crowther swear before. 'That's a very good question, Gerry, and the quick answer is, we don't know. Nobody does, or at least nobody was prepared to reveal the identity.'

'But who played them?'

I explained, and it was rather like updating someone who had been cast away on a desert island. 'In early 1968 a phenomenon burst onto the music scene. As far as I can remember, it was around March that the keyboard player you heard on those tracks reached the top ten with the first of four hit singles. Over the next eighteen months all four reached number one. The keyboard player called himself

The Mystery Minstrel, and for the most part he refused all gigs and concert offers. Even when he did agree to appear, on shows like Top of the Pops, he was always in deep shadow, and all the viewers could see was the silhouette. The story was that the sessions were pre-recorded, with only the few technicians and the show's producer on the set.'

'You seem to know a lot about this Mystery Minstrel.' Crowther commented.

'I was a journalist, remember. There was a lot of speculation in the national press, and it became every reporter's ambition to discover who the Mystery Minstrel really was. Nobody succeeded, though.'

Crowther snorted. 'That's probably because there would have been too many suspects to choose from. The way that person mangled those tunes, I'd guess anyone over the age of eight with the most basic knowledge of music could have played them – in most cases probably making a better job of it.'

'Don't be such a musical snob, Gerry,' Sheila told him. 'The question remains, where did they get that music from?'

'I wasn't certain until I heard all four,' Crowther told her, 'but there can only be one explanation. Do you remember that night in Chester?'

Sheila went bright red and glanced swiftly at her daughter. I'm not sure if any of the others caught that implication, but I think Crowther did, for he hurriedly continued, 'That was the night my hotel room was broken into and my case stolen. It had those four tracks in it.'

'What a shame there isn't another copy,' Eve suggested. 'Then you could challenge the authenticity.'

'But there is. Not another copy, but the fully scored version. Those,' Crowther gestured to the record, still revolving silently on the turntable, 'were only draft copies. The complete score included orchestral backing amongst other differences.'

'I assume you still have those?'

'Of course I do. I would never throw anything like that away. Too much hard work goes into writing them.'

'Where are they?'

Crowther looked at me for a moment, considering the implications of my question, I guessed. 'At the bank, along with my other documents.'

'Have you opened that box since you put them in?' To our surprise it was Charlie who asked.

'Only once, to get the anonymous letters out, why?'

'That's a shame. I remember my Dad telling me once that the bank keeps a record of every time you go to a safe deposit. If you hadn't been in since the date you placed them there, you could have proved beyond doubt that they were the authentic versions.'

Crowther smiled at Charlie. 'You are a very astute young man. I would probably not have thought of this had you not prompted me, but all my sheet music, both published and unpublished, is in an envelope. Also in that envelope are the deeds to Lovely Cottage and my will. I made the will in January of 1966, and took it straight to the bank with all my other papers. The envelope was dated, sealed and signed by me, then countersigned by the bank manager. He added the date once more in his handwriting, before the envelope flap was stamped with the bank's rubber stamp. That was all done at my insistence,' Crowther told us, adding with a wry, self-mocking smile, 'that was only three months after the Newcastle disappearing act, when I was at the height of the Crowther paranoia season.'

'And that envelope remains intact? You haven't broken the seals on it?'

Crowther shook his head. 'And to go back to what you've just heard, you're convinced those are all your work, but without the orchestral backing?'

'I am.'

'No other differences? On the first track, for example?'

Crowther gave me an odd look, but eventually agreed that the lack of an orchestral backing was the sole variance from what he'd composed. Although he and the others were convinced that those who claimed to have composed the piece, plus the Mystery Minstrel, must have been the ones who stole the music, I was suddenly smitten with doubt. There was one point where the track we'd just heard varied markedly from the version I'd heard on the radio. I'd no idea who it had been played by, but I now felt sure there was a second version out there. What added to my misgivings was that Crowther had not volunteered any information about what was missing from the tune we'd heard, when compared to the earlier rendition on the radio. With two possible suspects to pursue, identifying those responsible would be far from easy – and possibly highly dangerous.

'Haven't they to put their name on the label?' Trudi asked.

'They certainly do,' Crowther agreed. 'Good thinking, Trudi. The composers have to be identified, along with the performer. The names of those responsible for nicking my music should be on there.'

I reached across and lifted the record from the player. After examining the label, I looked at the others. 'I'm none the wiser. Do the names A and J Deva mean anything to you?'

As I glanced round, and was met with a set of blank stares, I realized that we were no nearer forward than we had been when the music started playing.

I was about to raise my point about the tunes we'd just heard, but Eve began to expound her theory. By the time she finished, I changed my mind and decided I would do some research first.

'Adam's theory is that whoever stole the music from

you, or whoever they passed it to, must have recognised the potential to make huge sums of money from it,' she told them. 'However, that couldn't happen with Gerry around. But if he was killed, in a tragic accident, say, that would leave them free to publish those tracks without being challenged to their rights.'

'I accept that,' Crowther replied, 'but I still have no idea who might be responsible.'

'We do, or rather I do,' Eve told him. She explained her theory regarding how successful Robbie Roberts had become. 'He started *Music Magic*.'

I could tell the name of the publication meant nothing to Crowther, although Sheila and Trudi clearly recognized it. '*Music Magic* is a monthly magazine devoted to rock and pop music,' Eve explained for Crowther's benefit. 'It's become highly popular with pop fans and now has a huge worldwide circulation. My point is that in order to set up something like that, Roberts would have needed a huge amount of working capital. The obvious source for that would seem to me to be the proceeds from a string of hit records.'

During the discussion that followed, no solution as to resolving the threat against Crowther and his family presented itself. We were still groping in the dark, the figures of the perpetrators as shadowy as they had been when we started out. And they still had us firmly in their sights.

Chapter Seventeen

It was an enormous relief when the insurance assessor arrived, inspected the damage and indicated that he would advise the company to authorise our claim.

Armed with that knowledge, Eve co-opted Sheila to assist in a series of shopping expeditions to boost the sales figures of a number of local furniture stores. I was invited along, as was Crowther, but we both sensed that the invitations had been issued purely out of politeness, and declined the offer, as did Trudi and Charlie.

Having moved my car to allow Eve to reverse her Mini out of the drive, we waved the women off, before setting out for Allerscar. There, Charlie and Trudi collected eggs, fed the hens, and helped Crowther harvest more of his crop of vegetables, while I was placed in charge of the hosepipe. It was a warm, dry spell of weather, and watering was essential.

As I watched Crowther working I reflected on how different this must seem to him, compared to his old career as a pop star. The contrast could not have been more marked, and even as I was considering this, I realized that to a large extent it only mirrored the changes in my own lifestyle.

The change from the plains and mountains of Africa, where danger was a constant companion, or the hustle and bustle of New York, to the peace and tranquillity of the Yorkshire Dales was as radical as could be imagined. Granted, many of my former companions had also changed roles, but most of them had remained within the news industry. Some had become political pundits, or correspondents dealing with specialist subjects like health or education. One, a particularly close colleague, with whom I'd shared several perilous missions in search of stories, was now a highly respected crime reporter for one of the big national dailies. What, I wondered idly, would Paul Faulkner make of the story I was watching unfold.

Even as I was dwelling on this, the idea came to me. It was a radical one, to such an extent that I momentarily lost control of the hosepipe. The cold shower I treated Charlie and Trudi to caused instant protests.

'Sorry,' I told them, 'something startled me.'

Trudi accepted my apology at face value, but Charlie gave me a searching look of disbelief. The only other witness, Trudi's father, said nothing, but his deep-throated chuckle spoke volumes. Having re-directed the hose pipe to its intended target, I thought some more of the notion that had taken hold of me. Like one of Crowther's seedlings, it took time to develop, and it was a couple of days later before I had thought it through in sufficient depth to present it to the others. We had just finished dinner when I addressed our little gathering. 'I've had an idea,' I told them.

Reaction was instantaneous. 'Quick, Sheila,' Eve said with some urgency, 'grab my car keys. We need to escape as fast as possible.'

Her alarm, fortunately, provoked more amusement than mass panic.

'What sort of an idea?' Crowther asked.

'I think we ought to go public with what we know.'

The idea was revolutionary enough to appal everyone in the room. After a long silence marked by universal expressions of shocked disbelief, Eve said, 'We can't do that, Adam. It would expose Gerry, Sheila, and Trudi to the sort of danger we're trying to protect them from.'

'That's not how I see it. Think about it this way; the

people who have demonstrated that they fear the affair coming into the open have been the opposition. They are obviously so terrified of exposure that they have taken extreme measures to avoid anyone talking to us.'

I watched them mull over my point of view, but was unable to gauge how well I'd put it over, so I continued, 'I think if we plan our campaign carefully and avoid mentioning any names in the early stages, we will actually provide more protection rather than exposing anyone to risk. In addition to everything else, I'm fairly certain they're unaware that Gerry's still alive, and in any event the idea that they might have been found out is sure to stop them taking further action. If they're unsure how much we know, anything that could tip their hand would be far too risky.'

'How do you plan to go about it?' Crowther asked. It seemed strange that he, of all people, was most receptive to the idea. I had expected him to be hardest to convince. 'I mean, if you don't mention names, it will hardly be of interest, will it?'

I explained in detail. When I'd finished, Crowther looked at Sheila for reassurance, and when I saw her nod, I knew I'd converted the two people most affected by the plan. Naturally enough, Eve wasn't as easily satisfied. 'Do you have anyone in mind for the job?' she asked. 'I'd hate it to appear having been mishandled by some of the gutter press.'

'I was thinking about Paul Faulkner.' I saw her eyes widen with surprise, and knew I was almost there. 'Paul is an old friend, and I know he's also an avid fan of pop music. This is just the sort of story he would love to write.'

Inevitably, it was Eve who threw a spanner in the works, even if it was only a temporary show-stopper. 'Before we do anything, ought we not to discuss what we're planning to do with Lew Pattison? He doesn't even know about the copyright theft, and I for one don't think

193

we ought to proceed without an expert opinion.'

Crowther looked at me, as if urging me to contest the issue, but I wasn't about to do so. The logic and common sense in Eve's remarks was unarguable.

Having acceded to Eve's suggestion, our next problem was arranging a meeting with Pattison. This time, our luck was in. Alice explained to Eve that she and Lew were planning on visiting us anyway. As Eve reported, 'Lew got back yesterday, and next weekend he wants to go to Harrogate to arrange something. It's to do with Trudi, but Alice wasn't sure exactly what "it" is. Anyway, Lew suggested to her that they come and visit us at the same time, so I said, yes, why not. Maybe we could do Sunday lunch. That would make it perfect. Here, in private, we could bring Lew up to speed on everything.

We told the others. 'Ooh, that'll be about my concert,' Trudi said, her excited expression reminding me yet again how young she was. She explained, 'The TV people want to do a special concert and I'm going to be one of the acts. I think they're planning on showing it at Christmas.'

Fortunately, Sunday was warm, dry, and sunny, perfect for our plans for alfresco dining. My stint in Africa had given me a liking for food cooked over a fire pit, and although the British climate gave few opportunities for barbecues, this summer had enabled us to take advantage of the good weather on several occasions.

As I had been placed in charge of cooking, Eve and Sheila were busy preparing salad, dips, and dessert, while Charlie acted as my assistant, not too onerous a task. Trudi volunteered to take the role of waitress, leaving her father the job of barman.

There was ample opportunity during the cooking process to bring Lew and Alice up to date with our discovery of the copyright theft. At one point Charlie and Crowther escorted them into the study to listen to the record I'd bought.

On his return, I asked Pattison what he thought. 'I remember thinking at the time what a shame it was to have spoiled such good tunes by getting a second-rate musician to record them. I assumed he or she must have been the songwriter, otherwise the record label would have insisted on somebody better.'

I chuckled. 'That was pretty much what Gerry said, but put it down to wounded pride. What you will be able to tell us far more accurately than anyone else, Lew, is how much they might have made from those records.'

'That's anyone's guess. It isn't as simple an equation as royalties on book sales. Every time one of those tunes is played, on a radio station for example, the composers are entitled to a small fee. The amounts may be tiny, but it's surprising how they add up. Tunes like those, that were so popular in their day, keep on getting played, as you discovered recently.'

'You must have some idea though, Lew,' Alice prompted him. 'Is it thousands, or hundreds of thousands?'

'The four Mystery Minstrel tunes all got to number one in Britain, and two of them reached the American top ten, I seem to recall. So I'd say you could be looking well into seven figures by now, possibly eight.'

I hadn't been giving Pattison lessons in how to stun an audience to silence. He didn't seem in need of teaching. He had a natural talent for it.

We had set up a table on the lawn, and as we ate, Pattison told us more about the concert that was to feature Trudi Bell. 'The show should have been in the can long ago, but the recording has had to be postponed a couple of times because the comedian who is down to act as compère has been ill. However, the TV company have signed up a stand-in, so if he can't make the next date, they'll go ahead without him. Which means, young lady,' he smiled at Trudi, 'that we're all set to go in three weeks' time.'

'Where is the venue?' Eve asked.

'The new International Conference Centre in Harrogate, where they held the finals of the Eurovision Song Contest earlier this year.'

Pattison talked to Trudi and her mother about the details of her appearance in the show, and at one point mentioned her new song. 'This will be the perfect occasion to unveil it,' he suggested, 'but I need to be able to talk to you regarding the fine details soon. Do I contact you here?'

'We should have our phone line installed next week and then we can return to Allerscar,' Sheila told Pattison. 'We've imposed on Adam and Eve's hospitality long enough.'

'Before that happens, Lew, I've had an idea how to bring this matter to a head.' I explained my plan for getting the copyright theft into the public domain, and could see Pattison was in favour of what I proposed.

'I know from experience,' Alice added her support, 'that anyone involved in this sort of crime fears the idea of their misdeeds becoming public more than anything.'

Late that night, as Eve and I were preparing to go to bed, she stopped in the middle of getting undressed. 'Damn!' she exclaimed, 'I forgot to ask Lew about that magazine.'

My attention was on the strip-tease. 'What magazine?'

'You remember, the one that guy Roberts founded, *Music Magic*.' Eve turned to face me, unhooking her bra as she did so.

'Oh, that one.' My mind was still not on magazines, or music tycoons. 'Ask him later.'

Eve realized the futility of further conversation and gave up the effort.

Getting approval to approach Paul Faulkner had been by no means an easy task. Actually getting to speak to the reporter proved even more difficult. Paul, it appeared, was now so important that the telephonist and secretaries at the newspaper where he worked had obviously been given instructions to act as his gatekeepers, preventing waste of time callers getting through to him.

In the end, following three abortive phone calls, I resorted to subterfuge and a little gentle blackmail. Having stated my name, I added that of the TV channel where I had previously worked. I then explained that if Paul wasn't interested in the story, I would have to approach another paper. I may have mentioned the name, which was that of their fiercest rivals. Quite accidentally, of course.

I was still uncertain of the outcome when the secretary gave me my opportunity by asking if I could explain what I wanted to speak to Faulkner about. 'Let me see ...' – I pretended to count – 'there have been three – no – better make that *four* murders so far, plus arson, attempted murder, and a giant financial fraud, possibly running into millions.'

There was a long silence, before she uttered the magic words, 'Hold the line, sir, and I'll put you through.'

A few seconds later I heard a couple of clicks, then, 'Paul Faulkner, who am I speaking to?'

'Strictly speaking, that should be "to whom am I speaking", Paul. And the answer is, Adam Bailey.'

'Adam, trust you to be so bloody pedantic. What's woken you from your rural slumber? I thought you were out in the wilds, in sheep-shearing country?'

Faulkner was obviously in an open office, otherwise he wouldn't have cleaned his sentence up.

'I am, Paul, and if you want the biggest scoop of your failing career, you'll catch the next train up here.'

As Faulkner had won the most prestigious award in journalism the previous year, the calculated insult made him chuckle. 'What's the story, Adam? My secretary gave me a fantastic tale of multiple murders et cetera. Has someone slaughtered Bo Peep and her flock?'

I told him just sufficient to whet his appetite, and it had the desired effect. 'OK, how do I get there? And where do I stay? Should I bring my own wellies, or is there a hire service?'

Two days later, I drove with Eve across to York to meet Faulkner's train. Eve had a reservation about involving the journalist in our scheme, but it wasn't the one I expected. 'This doesn't mean you're hankering after your old life, does it? I've heard about seasoned travellers getting itchy feet once they settle down, and let's face it, Adam, you've travelled more than most.'

I would have turned and stared at her in surprise, but that's hardly the most sensible thing to do when driving through the narrow lanes of our dale. The volume of traffic might not compare with rush hour in London, but then you rarely encounter combine harvesters in the capital.

'No, of course I'm not, Evie. Why would you think that? I have a lovely home in delightful surroundings. Added to which I now have a beautiful, intelligent, and loving partner. I think I'm as lucky as a man can get. Only a fool would wish to put even a fraction of what I have at risk.'

Having made the declaration, I risked life and limb by casting a swift glance sideways. The quick glimpse I had of the expression on Eve's face put me in mind of a cat. One from Cheshire.

During her recent shopping expeditions, Eve had discovered to her delight that her favourite café, Betty's, had a branch in the town. She suggested that we collected Faulkner and took him for afternoon tea. Not that I minded.

'OK, Adam, you've got me up here.' Paul bit into a choux bun as he spoke, careless of the consequences. He wiped cream from his tie before continuing. 'The buns are great, but we have confectionery in London, so what's the story? I don't think a critical review of Yorkshire patisserie is going to do wonders for the paper's circulation.'

Before telling him anything, we extracted a promise from Faulkner that he would not allow anything to go into print without first seeking our approval. Between us, Eve and I told him the full story from the moment Pattison came to visit us, omitting only the names of the group, the people involved, and of course Crowther.

'What we'd like to do, Paul, is take you to our place and introduce you to someone who is directly concerned, and demonstrate to you there and then what this is all about.'

'OK, why not?'

It was late afternoon when we arrived in Laithbrigg, and as we approached Eden House, Faulkner conceded that he could see the logic in my choosing to live in such delightful surroundings. 'Apart from the setting, Adam, I couldn't imagine anywhere further from the rat race, except perhaps the plains of Africa, and I suppose there's far less risk of being shot at round here.'

'I wouldn't put money on that,' Eve muttered, 'we seem to do nothing but attract trouble and violence.'

'I can't quite work out how Adam persuaded you to join him out in the wilds,' Faulkner told her. 'London has so much life.'

'Put it down to my natural charm.'

The outburst of laughter from the passenger seat was totally unwarranted, I thought.

There was no one in sight when we pulled up in the drive, which concerned me for a moment, but my fears were eased when Charlie opened the front door and waved a greeting. Faulkner looked at Eve's nephew for a second, before transferring his gaze to the pretty girl standing alongside him. 'Hang on,' he exclaimed, 'isn't that –'

'Trudi Bell? Dead right, Paul, and she has a part to play

in all this. Now you can understand how newsworthy this story is. Come along inside and we'll explain further.'

As we entered the building, I told him, 'By the way, when I was reciting that litany of crimes to your secretary, I forgot to add criminal damage to the list. Believe me, our house doesn't usually look like this.'

I introduced the reporter to Charlie and Trudi. 'Is everything set up?' I asked.

'Of course, Adam, just the way you asked for it. We're ready to go when you are.'

We steered Faulkner into the study, with Eve staying a couple of paces behind. She stopped in the entrance, ensuring the door remained wide open. 'I want you to listen very carefully, Paul,' I told him. 'I know you have a decent ear for music, but it is very important that you carry the melody you are about to hear in your mind for the next few minutes, OK?'

I nodded to Eve, who took a couple of paces back into the hall and waved her hand. Seconds later, the house was filled with the sound of an instrumental piece. Even with my limited knowledge, I could tell that the musicianship was superb, the work of a true maestro on the keyboard. When the last note died away, Faulkner was about to speak, but I held up a prohibitive hand, nodding to Charlie at the same time.

I think Charlie was relishing his role as the house DJ, for he placed the stylus on the disc with a flourish, and we listened as the tune was replayed. Hearing the two in such rapid succession, it was easy to tell that the recorded version was vastly inferior to the previous rendition. When it was over, I looked at Faulkner. 'Well, Paul, what do you think?'

'It's obviously the same tune, although the first version was far superior. Isn't it that hit by the Mystery Minstrel?'

'Yes, it is, and on the record, the songwriters are identified as A and J Deva. I've never heard of them, and I can vouch for the fact that whoever they are, they didn't write a note of that music. Would you like to meet the man who did? The man who has just played you the better version? The man everyone believed died seventeen years ago? Which, for your information, is three years before that record was released.'

Faulkner nodded, seemingly at a loss for words, which was almost a unique event. Eve stepped out of the room.

'Prepare yourself for a shock.' Eve returned right on cue, and as her companions followed, I told Paul, 'Allow me to introduce Sheila Bell, Trudi's mother, and the man alongside her is Gerry Crowther, former lead singer and keyboard player of Northern Lights.' I watched Paul grow more confused. 'Gerry is the actual composer of the tune you just heard, and he is also Trudi's father. None of which you can reveal just yet, OK?'

I have to admit that my talent for reducing an audience to stunned silence had never faced a stiffer challenge than that posed by Faulkner. My success was therefore all the sweeter.

Chapter Eighteen

The Admiral Nelson had six letting bedrooms, which were in the form of a terrace of chalets across the car park from the pub itself. I had arranged accommodation for Faulkner there. Despite the popularity of the pub as a bed and breakfast establishment, I'd been lucky enough to secure the last available room. That evening, as we entered the pub, I noticed that there seemed to be quite a lot of young customers in the bar, far more than usual, and many of the faces were unfamiliar to me. The landlord explained. 'Word seems to have got round about the identity of your famous house guest. Most of the local lads and some from Thorsby and Dinsdale are in here. I'm surprised they haven't been knocking on your door.'

I was intrigued to see how Trudi dealt with the situation. The solution she came up with was a simple one, and had me smiling with admiration at her ingenuity. As she was approached by first one, then another autograph hunter, Trudi appeared not to notice them. Instead, her attention remained fixed on her companion, as she stared with apparent adoration into his eyes. Immediately she had dealt with the request, sometimes even as she was handing the biro and paper back, she resumed her seemingly intimate conversation with Charlie. Even though he was obviously aware of her strategy, he played along with it. Only when we had entered the relative privacy of the restaurant and took their places at the table did they drop the pretence.

They walked the full length of the bar hand in hand, to

the obvious disapproval of Trudi's followers. Once the dividing door closed behind them, I heard Trudi tell him, 'Thank you for helping me, Charlie. It can get a bit oppressive. It's nice to be noticed, but sometimes you don't need all that attention.'

As we followed them to the table, I noticed that Trudi seemed in no hurry to let go of Charlie's hand, possibly, as a gesture of thanks, I thought. Nor did Charlie seem in the least upset by the arrangement.

Over dinner, we planned our strategy for going public with our story of the crimes we knew had been committed. Once Faulkner was in possession of all the facts in the case that we knew, I realized that it would be up to him how he wanted to play it. 'We have to maximise the impact for the readers, without giving it all away in one go,' he told us. 'One thing I will have to do even before we start putting the article together is obtain approval from our legal people. That's a much tougher assignment than it sounds. They're very twitchy about the paper being sued for libel, because judges seem to enjoy awarding large sums of damages against the media.'

He looked at Crowther. 'Going from what you told me earlier, I'd say it would be relatively easy to establish the provenance of the sheet music in your safe deposit, especially if it's signed and sealed. However, even doing that would need some careful arranging. I think we should make sure that when the envelope is opened, we have people present who can vouch for the authenticity of the paperwork and the occasion. In addition, we'd get a staff photographer up from London. Not for pictures that will be printed,' he added hastily, seeing the look of apprehension on Crowther's face. 'Not in the first instance, anyway. But they will be invaluable when you take the case of copyright theft to court, as I assume you will.'

He thought for a moment and then looked at me. 'I

think we can do this with a three-part article, make it a bit like a serial. We start with a scene setter to grab their attention, promising startling revelations in part two. Then we go for the meat of the story in the second section and finally the big revelations once all the facts are out there. That means Gerry's name and Trudi's parentage. It can be written as a bit of a tearjerker too, the father's missing years, that sort of thing. Then, if we can do it, we can name names, and make accusations. Do you think that will do the trick, Adam?'

I saw the look of mild distaste on Sheila's face. 'It sounds a lot worse than it will read,' I assured her. 'Paul is only expressing it the way any reporter would in-house.'

'Besides which,' Faulkner pointed out, 'if there's anything you don't like or feel uncomfortable with, you can veto it. Adam's made sure there are safeguards in place.'

'Before we begin, wouldn't it be sensible to obtain clearance from Lew Pattison and get his involvement,' Eve suggested. 'Not only might he have ideas about what he wants revealing and what he doesn't want to become public knowledge, but he's also bound to be able to provide more in the way of background.'

'Does he know about the copyright theft?' Faulkner asked.

'Yes, he was out of the country when we discovered it, but we brought him up to speed last week.'

'Adam means when *he* discovered it,' Crowther pointed out. 'He seems to have a flair for unearthing obscure facts.'

'You don't have to tell me that. He's like a pig rooting for truffles. It was a sad loss to the industry when he retired.'

Faulkner suggested his best plan would be to return to London, interview Pattison and obtain tacit approval from his editor for the articles before we proceeded further.

'And our lawyers,' – he grimaced – 'that will be the really hard bit.'

When we got back to Eden House later that evening, as we sat drinking a coffee before going to bed, I said to Crowther, 'If you're going to talk to Lew about Faulkner, would you ask him to try and find out about the other version of that Mystery Minstrel tune?'

'What other version is that?' Crowther asked. 'How many people have copied my tunes?'

'The version I heard on the radio is the only one I'm aware of. It definitely wasn't the same as that record.'

'How would you know?' Eve challenged me. 'You've said yourself more than once that you're hopeless where music's concerned.'

'Hopeless I may be, but not that dim that I can't tell the difference between the two different renditions of the same tune.'

'OK, clever clogs, what was the difference?'

I could tell that the four non-combatants in this scrap were enjoying the verbal encounter, and also that none of them thought much of my protestations. It was time for me to prove myself. 'Very well,' I told them, 'I'll set the record straight, if you'll stop needling me.'

I waited until the groans of protest at my dreadful puns died away before continuing. 'The difference couldn't be more marked. It was what attracted me to listen to the track on the radio. Not because of the keyboard playing, which was nothing special; not a patch on Gerry's. It was the guitar solo in the middle that grabbed my attention. I'm no expert, but I thought it was superb, truly outstanding.'

I was looking at Eve as I spoke, but out of the corner of my eye, saw Crowther, who had been lounging back in his chair, sit bolt upright. 'What did you say?' he demanded.

'I was talking about the guitar solo on the track I heard on the radio. Why, is it important?'

Crowther, whose natural complexion reflected his outdoor life, looked deathly pale. He stared at me in silence. For some reason, what I'd said had shocked him to the core. Sheila shook his arm gently, 'Gerry, Adam asked you a question.'

'You heard that tune played on a keyboard with a guitar riff in the middle?'

'Yes, that's right.'

'Then I'd love to know where it came from. When I wrote the original, I had it planned for a guitar riff, and I wanted Billy to play it. However, as you know, everything went pear-shaped and we never recorded it. In fact, Billy and I only played it through once, and we were on our own at the time. So, yes, please ask Lew to trace it, because I'd like to know who made the record, and where they got the music for it.'

'I was thinking earlier, when we were talking to Faulkner, that we haven't spoken to the other former members of Northern Lights. We talked to those we could around here, but no more than that. Nor any of the musicians Gerry took out of the line-up,' Eve added.

'It didn't help that two of them got murdered before we had chance to ask them pertinent questions,' I pointed out, 'and how can we be sure that wouldn't happen to the others if we approached them?'

'In that case perhaps it would be better to ask Faulkner to speak to them. He has no obvious connection to us, or to Gerry, or to Northern Lights. Besides which, as far as we know they're all based in or around London, which would be far more convenient for him than for us to have to trail back there again.'

I thought over Eve's idea, and developed it a little further. 'Perhaps if he visited Lew at his offices and chatted to members of his staff, like we did, possibly hinting at why he was there, and then made similar obscure remarks to the musicians, he might get lucky and provoke a reaction.'

I may have mentioned before that I seem to possess the knack of prophecy, but not always with the result I had in mind. Little did I know that I'd done it again.

I was up before eight o'clock the following morning, but Charlie beat me to it. When I went downstairs he was in the study, looking very much at home behind my new desk, which had been delivered the day before. He was reading what appeared to be the replacement files Harvey Jackson had sent us.

As I greeted Charlie, I heard footsteps on the stairs behind me, and turned to see Crowther was also an early riser. 'What are you studying?' I asked Charlie.

'You forgot somebody,' Charlie told me, rather obscurely. 'When you were talking about people who had it in for Mr Crowther, you forgot the woman who wrote those horrid reviews about Northern Lights.'

'Oh yes, I'd forgotten all about her.' I turned to Crowther. 'Among the stuff that Lew sent us there were some really vicious reviews of your gigs. The writer singled you out for the fiercest criticism. Do you remember them?'

Crowther shook his head. 'I never used to read reviews, and I certainly didn't move in the same circles as journalists. I tended to leave anything like that to Lew.'

'And of course he wouldn't show you any that were as unpleasant as those Charlie's looking for.'

'Certainly not, it would have been bad for morale.'

'Have you found them yet?' I asked Charlie, who was still turning documents over.

'No, not yet. I'll keep looking.'

'Do that, Charlie. When your aunt eventually manages to stagger out of her pit will you tell her I've taken Gerry over to Allerscar and that we'll be back for breakfast? We'll bring some eggs, so hopefully if she's up in time, perhaps she might condescend to cook for us.'

'No way am I passing her that message, Adam. I don't want to die young. You'd better write her a note. Alternatively, I'll just tell her where you've gone.'

It was almost ten o'clock when we returned, having called at the village shop in Allerscar for Gerry to drop some produce off. Eve was on the phone, and I could tell by her conversation she was taking to Lew Pattison, explaining Faulkner's involvement, and our plans for the reporter to conduct a series of interviews supposedly into the deaths of Mitchell and Thompson.

When she'd finished, she reported that Pattison was happy with the arrangement. 'We can brief Paul when we take him to catch his train,' I suggested. 'Lew can give him addresses and so forth.'

We walked through to the kitchen, where Crowther was chatting to Sheila and Charlie. 'Did you find those reviews?' I asked our junior detective.

'Yes, the woman's name is Diane Little. I told Aunt Evie, and she was going to ask Mr Pattison about her.'

'Oh yes, I almost forgot. Apparently, she still writes reviews, plus a showbiz gossip and scandal page. According to what Lew said, she seems to be able to access information and pick up bits of gossip other journalists can't get, and she's always spot-on. Lew said she has to be, otherwise she and the magazine would have been sued for millions before now. I don't know whether it's coincidence or not, but Diane Little now writes exclusively for *Music Magic*. And she still remains a mystery woman. Nobody knows the first thing about her.'

'Except that she's a fan of Dion,' Crowther interrupted.

We looked at him in surprise. 'Why do you say that?'

'I suppose it's entirely possible that Diane Little is her real name, but if she's gone to a lot of trouble to hide her true identity, what better way than assuming a false name?'

'You mean like you did,' Sheila suggested.

'Exactly like that.'

'Why did you say she might be a fan of Dion?' Eve asked.

'Dion recorded a single in the early sixties, *Little Diane.*'

We stared at Crowther for a moment before Eve spoke again. 'The fact that the name might be an assumed one could actually mean that the reviewer isn't a woman at all. Which would explain how the columnist got hold of all that gossip and inside information. I think Gerry has just given us a huge clue as to the journalist's identity.'

'You do? In that case you'd better share it with us,' I told her, 'because I for one am totally in the dark.'

Eve turned to Crowther as Trudi entered the room. 'When you used to record an album, I suppose you spent a fair amount of time between tracks waiting for the technicians to get things ready for you.'

'We did,' Crowther agreed, 'but of course things might have changed a lot since my day.'

'They haven't, Dad,' Trudi told him. 'Mr Pattison and Mr Jackson get a bit upset by the delays and complain how much it costs them to have musicians sitting around swilling coffee and filling in their football pools coupons.'

I saw the look that passed between Sheila and Crowther as Trudi called her father 'Dad' for the first time.

Eve continued, 'And I suppose they also exchange bits of gossip, which a session musician could easily pick up on, especially if he was listening out for them. A session musician who is known to be a fan of Dion's music. One moreover who hated Gerry Crowther. A man such as Wayne Barnett.'

'Evie, that is sheer deductive genius. What's more, it tallies with what Charlie said about Barnett. Those reviews would have been read by thousands of music lovers. There was nothing secretive about the way he criticised Gerry, which fits with Barnett's other actions.'

Our next task was to brief Paul Faulkner and get his agreement to our plans. 'One thing we ought to try is to get Pattison to drop a titbit of tasty but false information into Wayne Barnett's lap and see if it appears in Diane Little's column,' I suggested.

Eve shook her head in mock sorrow. 'You have an extremely devious mind, Adam.'

I smiled. 'It's most gratifying to be praised by an expert.'

'What sort of information were you thinking of?' Sheila interrupted hastily.

'I have to confess I've not thought that far ahead,' I admitted. 'Any morsel of juicy showbiz gossip would do, as long as we know it to be inaccurate. It doesn't even have to be scandalous; in fact it would probably be better if it wasn't, as it's being made up.'

'How about a planned American tour for Trudi?' Eve suggested. 'That would keep it in-house, so to speak.'

I thought this was a great idea, but one look at the expression of dismay on Trudi's face, mirrored by that of her mother, told me they didn't share my enthusiasm.

'Did you say something?' Sheila asked Trudi.

'No, Mum, I thought you must have told them.'

'I take it that's a touchy subject.' My insight is keen at times.

'It is, a bit. I'm afraid we can't use that. Lew Pattison is negotiating with promoters in the United States, so we dare not say anything until those discussions are concluded.'

'So there is going to be an American tour?' Eve asked.

'We hope so, but we won't know for a while. It will be sometime next year, all being well.'

'That's obviously out of the question then, but I'm sure Lew can come up with something else convincing.'

We'd been so absorbed in the events surrounding Crowther's reappearance that it came as a shock when Eve's sister Harriet rang from America, and I realized it had been over three weeks since we had heard from her. She began by apologizing for the delay in calling and asked how her son was.

'Charlie's fine,' I reassured her.

'Has he been behaving himself? I knew he must be tons better because of that practical joke he played on his sisters. Who did he get to impersonate a famous pop singer? Whoever it was, she certainly had Sammy fooled.'

'He didn't get anyone to impersonate her, Harriet. That actually was Trudi Bell on the phone to Sammy. She's staying here along with her mother and father.'

'Come off it, Adam, you can drop the pretence with me.'

'It isn't a pretence. I promise you, Harriet. It's far too long a story for a very expensive transatlantic phone call. We'll explain when you get back. I'll get Charlie for you.'

Harriet's conversation with her son took some time, leaving me to wonder how much her husband Tony would have to fork out for the call. When Charlie emerged from the study, he had a slightly anxious expression on his face.

'Something wrong?' I asked. See, insight again.

'Not really, at least I hope not. Would it be OK for me to stay a bit longer than planned? Dad's been given chance to bring the family back on the QE2, and that means they won't be home when we thought.'

'You didn't think that would be a problem, surely? Did you imagine we'd say no, you'll have to pack your bags and go back to the castle and spend the rest of your holiday on your own? Of course you can stay, Charlie, stay as long as you want.'

Charlie's frown vanished, to be replaced by a warm smile. I was surprised that my words had such a positive effect, until I realized that Trudi had appeared from the lounge and was standing behind me. I told them both about Harriet's disbelief, and her theory that Charlie had been playing an elaborate practical joke. 'She even accused me of being party to the deception.'

'That's going to make it even funnier when Trudi comes to visit us at the castle,' Charlie said smugly. 'I've invited her to come and look around. She's never been in a castle before. Trudi said she especially wants to see all the ancient bits, and I told her that my grandmother isn't really that old.'

'Don't believe him, he's making it all up. What I actually said was that I'd love to see the old chapel, and I was disappointed that the dungeons were blocked off. I'd have loved to have gone in there.'

I shuddered at the memory. 'You wouldn't say that if you'd spent any time down there,' I told her.

When Faulkner arrived at Eden House early that afternoon, he told us that he had been in touch with his editor, who had given cautious approval for our plan to expose the villains, but with one huge reservation. 'Everything will have to be run past our lawyers before publication. That's standard procedure, but they're very tough at the moment. We had to pay a huge amount out in damages last year after a story appeared that hadn't been properly vetted, so now they're insisting on belt and braces for everything.'

We explained our idea for him to conduct the interviews, and he saw the sense of the suggestion. 'I'm happy to go along with that; it will help give me a feel for the story. The other end of it, if you like. It's one thing talking to Gerry and Sheila about what happened in the past, but I need to get to grips with what's going on now.'

'Be careful, though, Paul,' I warned him. 'Whoever is behind this is both desperate and dangerous. Everyone here can vouch for that.'

Next morning, I drove Faulkner to the station. 'I can

see why you're so content up here,' he told me again. 'And I'm glad things have worked out for you. A lot of people couldn't understand why you chucked your job in and buried yourself away, but in view of what happened it seemed a logical thing to me.'

As he got out of the car, Paul said, 'I'll phone you with updates when I've spoken to everyone on that list. I reckon the guy Roberts will be hardest to catch if he's only a ninety-day resident in the UK, and I can't see the paper paying for me to go to the Bahamas or wherever. Still, you never know, I might get lucky.'

I was surprised when Faulkner rang next morning; even more surprised by his opening question. 'How good are you at Roman place names?'

For a moment I wondered if he'd been drinking, but that was totally unlike him. 'Not very good,' I admitted. 'In case you hadn't noticed, we gave up speaking Latin round here a few years back.'

'Very droll, Adam. I was looking through my notes on the train yesterday and I suddenly remembered that the Roman name for Chester is Deva. Wasn't it in Chester that Crowther's sheet music as stolen?'

'Yes, it was, and the supposed writers of the stolen tunes called themselves Deva.'

'Exactly, not that it gets us any further forward towards identifying them. Anyway, I've spoken to Pattison like you said and I'm due to visit his offices tomorrow. After that I've to try and locate the other members and see about talking to them. I'll call you again once I've done that.'

It was three days later when we heard from Pattison. After confirming that Faulkner had gone to his offices and spoken to all the relevant staff members, Lew told us the principal reason for his call. 'I was hoping to get Trudi to Harrogate tomorrow. We need to rehearse her concert appearance for one thing, and I want her to test the acoustics of the auditorium. However, we've hit a major problem. The keyboard player I had lined up to accompany her has been involved in a nasty road accident. He's in hospital, and won't be able to perform for several weeks, far too late for this show. The whole thing seems to be dogged by bad luck.' Pattison sighed. 'First it was the compère being ill and now this. The TV people are getting extremely twitchy. They're threatening to scrub the whole project unless they can get it in the can by the end of the month, and I'm at a loss to know what to do. There are other players about, but nobody I consider suitable.'

As Pattison was talking, I had an idea. 'Let me call you back, Lew. I need to chat to Trudi. In the meantime, I'd like you to do me a favour. Is it possible to find out how many different versions of a tune have been recorded?'

'Yes, it's quite easy if you know how.'

'In that case, here's what I'd like you to find out for me.'

Having explained what I needed, I hung up and walked through to the dining room, where Eve had just finished serving our guests their breakfast. I explained the problem surrounding Trudi's concert, and Pattison's despair at finding a replacement instrumentalist. 'Of course, there is one simple solution,' I added casually, 'and it's so obvious I can't understand why nobody else has thought of it.'

'And what might that be?' Eve asked, a trifle sarcastically.

'Well, I'm no expert, but I'd have thought who better to play the music than the composer.'

As soon as I said it, I realized I'd lost none of my talent for silencing an audience. Eve looked surprised, Sheila dumbfounded, and Crowther horror-struck by the suggestion. Only Charlie, and to a lesser extent Trudi, seemed to approve of my idea.

Eventually Sheila found her voice. 'What do you think, Gerry? I have to say Adam has made a good point, and it would be good for you to be on-stage with Trudi.'

'I can't do it, Sheila. I've been away too long. Besides which, if I appear in public all that will start up again, and I can't risk anything happening to you, or Trudi. I would never be able to live with myself if they harmed you.'

It seemed to me, it was at that point that Sheila took charge of Crowther's life and managed it much as she had Trudi's. 'It already has started, Gerry,' she told him. 'And the only way to stop them has already been instigated. Once they know the truth has been discovered, they won't dare risk anything for fear of giving themselves away. Apart from all that, they've robbed the three of us of almost twenty years together. I'll be damned if I let them spoil one more day.'

Trudi added her voice to that of her mother, which I think left Crowther with no choice. 'Please say yes, Dad. Mum's right in what she says, and besides, I'd rather have you play for me than some stranger. I'd be proud to be on stage with you.'

It was fascinating to watch the persuasion tactics and their effect on Crowther. As his expression changed, I knew what he'd decided long before he spoke. 'OK,' he agreed, 'you'd better phone Lew back and ask him what time we've to be in Harrogate for rehearsals.'

The rest of the day was spent at Allerscar, where Charlie and I tended Crowther's gardens, assisted by Eve and Sheila, whilst father and daughter rehearsed in the makeshift studio.

On our return home, I went upstairs and hauled out the battered cabin trunk that had accompanied me on many of my travels, but which was now a resting place for much of my memorabilia from childhood and my former career. I found what I was looking for and removed it. I decided to wait before revealing it to the others.

Chapter Nineteen

The next few days were hectic. Early starts involved ferrying Crowther to Allerscar where the two of us would sort out his vegetables and the chickens, before returning to Eden House to collect the others for the journey to Harrogate, where Gerry and Trudi continued rehearsing. After the second visit, which Sheila and Eve used as an excuse to go shopping, dragging Charlie along, while I watched the rehearsal, we gathered in Betty's Café – where else? I asked how the expedition had gone.

'Sheila enjoyed it, and so did I, but Charlie was bored silly until the last shop we went to. That really interested him, didn't it?'

Charlie, who had just that second taken an enormous bite from a caramel-iced choux bun, nodded agreement rather than risk spraying the assembly with a liberal coating of cream.

'What was so special about that shop?' I asked.

Eve explained about the antique shop they had ventured into, looking for a replacement mirror. It was the name of the shop that intrigued Charlie, coupled with what he saw in the window. As she spoke I was distracted by a stray thought, to such an extent that I failed to respond to a question until she prompted me. 'What do you think, Adam? Is it a good idea, or not?'

'Er ... yes, I think so. Sorry, something you said reminded me that we haven't heard from Paul Faulkner yet. He promised to report progress, remember?'

'Oh, yes, so he did. Perhaps he's been put onto another

story, or hasn't been able to interview the band members yet.'

'It isn't like Paul not to let me know, though. I'll phone him as soon as we get back to Laithbrigg.'

When I made the call, instead of speaking to Faulkner, I was put through to the paper's editor. Our conversation was brief and to the point. I put the phone down and stood for a moment, staring at the study wall, before rejoining the others in the lounge. As soon as I entered the room Eve could tell that something was wrong. 'Trouble, Adam?'

I nodded. 'My call was re-routed to Faulkner's boss. Paul was attacked the night before last. He's in hospital, unconscious, and they're not sure whether he's going to make it or not.'

My attempts to reassure Gerry and Sheila seemed unconvincing. In my own mind the attack seemed far too opportune to be coincidental. However, I didn't have long to ponder the motive, because a few minutes later the doorbell rang, and after she answered it, Eve called me through to the study.

I was surprised but not shocked when I recognized our visitors. Detective Inspector Hardy was accompanied by Johnny Pickersgill. 'I've had a phone call from the Met,' Hardy explained. 'They're investigating an assault on a reporter by the name of Paul Faulkner and they asked me to come and talk to you, because when they checked his belongings they discovered your visiting card in his pocket. Would you care to explain how he came by that?'

Although Hardy's words could have sounded accusatory, his tone was friendly. 'Simple enough,' I replied, 'I gave him it.'

Hardy smiled. 'OK, I didn't put it very well. Why did you give him it?'

I brought him up to date with developments, explaining the significance of the copyright theft. When I told him Pattison's estimate of the amount the thieves might have obtained from the record royalties, Hardy's eyes widened with surprise, and I heard a soft whistle of astonishment from Pickersgill. I told them of our plan to flush out those responsible, and Paul's part in the scheme. 'Whether that's the reason for the attack on him, I couldn't say. I spoke to his editor a few minutes ago because we hadn't heard from him, and he told me Faulkner's very ill.'

'We may never know the reason for the attack,' Hardy said. 'The officer I spoke to said there had been a number of death threats made against him over the years. You can't write about criminals and expect them to be pleased. One thing I can tell you is that his condition has improved slightly. Although he hasn't regained consciousness, he's off the danger list. The medical people aren't in a hurry to wake him up. They say patients often need time for their brain to recover when there have been head injuries. What does concern them still is how much he'll be able to recall, and whether there will be any permanent damage.'

'That sounds to me like an attack with a blunt instrument.'

Hardy agreed. 'That was what I was told. It sounds as if he had a lucky escape. The attackers were disturbed by a man who was walking past the alleyway when the assault happened. He challenged them, which was brave of him, and they ran off, otherwise there might have been a totally different outcome.'

Something in Hardy's words chilled me, but first I concentrated on another aspect of what he'd said. 'You mentioned attackers. Does that mean there was more than one?'

'Apparently so, although the witness can't be sure, because it was pitch black, and everything happened so quickly. He may have been wrong. There might only have been one other person besides Faulkner in the alley, but he thought there could have been two.'

'Did the officer you spoke to tell you where the attack

took place? A precise location, I mean?'

Hardy shook his head. 'No, he merely said it was in an alleyway. Why, is that important?'

I could see Eve was also looking puzzled. 'It might be. Let me explain. When all this started, we were given a lot of background information about the people surrounding Gerry Crowther. One of the members of Northern Lights was murdered in London.' I went on to explain the circumstances surrounding Billy Quinn's death. 'His body was discovered in an alleyway near a nightclub. It would be far too much of a coincidence if the alley where Faulkner was attacked and Quinn was murdered was one and the same, don't you think?'

Hardy promised to make enquiries and keep us posted on any developments.

After he left, Eve made a phone call to Pattison, which yielded more information. 'Apparently Faulkner went from Lew's place to the offices of *Music Magic* with a view to talking to Roberts. He must have found out that Roberts was in the country, and later that day, Lew got a phone call from Roberts demanding to know what was going on. Lew said he sounded extremely agitated, but wouldn't explain what had upset him. I think it's extremely significant that Roberts just happens to be in the country when all this is happening, and Faulkner interviews him, then a few hours later is found almost beaten to death.'

'That may be so, Evie but it isn't by any means conclusive. For all we know, Paul could have gone from *Music Magic* to interview the others on his list, and one of them could have turned nasty. Alternatively, as Hardy said, it could be someone else with a grudge against him.' As I was speaking, another thought struck me. 'We must also take into account that it was Faulkner's visit to Lew's offices that sparked the attack. What it shows is that if the attack is related to this case, the culprits are getting increasingly desperate to cover up their crimes.'

'And we're still no nearer to finding out who they are. What can we do to change that?'

'It would have to be something truly dramatic to force their hand, but don't ask me what, because I haven't a clue.'

A couple of days passed before the idea came to me as to how to force those responsible into the open. In the meantime, news that Paul Faulkner's condition was continuing to improve was balanced by learning that the alley *was* the same one where Billy Quinn had been murdered. Knowing that the attacks were linked gave impetus to my scheme, which I put to Eve, Sheila, and Crowther at what I mentally referred to as a management meeting.

Although at first horrified by the plan, Crowther soon accepted the necessity, especially when I pointed out that if we were successful, it would free him, Sheila, and Trudi from any further threat. 'Look at it this way,' I told him, 'once they know you're still alive, and that you're aware of everything they've done and why they did it, there will be no mileage in trying to attack you.'

It was logical, and Crowther accepted that logic. What I failed to take into account was that desperate men don't think or act logically.

I left it to Eve to sort out the details with Pattison, who would also have to negotiate with the TV company on our behalf. 'What we need,' I told her before she made the call, 'is for Lew to invite all the ex-members of Northern Lights plus members of his own staff to the concert recording in Harrogate. If he offers them complimentary tickets, plus rail fare and accommodation, that should get them all there.'

'Anything else, apart from spending Lew's money for him?'

'Yes, ask him to follow through with our idea by dropping a bit of false information Barnett's way. If it appears in this week's issue of *Music Magic* it will confirm what we suspect to be true.'

As Eve was talking to Pattison, I walked through to the lounge and handed Crowther a parcel.

'I dug this out the other day and thought you might want it for the concert.'

He unwrapped it and held up the jacket for Sheila and Trudi to inspect.

'That's brilliant,' Sheila told him. 'Where did you find it, Adam?'

'I bought it many years ago when I worked in New York.'

'Try it on, Dad,' Trudi urged him.

'We're pretty similar in build, so hopefully it should fit.'

Crowther stood up and put the jacket on. As I'd hoped, it fitted perfectly. He turned, like a model at the end of the catwalk, revealing the rear of the garment. The iconic image of Buddy Holly was as identifiable now as it had been twenty years ago. Nobody with any knowledge of Gerry Crowther seeing that jacket could mistake the implication, even before the announcement was made.

'I've had another idea about the concert. I think I should do the introduction,' I told them as we waited for Eve to join us. 'What do you think? Will it work? And will the TV people agree? Eve's putting the idea to Lew right now.'

'Lew Pattison will get them to agree,' Sheila told me confidently. 'He's got them eating out of his hand. Nobody but Lew could have got them to put up with the delays to the concert recording.'

Pop magazines such as *Music Magic* were not exactly high on the reading list at Eden House. Not in the normal course of events, that is. However, having ordered a copy from the village shop, much to the surprise of the owner, I sent Charlie to collect it on the day of publication. The journey to the far end of the village must have been fraught with terrors I obviously wasn't aware of, for Charlie apparently needed the protection of someone to accompany him on the walk. Luckily, Trudi volunteered for the dangerous mission.

We'd left it to Pattison to provide the requisite item of spurious gossip, and his phone call the previous day confirmed that he had engineered an 'accidental' encounter with Wayne Barnett and passed on a tasty morsel of false information.

Sure enough, when the youngsters returned, we scanned the magazine and there, right at the top of the page containing Diane Little's Show-Biz Round-Up, was the titbit we had been told was likely to be reported. 'Country and Western Legend to team up with Punk Rock Group for UK tour' the headline read.

Pattison had consulted the American singer in question, who was in London at the time, and the man, who was one of Lew's biggest overseas clients, had readily agreed to go along with the deception. 'He thought it sounded like terrific fun,' Lew told us. 'His actual words were, "I've had enough shit dumped on me by reporters over the years, it'll be great to get a bit of revenge". I think he'd relish the chance to confront Barnett over the story, but I won't allow that.'

Now that we had established beyond doubt that Wayne Barnett and Diane Little were one and the same person, we more or less discounted him from our list of suspects, which left us with four. Neville Wade and Pete Firth I considered to be long shots, the favoured ones being Robbie Roberts and Tony Kendall. 'The one thing that does concern me though,' I told Eve, 'is Pete Firth suddenly vanishing from home. I could understand it if he'd been tempted by another woman, or gone on a drink or drugs binge, but I think Julie keeps him on too tight a rein for that to happen. Besides which, she told me Pete's visitor had put the wind up him somehow. I think I'll give her a call and see if she's heard from our mobile DJ.'

The resulting telephone conversation did little to allay my disquiet, in fact it increased it. 'She admitted that she's heard from Firth,' I told Eve. 'She wasn't going to say anything, but I threatened to call the police and report Firth as a missing person if she didn't tell me what she knew. However, I'm by no means convinced I heard the full story. All she was prepared to say was that Pete had phoned her a couple of times, and that she was hoping he would ring again in the next couple of days.'

'What did you say to that?'

'I told her that when Pete phones she can tell him it's quite safe for him to come home now, and if he doesn't believe me, all he has to do is wait a couple of days and then call me. I also told her that in the meantime I was arranging for a couple of invitations to be sent, one for her and one for Pete, to attend Trudi's Harrogate concert. By then, I said, we believe this will all be over.'

Eve's eyes widened at my final statement. 'That was a bit presumptuous, wasn't it?'

'I don't think so. We have our eyes on the main targets now, and besides which, once Gerry makes his reappearance, that, together with my announcement, should put an end to the danger.'

'I still think Roberts has to be number one on our list,' Eve told me, 'you don't start up a magazine like *Music Magic* without a substantial investment, and Roberts didn't have that sort of money, by what we can gauge.'

'What about your other contender? Are you ruling out your Harrogate antique dealer?'

'He's Charlie's, not mine. He spotted the name Kendall on the premises,' she pointed out. 'But, no, I'm certainly not ruling Kendall out, even if he is the same person as the shopkeeper in Harrogate, which I think is a long shot. Let's face it, Kendall isn't exactly an uncommon name.'

'I agree, and I think the chances of a former musician becoming the owner of an antique shop in the centre of the area where all this has been happening are somewhat remote. Tony Kendall is just as likely to have become a tourist guide in the Kalahari desert or a missionary working in the Amazonian rain forest.'

Eve stared at me for a moment, which seemed longer to me. Her gaze was one of the piercing ones that always makes me uncomfortable. 'All right,' she admitted, 'so my idea was a wild one, but you never get them, I suppose? There's no need to pour scorn on it simply because it wasn't the product of your over-heated imagination. Or were you rehearsing prose for a change in career, moving from crime fiction to fantasy, perhaps? The Kalahari desert indeed!'

To this day, wild ideas are known in our house as 'Kalahari dreams'.

When Pattison had phoned to tell us about the deception he'd set up, he also informed us that he had told Harvey Jackson to arrange security for the concert, to supplement that provided by the venue. 'I'll be coming up to Harrogate the day before to supervise the arrangements and liaise with the TV Company,' he told us.

Despite the precautions he'd put in place, I was uneasy, and told Eve so. 'Being of a naturally cautious nature I think it would be sensible to tell DI Hardy what we're up to with Gerry, and ask if it's possible for a police presence in the amphitheatre too. It may prevent trouble and, who knows, with a bit of luck they might be in a position to make an arrest.'

'I think pretty much all of what you said makes perfect sense,' Eve replied. She paused then, but I knew there was more to come, and waited in trepidation. I wasn't disappointed. 'The only thing I would take issue with is your opening statement,' she said with a smile that combined sickly sweetness with a touch of venom. 'To describe yourself as "being of a naturally cautious nature" is one of the most outlandishly preposterous claims of all time. How long have I known you? Less than two years, and in that time I've been tied up and left to die in a dungeon accompanied by a pack of hungry rats who had me on their menu as their tastiest meal for centuries, then kidnapped at knife-point and held prisoner by a triple murderer, and only a couple of weeks ago had my home wrecked as a warning to keep our noses out of other people's business. All this because of you and your so-called "cautious nature". If that's a representative sample of the after-effects of you behaving cautiously, heaven help me if you ever become reckless.'

I stared at Eve admiringly. 'You really have a superb way with words. I think you should take over the writing and I'll go into partnership with Gerry Crowther growing peas and beans.'

Later that morning, as I was enjoying a quiet half hour in the study with the door closed, pretending to work, I picked up the magazine that had been left on the dresser. This time, instead of heading straight for the Diane Little article, I read the whole of the paper. I don't know if I'm unusual in this, but with newspapers and magazines I often start at the back page, then work my way to the front. I think this might stem from my interest in sport rather than politics or economics. I bypassed the Diane Little column and eventually ended up reading the editorial. As I reached the final paragraph, I stopped reading and began to cast my mind back to the facts we knew. I read the paragraph again, to make certain I had understood before going in search of Eve. Following the pungent smell of raw onions, I found her in the kitchen. Eve was chopping vegetables for the casserole she was cooking for the evening meal.

'Have you a minute to take a look at this?' I asked, putting the magazine on the worktop. I pointed to the editorial. 'Concentrate on the final paragraph.'

Eve read it through and then looked up, her surprised expression telling me the significance hadn't been lost on her. She was about to speak when the phone rang. I went to answer it, meaning to get rid of the caller as quickly as possible so as to return to our interrupted impromptu meeting. However, when I heard the caller's voice, my plans changed abruptly.

Ten minutes later I returned. Eve stopped work and turned round, a carrot in one hand, a kitchen knife in the other. 'Who was on the phone?' She gestured down the hall, using the carrot to point with, which was a mild relief.

'Pete Firth, he rang because Julie passed him my message. He still didn't want to talk, but he admitted he was scared, both by his visitor, and by what happened to Mitchell and Thompson.'

'Did he say who visited him?'

'He implied it was Steve Thompson, but he wouldn't tell me outright. Anyway, he's going to think about whether to attend the concert or not.' I gestured to the magazine. 'What do reckon to that? It seems to eliminate one more suspect, don't you agree?'

'I do, but where do we go from here?'

'I think we should phone Hardy and get him to look at that, then we can try and get him to investigate your other theory.'

Chapter Twenty

DI Hardy looked at the article for much longer than the time needed to grasp its meaning, by which I realized that he hadn't grasped its importance. I explained, 'It states in the final paragraph that *Music Magic* has recently celebrated its sixteenth anniversary and that the circulation continues to increase. All very nice, but the point as far as we're concerned is the date the magazine went on sale for the first time. Sixteen years ago would make in 1966. Our theory, or rather Eve's, was that Robbie Roberts, the former Northern Lights musician who founded *Music Magic*, got the working capital needed by filching music written by Crowther and recording it, creaming in the royalties. However, the Mystery Minstrel didn't appear until 1968, by which time this magazine was well established.'

'So on that basis, you think we should discount Roberts as a suspect?'

'Perhaps not entirely. Don't have him down as a non-runner; just lengthen the odds against him.'

'OK, who do I chalk up as favourite?'

I looked at Eve. This was down to her. She'd been the one who had devised the plan she was about to put to Hardy. 'Our prime suspect is now a man called Tony Kendall. He was the Northern Lights keyboard player until Crowther joined the group. There wouldn't be room for two members playing the same instrument, so Kendall had to go. This would have left him very bitter, I guess. Added to that, from what people have told us about him, Kendall is the type who worshipped money, and would go to any lengths to get it.'

Eve paused for a second, gathering her thoughts, then continued, 'I asked Crowther whether Kendall might have heard him playing one of the pieces that were later recorded by the Mystery Minstrel and realized the potential. Crowther isn't sure. He only played it through two or three times, because he wasn't satisfied with it. The alternative is that if Kendall saw the sheet music lying around, that could have been enough to inspire him to steal it.' She stopped and looked at me. I knew my cue and took up the story.

'We have a few problems regarding Kendall, though.'

'What might they be?'

'The first is that as far as we can tell, nobody has seen Kendall since the day he left Northern Lights. I say, as far as we can tell, because we do have one idea, but it's a fairly long shot, and we have nothing to confirm it as yet. The second, is that even if we locate Kendall we have absolutely no proof. All we're working on is guesswork and supposition.'

Hardy chuckled. 'They seem to have worked well enough for you in the past.'

'The other stumbling block,' I added, not wanting to make things too easy for him, 'is that we're fairly certain that Kendall, or whoever is responsible, isn't working alone. We believe they have an accomplice, someone working within Pattison's company, and that person has been passing information about our activities. What we don't know is who that person is.'

'Any other problems?' Hardy smiled, robbing the question of any hint of sarcasm. 'Not that those aren't big enough.'

'No, I think that about covers it.'

'What was your idea?'

I handed the conversational baton back to Eve. 'When

we were in Harrogate the other day I went shopping with Sheila Bell. In the process we went in a shop named Kendall Antiques and it made me wonder if that was the same Kendall.'

Hardy looked sceptical.

Eve explained her reasoning before I asked. 'I seem to remember you had fingerprint evidence from the car involved in Thompson's death, is that right?'

'We do, and DS Middleton from Leeds also matched it to a single print found in Mitchell's garage.'

'Even better, because Eve has an idea as to how to prove one way or the other if it is the same Kendall, and if he is behind the murders.'

Eve, explained. 'I thought that if someone were to go into the shop with an item and ask for a valuation for insurance purposes, they would be able to walk out with a sheet of paper with Kendall's prints on, ready for comparison. We would have gone ahead and done it, but for one of the problems that Adam outlined. If we're right, and one of the conspirators works in Pattison Music and Management, and they happened to be around when we went in, they'd be certain to recognize us, and the game would be up.' Eve gave Hardy little chance to ponder over this before continuing, 'However, they wouldn't get suspicious if a stranger walked in.'

'I suppose I could get someone to do that. Which, I guess is the reason you asked me here.'

'Only part of the reason,' Eve replied.

Hardy thought for a moment. 'So where do we find an antique? It would need to be something valuable, something worth insuring as a separate item.'

'I thought of that too. The sign actually said *Kendall Antiques: Fine Arts and Antique Jewellery*.' Eve reached across and took a jewel case from the dresser drawer. She opened it and laid it on the table. 'How about this?' she asked.

Hardy stared at the necklace with admiration. The perfect ovals of the rich, red stones stood out sharply against the brilliant translucence of those gems surrounding each one. He gestured towards the jewellery. 'Are those what I think?'

'Rubies in a diamond setting,' Eve confirmed. 'They were commissioned by my great-grandfather as a wedding gift for his young bride. My great-grandmother also had another one which he had made for their silver wedding. That one was passed down to my sister. It has sapphires instead of rubies though.'

'We don't have much time before the concert,' I pointed out, 'and it would ease Crowther's mind considerably if we were to get this resolved before he goes on stage. Which reminds me, we were going to ask you if you would like to go along in an official capacity, together with DS Middleton and one or two other officers. That way we might wrap the whole business up.'

'That sounds like a good plan. I think it best to appoint officers rather than ask for volunteers, though. I don't want to get knocked over in the rush. I'll leave this necklace here and ask Johnny Pickersgill to take it through to Harrogate tomorrow, get the valuation, take the document to the fingerprint guys, and return your jewels.'

The day before the concert, when I was on my daily run to Allerscar in my role as gardening assistant, Eve took a phone call from Lew Pattison. 'He wants you to travel to Harrogate,' she told me. 'Apparently the TV producer is keen to talk to you, to discuss your part in the concert.'

'What did you tell him?'

'I said that wasn't possible. I told Lew you were already behind with work on your next book, and that was because you'd been spending far too much time looking after his clients and dealing with their problems, as well as acting as host for them. I said your publishers were getting twitchy about you meeting the deadline they set you for delivery of the manuscript.'

I stared at my intended with admiration. She looked so innocent and guileless, it was virtually impossible to believe her capable of uttering such a tissue of lies and half-truths. 'I don't have a deadline to meet,' I pointed out weakly.

'I know that, and you know that, but Lew doesn't. If that TV producer is so desperate to talk to you, let him drive here from Harrogate. I don't see the need, myself.'

'Did Lew give any indication of what the man wants from me?'

'None whatsoever. I told him they could either phone you or come here. Alternatively, they'd have to wait until tomorrow. That can't have been satisfactory, because he rang back a few minutes later to inform me that they will be coming here later today, and to make sure we're in. I told him I couldn't give any guarantees, they'd have to take their chance. To be honest I was a bit annoyed with Lew. He's not usually that inconsiderate.'

'Maybe he's feeling the pressure. This is a big event, after all.'

'There are other ways of dealing with pressure than taking it out on other people, though.'

Pattison's car pulled up outside Eden House just as Eve was on the point of serving dinner, which caused her to suffer a distinct sense of humour failure. I think Pattison could tell she was fuming, because he promised not to keep us a minute longer than was absolutely necessary. Unfortunately, I don't think his companion, who I judged to be in his mid-to-late-twenties, was listening, or if he was, he paid little heed.

He took me through every aspect of television appearance, speaking slowly and reiterating several points, as if talking to someone for whom a TV set is a novelty. I listened, my increasing frustration wearing away at my patience, until he began to lecture me on the art of talking to camera. 'Many people find the experience too stressful to cope with,' he said, 'which is why I wanted you to come through to Harrogate so we could have a trial run, so to speak. Just to get you familiar with the technique.'

'I'm immensely grateful for your thoughtfulness.' As I spoke, I saw Eve wince at my sarcastic tone. 'Just how stressful do you think speaking to camera with an audience of a thousand people can be? Tell me how you think it compares, for example, to recording a live news report with mortar shells exploding all round you, machine gun bullets flying past, and your cameraman having to stop shooting in mid-sentence because he's been hit by shrapnel?'

'Er ... no ... I don't suppose it does compare. Have you done that?'

'I have, and when you've spent as many hours talking to camera as I have, perhaps you will appreciate that it holds no terrors for me.'

I dare not look at Eve, so I glanced at Gerry and Sheila instead. That was a mistake, because Crowther was biting his lip, while Sheila was examining the wallpaper intently. To give him his due, the producer realized his mistake and apologized, and a few minutes later they departed. Before they left, Pattison assured Gerry that he had organised personal security for both him and Trudi at the venue. 'Or rather, I got Harvey Jackson to sort it out. You remember Harvey, don't you?'

'Yes, he was a friend of Billy's, I'd heard he was still with you,' Crowther said.

'There will be quite a few from the old days there tomorrow. Harvey's secretary, Judith Lane, for one, plus Melissa Norton, Graham Stead, and Barry Walker.'

'You must pay them well, to keep them all this time.'

'Please tell them that.' Pattison turned to me. 'I did what you asked, Adam, or rather I got Graham to do it. He checked that tune out, and the only recording of it in existence is the one by the Mystery Minstrel. We'd better get off now. I left Alice at the hotel, and we haven't dined yet.'

'Neither have we,' Eve reminded him.

I was still standing in the middle of the room, in a state of shocked silence as Eve ushered them through the front door. What Lew had told me made no sense. If no other recording of the tune existed, how come I'd heard a different version on the radio? I was sure I hadn't been mistaken, but now I was beginning to doubt both my memory and the evidence of my own ears. The version I'd heard on the radio was too dissimilar to that on the record I'd bought for me to have been wrong.

'Now perhaps we can have dinner. I only hope it hasn't been spoilt,' Eve remarked acidly.

She was still speaking when the doorbell rang. Charlie's giggle earned him a murderous glare from his aunt, who wheeled and marched down the corridor towards the front door like an invading soldier. I feared for the safety of whoever was on the other side of it. She flung the door open and paused, her aggression almost visibly draining away as she stared at the amiable face of our village policeman, who looked somewhat taken aback on seeing the virago in front of him.

'Sorry to intrude,' he told her. 'Is this a bad time? Only, I wanted to return your necklace as soon as possible.' He led out the jewel case.

'Sorry, Johnny, I was on the point of serving dinner. Do you want to come in for a minute?'

He stepped through into the hallway. 'I won't keep you. I only wanted to give you this, and to let you know the mission was successfully accomplished. I got a valuation letter with the man's prints on it. It's gone off to the fingerprint guys for checking. While I was there, I had a look round and spotted the old musical instruments. I think young Charlie could be on to something.'

'Can you describe the man who gave you the valuation letter?'

The interruption came from Crowther who had followed Eve. Pickersgill turned to look at him for a moment. 'Fairly ordinary, about your age and size.'

'What about his hair?'

'The lighting in the shop was so poor it would be difficult to say. Mid-brown, I think, neatly trimmed, that's about all I can remember.'

'In that case I don't think the man you saw was Tony Kendall. He was already losing his hair when I knew him, and that's nigh on twenty years ago. He'd be bald as an egg by now, I reckon. What do you think, Sheila?'

She shook her head. 'I never actually met him. I think I saw him on stage with Northern Lights once, but by the next gig I attended, he'd left the group.' She smiled. 'I wasn't your groupie at that point, remember.'

Johnny was about to leave when he turned and said, with concern, 'By the way, I hope you actually do have that necklace insured. According to the bloke who examined it, it's worth well into five figures. I'll get you a copy of the valuation if you need it.'

'Thanks, Johnny, but that won't be necessary.'

Later that evening, I was sitting in the study making some plot notes for the next book I'd got planned, when Crowther entered the room.

'Am I disturbing you?' he asked.

'No, I'd just about finished.'

'Oh, good, because I wanted to ask you something.' He hesitated for a moment, as if choosing how to continue. 'When Lew told you about that tune, I could see it disturbed you in some way. Why was that?'

'I still don't believe what I heard on the radio was the same as what's on that record.' I gestured towards the record player.

'Could it have been someone playing live?'

'No, it wasn't that sort of show.'

'You said before there was something special about it. Something to do with the guitar?'

'It was the way it was played. I definitely heard it, and there isn't one on the recorded version.'

'What sort of guitar was it?'

The question was ordinary enough, and my answer was straightforward. I certainly couldn't have predicted the effect my reply would have on Crowther – and on me. 'That's easy, because you don't hear them often these days. It was a Hawaiian guitar.'

Gerry clutched the back of a nearby chair for support, and I noticed his knuckles were white with the tight grip he had on the wood. 'What's wrong?' I asked.

'When I composed that tune, I wrote the riff for a Hawaiian guitar. As far as I'm aware, the only other person who knew that was Billy Quinn.'

'Did he use a Hawaiian guitar when you and he tried the song out? Perhaps someone else, the thief perhaps, overheard it played that way and copied it.'

'If they'd done that, surely they would have put it on the record. It's too good to leave out. Besides which, we didn't have access to a Hawaiian guitar when we played it. The only reason we gave it a run through was so I could tell whether it was worth continuing with.'

I smoothed the hairs on the back of my neck down. If there was a logical explanation, I certainly couldn't think of one. And neither, to judge from his expression, could Gerry Crowther.

Chapter Twenty-one

We'd been asked to report to the venue by 10 a.m. next day, which made for a very early start, for me and Crowther. We took Charlie with us to help speed up the work. The task of ferrying him to and fro was becoming a bit of a chore. Admittedly the fresh produce and newly laid eggs were more than welcome, but I'd be glad when the matter was resolved and our lives could return to normal. I'm not averse to company, or to having guests in the house, but it seemed as if Eve and I had barely any time to ourselves.

Mind-reading was something I've never been proficient at, but perhaps Crowther sensed some of what I was thinking. 'I'm sorry, this must be an awful bore for you. It can't be easy being landed with the three of us, and having all this to do as well. To be honest, Adam, I'll be glad when tonight's over with. Perhaps then, Sheila and I can start our life together and I can get to know my daughter properly. So, if I feel that way, you and Eve must be really frustrated at the unwanted company.'

Naturally, I protested, but how much of what I said he believed is another matter. We got the chores out of the way as quickly as possible and returned to Eden House before eight o'clock, with Crowther nursing a tray of our breakfast on his lap.

The process of filming a performance such as the concert Trudi was to appear in was new to me, despite my former career. My filming had been unrehearsed, on the spot, often with events unfolding in the background, and little chance for more than a single take. The spectacular, which was the TV company's description, not mine, featured a combination of established stars, some household names, plus up-and-coming talent such as Trudi. All the acts were to be introduced by a comedian, whose role as compère befitted his status as a household name.

His task was made more difficult by the number of retakes, involving panning shots, tracking shots, sound level changes, lighting modification, and any number of other difficulties that prevented perfection. Despite the comedian's undoubted talent, the whole process soon became tiresome, and after a particularly trying half hour, where every aspect of filming one act went wrong in turn, I nudged Eve. 'Let's get out of here while they're setting up the next take,' I whispered. 'If I hear that joke about the three men in the desert one more time, I'll scream. I vote we go for some lunch.'

Accompanied with some reluctance by Charlie, who was clearly anxious not to miss Trudi's rehearsal, we left the venue and headed towards town.

One of the disadvantages I'd found from living in a village was the unavailability of a fish and chip shop. In suggesting we have this delicacy for lunch, I was conscious that we should not be absent for too long, in case I was called on to rehearse. 'Good idea,' Eve agreed, 'but perhaps on the way I could show you that antiques shop.'

'And that's another good idea, but we'd better not be seen walking past in case someone recognizes us. We wouldn't want to put the villains on their guard if it does happen to be connected.'

'You still don't think it's the same Kendall, do you?'

'I'm not saying that. It could well be, but equally, it could be someone totally different.'

'One good thing, from our point of view – literally, is

that the shop is close to a road junction, so we'd be able to observe the front of the building from the street corner without being visible from inside.'

Less than five minutes' walk brought us to where Eve indicated the shop. 'It's along that road to the left, about four doors down.'

We reached the junction. Fortunately traffic was quite heavy, giving us chance to look round, whilst apparently assessing whether it was safe to cross the road. I looked towards the shop, but before I had chance to take in more than the name, Eve dragged me back by one arm, doing the same to Charlie with the other. 'Quick, inside here,' she hissed urgently.

We were standing in the entrance to a barber's shop. She thrust us through the door and tugged at our sleeves. 'Turn to face the inside of the shop,' she ordered.

'Why, what's wrong?' I asked as I obeyed.

Eve peered cautiously from between me and Charlie, who looked as perplexed as I felt. After a moment, she relaxed. 'It's OK, she's gone now. Didn't you see her?'

'See who? I didn't get chance to see anyone.' I looked at Charlie, who shrugged.

'Coming out of the antiques shop. It was Pattison's secretary, Melissa Norton.'

'I didn't see her. You dragged us in here before I noticed anyone or anything apart from the shop sign. Are you certain it was her? You couldn't have mistaken her for someone else?'

I was on the receiving end of one of Eve's withering glances. Her tone was as icy as her expression. 'Of course I'm certain. I think that more or less proves the connection, don't you?'

'Unless she was buying a whatnot for her Aunt Agatha.'

The stare got even colder, but before Eve could respond, the shop owner came forward to greet us. I hadn't particularly needed a haircut, but couldn't at that precise moment think up another excuse for having entered the shop. After an expensive but admittedly professional trim, I suggested we head for lunch.

'Did you see the woman, Charlie?' I asked.

He shook his head. 'I wouldn't have known her even if I had. I wasn't with you the day you went to Mr Pattison's offices.'

'One thing I did notice, before you manhandled me into the shop,' I told Eve, 'is the sign over Kendall Antiques window. According to that there are branches in Harrogate, London, and Cheltenham.'

'Sounds like a profitable business.'

'That's true, but the point is, all three of those are very expensive places to set up a business.'

'Oh, I see what you mean.'

'The cost of renting a shop, plus the local rates would be steep compared to other places. And that's before you stock it.'

'Wouldn't that be the same everywhere?' Charlie asked.

'Not necessarily, because the sort of items offered for sale in an upmarket place like this would be dearer to buy than a town where the residents aren't as well-heeled. And the more expensive the stock, the more of your working capital is tied up until it sells, and then you've to replace them. It's a vicious circle.'

I thought about the sighting, and it more or less convinced me Eve was right in her assumption. There could be little chance of an innocent reason for Melissa Norton going into Kendall Antiques. She had to be his accomplice. It must have been through her information that he realized the danger posed by us asking questions about Northern Lights and Crowther, and the potential threat should either Mitchell or Thompson talk about their part in events years ago.

'We ought to tell Hardy, don't you agree, Adam?'

We'd reached the fish and chip shop and were waiting for a table to come free in the restaurant area. 'Certainly, but not until we've eaten.'

Getting hold of Hardy proved harder than we'd hoped. Holding a meaningful conversation with officers at Dinsdale police headquarters, whilst feeding coins into the public call box, proved both frustrating and unrewarding. Eventually, as my stock of change was dwindling towards zero, I was told that Detective Inspector Hardy was out of the office, and that they couldn't tell me when he would return.

'That was a complete waste of time and money,' I said when I emerged from the phone box, allowing the heavy door to slam to behind me. I explained what little I'd learned. 'Why don't you phone Johnny Pickersgill,' Eve suggested. 'Ask him to contact Hardy and tell him what we saw. It's got to be better than feeding coins into that all day.'

Unfortunately, Pickersgill wasn't at home either, but I left a message as best I could. His wife took delight in telling me that she and Johnny would be attending the concert. 'There were some spare tickets, and DI Hardy wants us there. Apparently, as the concert recording has been cancelled a couple of times, the TV people are desperate to fill the seats so that the whole thing looks and sounds better. I'm really looking forward to it.'

'What should we do now?' Eve asked as we wandered through the town centre.

'I think we ought to go back to the Centre, but keep a low profile for the time being. Without a police presence as back up, we could risk putting ourselves in danger, or tipping off Kendall and Melissa Norton.'

'Maybe we should leave it a while before going back,' Eve suggested. 'I think I'd be uncomfortable if that woman is there, knowing what we do.'

'OK, we'll continue, but as long as you promise all we're doing is window shopping.'

Out of my eye corner I saw Charlie grin. 'Something funny?' I asked.

The cold tone in my voice didn't deter him. 'No, I was just thinking it was like being out with my mum and dad.'

It was a pleasantly warm afternoon spent wandering around. Charlie asked to visit the sports shop, but eventually, conscious that the producer would want me at some stage for a sound check, we ambled back to the Conference centre. We walked into the foyer, arriving in the middle of a minor crisis. It was clear that Lew Pattison was extremely angry by the ferocious scowl on his face. 'Something wrong?' I asked, displaying once more my talent for stating the obvious.

'There's been a king-sized mix up over the security arrangements for Gerry and Trudi,' he growled. 'The men were supposed to have arrived before now. I don't know what the hell's gone wrong. I've got Harvey Jackson and Barry Walker standing guard over Crowther, with Sheila and Graham Stead as Trudi's minders. Left to myself I wouldn't have bothered, the Centre staff are quite capable, but Gerry threw a wobbler and threatened to pull out, taking Trudi with him if I didn't sort something out.'

He glared at us as if it was our doing, which I thought was somewhat ungrateful. 'Have you found out what's happened to the security men? Could they have been stuck in traffic, perhaps?' Eve asked.

'No, that's another problem. I rang the company and the receptionist told me the only person who could tell me isn't available at present, but if I ring back in another hour he should be out of his meeting. Normally I'd have Melissa or Judith dealing with this, but both of them seem to have gone walkabout. I don't suppose you've seen either of them on your travels, have you?'

I was about to reply; to tell him we'd seen Melissa

Norton in town, but Eve warned me off with a slight shake of her head. 'Didn't I say this concert was jinxed?' Lew asked despairingly. 'I was wrong, fated is more like it.'

We uttered polite meaningless words of consolation, and left Pattison to fume as he awaited news from the security company. Inside the auditorium, we sat down to watch the rehearsal, which seemed to have made little progress during our absence. Our enjoyment of a talented singing duo was brought to an end when Alice Pattison appeared behind us. She tapped Eve on the shoulder. 'Lew wants to talk to you,' she whispered. 'It's urgent, and he's really upset.'

We followed her out of the auditorium, trying our best to do it silently. I hoped our departure wouldn't be noticed, or taken as criticism of the singers on stage. Outside, Pattison was pacing up and down, at little short of a march. 'I've just got hold of the managing director of the security firm. He was the one who took the order in the first place.' He paused, and his expression got even grimmer, if that was possible. 'He was also the one who took the phone call cancelling the men who were supposed to be here for tonight's show.'

'How come?' Eve asked. 'Who rescinded the order?'

'He told me it was a woman, and that she said her name was Melissa Norton, and that she was my secretary. I can't believe that Melissa would have done such a thing. Why on earth would she do that? If I don't get a convincing explanation she's about to become my ex-secretary.'

'Have you asked her about it?'

'No, that's another thing, she's disappeared. I tried the hotel where my people are booked in, and she isn't there.'

'I think we know why,' Eve told him. 'We didn't mention it earlier, because we were waiting for the police to get here.' She recounted our near meeting with Pattison's secretary. 'She was definitely coming out of the antiques shop, which we assume must belong to Tony

Kendall. I think that proves beyond doubt who his accomplice within your firm is.'

'Are you telling me that Melissa was involved in all this violence? All the deceit? I don't believe it. I could quite easily imagine Kendall doing those terrible things. I could imagine him stealing Gerry's music and passing it off as his own, but I can't for one moment see Melissa being involved.'

Pattison looked from one to the other of us, seeing no support for his backing of the woman who worked for him. Even Alice seemed unconvinced by his protestations. It was, we knew, another classic case of someone being too close to the accused, and being unable to believe they could be wicked. If I had one niggling doubt, it was because I felt there was something that didn't quite fit. One piece of information that was wrong, but I couldn't at that moment put my finger on what it was.

'One thing,' I told him, trying to put a positive slant on what we'd heard, 'if neither of them is here, there's no immediate threat to Gerry or Trudi. Hopefully, by the time the audience begins arriving for the recording, Hardy and his men will be on site, and they will have all the protection they need.'

For once, it seemed my prediction was proved accurate, which made a pleasant change. We returned to the auditorium, in time to see Trudi perform the first of her songs. During the whole of the time they were on stage, Crowther stayed in deep shadow behind his keyboard. Obviously the producer had given detailed instructions to the lighting team. After a while, I was called to the front of house, and went on stage. I went through a sound test, commending Trudi, and introducing her backing instrumentalist, with the immortal line, 'Let's have a big round of applause for Mickey Mouse.'

'I thought you were going to give the game away,' Crowther told me as we went backstage. 'Mickey Mouse, indeed.'

'It's the ears, Gerry.'

I was relieved when Hardy, with a party of a dozen men and women, all smartly dressed, entered the auditorium shortly after the rehearsal of the finale had ended. I recognized Johnny Pickersgill and his wife amongst the group, but the rest were strangers. Having introduced us to his wife, Hardy explained, 'There are seven male officers, plus four policewomen, all with their partners.'

'How will we recognize them in an emergency?' Eve asked.

'Good question, but I thought of that. All the male officers are wearing a buttonhole.' Hardy indicated his lapel, which sported a white rose. 'The women all have a brooch of some description pinned to their dress.'

'That works for me, let's hope it isn't necessary.'

'I have news for you,' Hardy told us. 'Our fingerprint people confirmed that the prints on the valuation Pickersgill got from the antiques shop match those from the hit and run vehicle. So it seems that your theory was right and the shop owner is Tony Kendall. We have obtained an arrest warrant for him on suspicion of murder.' Hardy paused before delivering the bad news. 'Unfortunately, when we visited the shop to execute the warrant, there was no sign of him. The girl who was in charge told us he had left soon after lunch. He told her he was going on a buying trip and would be away for several days. Apparently this is quite a regular occurrence, so she thought no more about it. He didn't indicate when he'd return.'

'If he does return. It sounds to me like he's done a runner.'

'You may be right,' Hardy agreed, 'perhaps John Pickersgill's acting isn't as convincing as we'd hoped. It could be that his visit to the shop aroused Kendall's suspicions.'

'Maybe not,' Eve told him. 'It's more probable that someone tipped him off that we were on to him. We tried to get word to you. Adam and I went for a walk earlier and we were close to the shop when we saw someone coming out. They could have recognized us and warned Kendall.'

Hardy didn't miss the implication. 'Someone?'

Eve explained about Melissa Norton and told Hardy about the missing security men. 'It sounds as if another of your theories has been proved accurate,' Hardy remarked. 'If you keep this up I'll be out of a job. Now, I want to have a word with that producer chap. I'm going to try and get our people scattered around the first few rows, close to the aisles if we can.'

As he walked away, one of the many assistant producers summoned me. 'We need everyone who is appearing in the show to be in their dressing rooms. They'll be letting the audience in soon, and we need you for make-up and stage clothes.'

'It's like *Sunday Night at the London Palladium*,' Eve told me as I kissed her. 'Be careful, Adam. There could still be danger, and we still don't know what Kendall looks like.'

Along with the rest of the performers, having left the auditorium, we were in effect sequestered. It was of some comfort that the venue's security officers were on duty. This would prevent any unauthorised person from getting backstage. The disadvantage of that was that it also excluded Hardy and his officers.

As I approached the dressing room I was sharing with the compère and Crowther, Lew Pattison emerged from the one next to it, which I knew was Trudi's. He confirmed that Trudi was OK, and that she currently having her hair done, supervised by Sheila.

I told him that Hardy and his colleagues were in the

audience and repeated what the inspector had told us. 'It would be useful if they had a more up to date description of Kendall to work with.'

Pattison shrugged. 'There was nothing unusual in his appearance, as I recall. You have to bear in mind that it's almost twenty years since I last saw him, and even then it was only an occasional meeting. About the only thing I can remember is what I think Gerry's already told you, the fact that Kendall was losing his hair rapidly. By now he must be completely bald, I guess.'

'Will you remind Hardy of that when you go out front, it could prove useful.'

'Of course, and speaking of that, I'd better be going. I want to have words with Melissa if and when she arrives.'

'Do you think she'll turn up?'

'I have absolutely no idea. I still can't believe her capable of doing what's she's supposed to have done, so heaven knows if she'll have the nerve to show her face. Unless she thinks we haven't cottoned on to her. I'm not even sure what possessed her to ally herself with Kendall.'

'Perhaps she's in love with him.'

'Melissa? I suppose it is possible, but to the best of my knowledge, she didn't have much to do with Northern Lights, and her only contact with them was in the latter stages, just before Gerry disappeared.'

'Why was that?'

'Melissa didn't join the firm until then. She came to us straight from leaving school.'

'But that means Kendall would have already left the group, doesn't it?'

'Yes, but what's your point?'

'How did she meet him? How did they get together if he was no longer on the scene?'

'I've no idea, and we can't very well ask her point blank, can we?'

'No, I suppose not.'

Pattison was about to leave when I remembered a question that had been puzzling me for some time. 'Do you have any idea how Robbie Roberts got the money to set up that music magazine? We had him down as prime suspect for long enough, until we worked out that the dates didn't fit.'

Pattison looked a trifle sheepish. 'Actually, I should have said. I lent him the money. He came to me after he left the group and instead of ranting and raving like the others had, he put the business proposition to me. I thought it worthwhile gambling on, and by heavens he's proved me right. Robbie is a very shrewd operator, and what he doesn't know about business isn't worth knowing. I've had an excellent return on that investment and a couple of others he brought me too. He's coming to the concert. He and his wife will be sitting with Alice and me, so I'll introduce you later. He's the only one I can think of, apart from Neville Wade, who doesn't bear Gerry a grudge.'

Chapter Twenty-two

As the opening music faded and the compère walked out on stage and began to introduce the opening act, a highly popular dance troupe, I listened to the announcement that was piped throughout the corridors by various speakers, before entering the dressing room. I walked into the aftermath of what I guessed had been a blazing row. I hadn't realized from my earlier brief inspection of the room that there was a connecting door to that occupied by Trudi, but Sheila had obviously found it, and she and Trudi were now confronting Crowther. The atmosphere was tense, almost visibly so.

Although there was silence, I guessed it had only been the sound of me opening the door that had put an end to the words that had been exchanged. All three turned and looked at me, and from their expressions I could see my interruption was less than welcome. 'Something wrong?' I asked. Working that out hadn't taken rocket science.

The atmosphere, if anything, got even icier. It was some seconds before my innocuous question provoked a response. 'Stage fright,' Sheila told me tersely. 'Gerry has chosen this night above all others to develop a phobia about appearing in public. It never used to worry him.'

Crowther looked at me, whether because he was appealing for help or because he couldn't look Sheila or Trudi in the eye, I wasn't sure. 'I can't do it,' he tried to explain. 'I thought it would be OK, but I've been away too long.'

'You're not the only one,' I pointed out. 'I've not been

away as long as you, admittedly, but all my previous TV appearances were done without a large audience, any audience.' A random memory prompted my next remark, which in some bizarre way lightened the mood. 'Unless you count the news report I did surrounded by a couple of hundred goats and a dozen camels. Seriously, Gerry, if you don't do it tonight, you never will be able to do it. And if you don't appear this evening there's a strong chance those responsible for the murders will get away with it and you'll spend the rest of your life looking over your shoulder. You owe it to a lot of people to appear in this concert. To the victims and those close to them, to Lew Pattison and the TV people who have shown faith in you, but most of all to Sheila, to Trudi, and to yourself. Ask yourself this, Gerry, if Trudi was to have a little brother or sister, you'd want them to grow up to be proud of their father, wouldn't you?'

Sheila was watching Crowther carefully, and saw the bemused expression on his face at the notion of fatherhood. 'Why not, Gerry? We're not past it by any means, and I feel sure Trudi would like the idea.'

'Dad, I am already proud of you,' Trudi told him. 'Proud of your courage, and the sacrifice you made for Mum and me, even though you didn't know me. It must have been a heart-breaking decision, to have to turn your back on everything you loved. To forego your music, tear yourself away from Mum, and forfeit all hope of watching your family grow. That was a brave and selfless act, and I cannot imagine how lonely and scared you must have felt, but it didn't deter you. Tonight, you won't be alone. I will be on stage with you, and so will Adam, and Mum will be in the wings right alongside you for extra support.'

Crowther smiled ruefully. 'Or to make sure I don't do a runner?'

'Anyway, I have some good news. Hardy and his men are here. They've identified the villains and we think they know the game's up, so it's unlikely they'll risk coming anywhere near.'

Between us we coaxed and cajoled Gerry into a better frame of mind. He took a deep breath and told Sheila, 'I will not run the risk of losing either you or Trudi again. I don't care what it costs, I will go on stage tonight. As long as you're there to hold my hand.'

'I'll be there, Gerry. Tonight, and always,' Sheila assured him.

We had been subjected to the ministrations of the make-up artist and donned our stage clothes when, during the first interval, the producer came to our dressing room. He explained that the delay was to change scenery, and was scheduled to coincide with an advert break when the show went out. 'I want to ask a favour of you,' he told Crowther, 'and Adam can help too. When Adam does his big announcement, I want one of the cameras to pick out the old members of the group and provide close-ups of their reactions. To do that I need the cameraman to know where they are seated. Will you come onstage and point them out for us?'

Crowther looked terrified at the prospect, but the producer reassured him. 'You won't be visible to the audience. All they will see is the camera lens poking through the gap in the curtain, and I very much doubt if they'll notice that. You'll be able to view them through the camera monitor.'

'Adam may be more use than me. I haven't seen any of them for years, apart from Neville Wade.'

'I've only met Firth. However, I do know where Roberts will be sitting.'

We all went onstage, where the cameraman was already waiting for us. Crowther stood to one side of the technician, whilst I peered at the monitor from the other side. As he panned the first few rows of the audience, I picked out Roberts almost at the same time as Crowther exclaimed, 'That big guy with the floral bow tie, I bet that's Robbie Roberts.'

I looked at the man who was seated alongside Alice Pattison. 'I think you're right. Lew said he would be with them. And look one row back, Gerry, that's Pete Firth.' As I pointed him out I added, 'You might recognize the woman with him. That's his wife, Julie, who you knew as Julie Solanki.'

'She's wearing well, a lot better than Pete, but then she was always a good-looking girl.'

That remark earned him a sharp dig in the ribs from Sheila. Crowther grinned ruefully, and resumed his inspection of the audience. 'There's Nev,' he said, gesturing to the image on the screen. The producer made another note on the pad he was carrying, and as he did, I noticed Melissa Norton in the second row. Alongside her was a man of around Crowther's age, although it was difficult to assess how old he was, because he was completely bald. 'Is that Tony Kendall?' I indicated the figure in the centre of the monitor.

'I very much doubt it, unless he's had plastic surgery. The shape of his face is all wrong. What made you think it was him, the lack of hair?'

'That and the woman he's sitting with. That's Melissa Norton, Lew's secretary.'

Crowther looked a second time, 'Oh yes, so it is. I remember her vaguely.'

I smiled, wondering if he was trying to avoid another blow to the ribs. However, our failure to identify Kendall in the audience concerned me slightly. Despite what Hardy had said, and our own earlier thoughts, the fact that Melissa Norton was there suggested that Kendall might also be desperate enough to risk appearing at the concert. There was little time to reflect on this, however, because we were ushered back to our dressing room. My mind was almost exclusively occupied by what I intended to say as I straightened my bow tie. Crowther looked much less formal. His attire was a pair of black jeans and T-shirt, over which he would slip the Buddy Holly jacket just before going on stage.

I had chance for a quick word with the compère before he went back to introduce the next act. I'd noticed when we looked through the camera monitor that Eve's seat was vacant. 'Do me a favour. See if there's a redhead sitting in the aisle seat on row three, will you?'

He eyed me with world-weary suspicion. 'I suppose that means you've got plans for her tonight?'

'I hope so. She's my fiancée.'

'Oh, OK, I'll check.'

He returned a few minutes later, having announced the duo we'd heard rehearsing earlier. He gave me the thumbs-up sign. I relaxed, knowing that if Eve had resumed her seat, everything out front must be OK. All too soon for my liking we were summoned to the side of the stage. As we stood waiting in the wings, one of the many stagehands touched my arm and beckoned me away from the glare of the footlights, where even the most sensitive of microphones wouldn't be able to pick up our whispered conversation. 'A woman gave me this note to pass to you.'

He passed me slip of paper, accompanying the gesture with a salacious grin that suggested he knew exactly what was going on. I sighed wearily. 'I suppose that means I'll have to take her to bed again tonight. Honestly, some women are insatiable. The price of fame, I suppose. I guess I'll just have to marry her.'

I saw his look of surprise and dismay and turned away, both to read the note and hide my smile. I opened the paper and all humour vanished as I read what Eve had sent me. 'M denies cancelling guards. She says JL asked her to deliver tickets. She gave them to young girl.' She'd signed it with three kisses. Eve, it appeared, was becoming sentimental. Suddenly, although we were only a few yards apart, I missed her, and wanted her beside me.

I returned to the side of the stage, pondering what I'd learned, and whether to tell Gerry or Sheila that the mole inside Pattison's company was Judith Lane and not Melissa Norton. As I pondered my decision, I suddenly recalled the label on the Mystery Minstrel's record. The composers had been named as "A & J Deva." Anthony and Judith, from Chester. The clue had been there all along, staring us in the face, but none of us had the wit to work it out.

I was still mentally kicking myself for my stupidity when Crowther touched my arm. He leant over and whispered, 'Look at the far side of the auditorium. Three rows back, near the side aisle there's a blonde woman. The man sitting alongside her could well be Kendall, were it not for the fact that this bloke has a full head of hair.'

I looked across and located the woman. I gasped slightly. It was Judith Lane. At that point I knew why no one had recognized Kendall. 'Was he very self-conscious about his hair loss?' I asked.

Crowther smiled slightly. 'You could say so. I remember him buying all sorts of weird preparations to try and restore it. Some of them stank to high heaven, but none of them did any good.' He stopped suddenly and peered at me. 'Is that what you think? That he's either had a hair transplant or that's a toupee? It would be just the sort of thing he would do.'

I nodded, then looked round for someone to pass the message to Eve, or to DI Hardy, but even as I did so, the song came to an end, and the audience began to applaud as the duo took their bows, preparing to leave the stage. It was too late. Allowing only time for a swift scene change, Trudi would be summoned any second now, and Crowther would be stationed behind his keyboard. Both of them in vulnerable positions for someone desperate enough to harm them. Worse than that, they were defenceless, and short of stopping the show to warn Hardy, there was nothing I could do to protect them.

To my side I spotted the stagehand and grabbed him by the arm. 'This is urgent,' I whispered. 'The redhead who gave you the note.' He nodded. 'Go to her now and tell her end of row K. She must tell Hardy. Have you got that? Row K, tell Hardy.' He looked thoroughly confused but nodded again. 'Go on then, now!' I urged.

I'd already heard the producer telling one of his assistants that because they were behind schedule they would have to insert the final ad break afterwards. All too soon the curtain was down, the stage re-set, and the lights went up again. The backdrop had changed, to display a set of twinkling bright lights scattered in a haphazard pattern through a swirl of green haze. I guessed it was the set designer's attempt to reproduce the Aurora Borealis. Someone, in the production team, I thought, had a weird sense of humour.

There was no time to dwell on this, because the compère was already centre stage and beginning to introduce Trudi. I forgot everything that had gone on. My only task now was to concentrate on what I was going to say when my turn came to walk out there.

I knew that Trudi was going to sing a medley of her previous recordings, after which I would go on and introduce Crowther. After that, he would play the Mystery Minstrel hit, and she would close the show with the song Gerry had composed for her. It would be ten minutes or so before I had to walk out there. Never has ten minutes passed so slowly.

At last, the music died away, and I waited for the applause to die down before walking to the centre of the stage. Trudi turned and welcomed me with a warm smile. Any resemblance to the shy youngster who had been staying with us was gone. The moment she had walked on that stage she had donned the invisible cloak that all great entertainers wear, the air of a true professional. I kissed her lightly on both cheeks in the entertainment industry manner, which made her giggle slightly. Then I turned to the audience as she retired to stand alongside her father in the shadows. I unhitched the microphone.

Chapter Twenty-three

'Good evening. My name is Adam Bailey. The reason I'm here on this stage tonight is to tell you a story. A story that not only involves Trudi, but one that has had a massive influence on her young life. Some of you in the audience may know parts of what I'm about to reveal, but very few of you know it all. I feel sure there are those of you watching who might have been puzzled by the producer's choice of the Aurora Borealis as a backdrop for Trudi's performance. The reason for that will soon become clear.'

I was aware, subliminally, of a slight restless movement in one or two of those sitting in the front rows, and knew that certain members of the audience had already made a connection, albeit without knowing what I was about to reveal.

'My story begins in the 1960s, before Trudi was born.' As I spoke, I risked a glance into the audience, and was relieved to see that Eve was still in her seat. She looked nervous, which for some strange reason relaxed me. 'At that time a young and highly talented musician was beginning to make a name for himself and his group within the booming British pop industry. They were tipped for huge international stardom. The man I am describing was far more than a talented performer. His ability stretched beyond his singing, beyond the instrument he played so well. In addition to these, he was a superb composer and songwriter. Although the many well-known temptations for pop stars were strewn in his path, he ignored them. He preferred to remain true to the girl he loved, the girl who had been his childhood sweetheart.'

I paused, this time for dramatic effect, before getting to the crux of the tale. 'They conceived a baby girl together. However, before the child was born, the father disappeared, vanishing suddenly and dramatically into the cold fog of a winter's night after the group had performed a gig in Newcastle. A long time later, a body wearing his trademark jacket was recovered from the Tyne. Everyone believed him to be dead. It was assumed that he had committed suicide by jumping from the Tyne Bridge. Both those facts are untrue.'

I had to stop once more, but this time it was to allow the audience to settle. The gasps of shock and disbelief from those who knew or guessed what and who I was referring to died away slowly. 'For several months prior to his vanishing act, he had been the victim of a series of carefully contrived attempts on his life. In some of those incidents, only luck and the intervention of others saved him from those murderous attacks. When the threats extended to his lover, and thereby to his unborn child, he made a courageous but painful decision. He argued that if he was no longer around, there would be no reason to attack those close to him. So he elected to disappear. He chose to forego the music career for which he had worked so hard, and the success that undoubtedly awaited him. He chose to abandon his girl and their child to prevent them coming to harm.'

This time I had to pause for breath, because despite my attempts to be dispassionate, the emotional content of the tale was having its effect on me. 'Despite his careful preparations, his plan was upstaged, and due to an unforeseen twist of fate, those who were stalking him with murder in mind chose the wrong victim, a fact he didn't know until long afterwards. Recently, I have been helping police investigate the events that took place back then, and together we have discovered the motive behind this cruel vendetta. It was a sordid one, but as the police officer in charge told me, they most often are. The motive was greed. Nothing more than that, but it has already cost the lives of four people and caused years of separation, loneliness, and heartbreak.'

I moved on to the climax of the story, and my next words gave Gerry the cue to begin playing, very softly, what must have seemed to those listening and watching nothing more than incidental music. 'The reason for all this was that our musician had composed a set of instrumental pieces, the sheet music for which had been stolen. The thief recognized the huge earning potential. However, he could not perform them or present them as his own whilst the real composer was alive to challenge him. So he set out to kill the man who stood between him and his fortune. The killer thought he could present the works as his own, hiding his true identity by recording them under the name of the Mystery Minstrel.

'Now that masquerade can be exposed, because we have the genuine article here tonight.' As I spoke I moved away from the front of the stage and off to the right, making a sweeping gesture with my right hand. Taking his cue from my gesture, the lighting director hit the spotlight, which illuminated Crowther. He was standing with his back to the audience, who could clearly see the iconic image on the back of the jacket. Conscious that the recording was still ongoing, I ended by saying, 'I am referring of course to Trudi Bell's father, the genius behind Northern Lights: Gerry Crowther.'

Gerry must have turned the volume on his instrument to maximum, otherwise it would not have been audible above the pandemonium in the auditorium, where cheering, clapping, a hubbub of conversation all mingled with the notes. The dais on which he stood revolved and he was facing his audience. As he played the middle section, using the Hawaiian guitar effect on the keyboard, I felt a momentary cold shiver run down my spine. I looked towards the seats where the man who looked like Kendall and Judith Lane had been sitting, and saw they were empty. This panicked me momentarily, then, to my relief, I saw Kendall, his toupee hopelessly askew, being marched towards the back of the auditorium by a quartet of burly but immaculately dressed men sporting buttonholes.

As Trudi walked forward I handed her the microphone, took her hand and led her centre stage. She squeezed my hand before I stepped away, leaving her standing for a moment waiting for the sound to die down. 'I would like to end by singing my latest recording. It is a song that means more to me than any other, not only because my father wrote it, but because it reunited him with my mother and brought him into my life. It is even more special because he is here with me tonight.'

Instead of remaining centre stage, she walked across to the keyboard, choosing to stand alongside Gerry, sharing the limelight with him. I watched, treasuring the moment, for it gave a feeling of satisfaction to see the happy outcome to all their tribulations. Gerry played the opening bars of the intro using only his right hand, gesturing to the wings with his left. With some reluctance, Sheila emerged onto the stage.

He had to play the intro a second time, because the first rendition was drowned by the cheering, whistling and clapping of the audience. When Trudi began to sing, however, you could have heard a pin drop in that auditorium. The ballad's message was a poignant tale of separation and heartbreak spanning years. For those who had just listened to my tale, the relevance was heightened, and I could see the lyrics were affecting the audience.

When the song ended there was a momentary silence, then another storm of applause. Instead of taking a bow, Trudi walked to the rear of the keyboard and stood with her parents, all three of them smiling broadly. That is another image I will treasure.

The idyll was rudely interrupted as a figure hurtled from the wings behind me and crossed the stage. The normally immaculate Judith Lane was barely recognizable in this avenging fury. The long-bladed knife in her hand was far too identifiable.

She reached the trio faster than anyone could react, or even cry out a warning. Her initial target was Trudi. Whether that was design, or because the girl was closest, I couldn't say. As she raised the knife to deliver a fatal blow, another figure emerged from the wings. Far too late, I thought, but as I watched, still horror-struck, I saw the newcomer raise one hand; saw something fly from it, and saw the object strike Judith on the temple. She staggered, then crumpled to the floor, and a split second later, a quartet of women descended on her. The women police officers handcuffed the semi-conscious attacker and dragged her away.

Amid the ensuing chaos and melee of television personnel, I sought out Trudi's saviour. As Charlie advanced, somewhat diffidently, onto the stage to retrieve the cricket ball he'd bought that afternoon and used as a weapon, I shook him by the hand. 'Well thrown, Charlie, I reckon your fielding practice just paid off, big style.'

Charlie grinned, still a little overcome at being the focus of attention. A moment later, as Gerry shook him by the hand and Sheila hugged him, they thanked him for saving their daughter. Then Trudi came forward and kissed him warmly. No peck on the cheek either, but full on the lips. Charlie's confusion was all but complete, but when I pointed out the TV cameraman who was recording everything, his embarrassment went into overdrive. He muttered something and turned back to the wings, where Eve joined us.

He looked at me, his face troubled. 'Adam, they won't show that last bit as part of the concert, will they?'

'You mean the part when you got to snog a famous singer? I don't think so.'

He nodded. 'Thank heavens for that, I'd never live it down at school. The guys would be so jealous they'd tease me forever.'

'No, I don't think they'll wait until the concert is televised. My guess is that it'll be on tomorrow's national news bulletins and every newspaper front page.'

As the Crowther clan, which was how I had got used to thinking of them, joined us in the wings, DI Hardy also arrived. 'I think it's safe to say that your problems are now behind you,' he told Crowther. 'I'm sorry we were unable to prevent the attack. It's a good job this young man was on hand to spot the danger and act.'

'How did the woman get backstage?' Eve asked.

'The security guards were called away by a fake message purporting to come from the centre manager reporting a disturbance in the foyer.'

Charlie explained, 'I heard the stagehand speaking to Aunt Evie and he pointed out where the woman and Kendall were sitting. Before he was arrested, I watched her leave her seat and when I saw her deliver a note to the security man I knew she was up to something so I followed her.'

The next couple of days were marked by a whirl of activity. Having given statements to the police, we were told that Tony Kendall and Judith Lane were being charged with offences ranging from murder downwards. We returned to Laithbrigg, having spent several hours helping Crowther to select a new car, which would be delivered to his house in a few days' time. Once we were back at Eden House, Sheila supervised packing operations, as she, Gerry, and Trudi would be returning to Allerscar.

A week later, Eden House was once again filled with visitors. First DI Hardy arrived, his purpose to update us on their intended prosecution. He had barely entered the house when another car arrived. Crowther, it seemed, was getting used to driving again. After Eve let Gerry and Sheila in, they joined us in the lounge, which thanks to Eve's refurbishment was now presentable again. Trudi wandered into the garden in search of Charlie.

'You've saved me an extra journey,' Hardy told them. 'When we searched Kendall's flat we found a selection of highly valuable paintings, antique furniture, ceramics, and jewellery, which he confessed he had bought for himself, not for the business. We also found these.'

He reached into his brief case and removed four sheets of paper, which were enclosed in clear plastic wallets. 'Can you confirm that this is your signature?' he asked Crowther, pointing to the top corner of one of the pages.

I peered over his shoulder and saw that the item was a page of sheet music. 'Good heavens!' Crowther exclaimed, 'Where did you get those?'

'They were locked in Kendall's safe. I can't let you have them back yet, not until after the trial.'

'The last time I saw them was in a hotel room in Chester.'

'Are you going to be able to make the charges against Kendall and Lane stick?' I asked.

Hardy smiled. 'That won't be a problem. It was like an aviary in the station when they started singing. To sum up what we've learned, I'd say Kendall was besotted by money and would stop at absolutely nothing to get it, and Judith Lane was besotted by Kendall and would stop at nothing to get *him*, and keep him.'

'Was greed the sole reason for trying to kill Gerry?' Eve asked.

'No, Kendall was furious because the way he saw it, Mr Crowther had denied him access to the two things he wanted in life: fame and fortune. He'd already decided to kill him. Somewhere in the process he hitched up with

Judith Lane, who he knew from Pattison's company. She supplied information that enabled him to track Mr Crowther's movements.

'The plan changed after Kendall overheard Mr Crowther and Billy Quinn playing one of those tunes.' Hardy gestured to the documents. 'He knew right off that what he was listening to would be a monumental hit. He decided that killing Mr Crowther would have to wait until he'd got his hands on the music. Then, with the real composer dead, he could pass it off as his own and reap the rewards. However, there was one major stumbling block. Kendall realized that a musician of Billy Quinn's calibre would be bound to recognize it immediately, if he heard it, and would know that it had been stolen. So Quinn would have to die as well.'

'We thought it was because Quinn knew Carl Long had the jacket, but Kendall set out to murder Gerry and Billy Quinn purely for the money? That is unbelievably callous,' Eve said.

'The rewards were too high to resist, certainly for someone who worshipped money the way Kendall does. Once he'd read all four pieces he knew they would earn him a small fortune.'

'Why did he kill Jimmy and Steve?' Crowther asked.

'Jimmy Mitchell saw him near the keyboard at the venue when you were almost electrocuted, and Steve Thompson spotted him on the building site when you were almost killed by that falling girder. Kendall told us the two of them got together and realized that he must be behind whatever was going on.'

'Those two were always as thick as thieves,' Crowther interjected.

'Yes, and when they tried to blackmail Kendall, he was desperate, but thanks to Judith Lane he managed to turn the tables on them. She got hold of some suppressed paperwork concerning the rape of two underage girls which was allegedly carried out by Mitchell and Thompson. Kendall threatened them with exposure, not only to the police but also the press. That kept them quiet long enough for Kendall to perform as the Mystery Minstrel, reap the rewards, and vanish from the music scene. He resurfaced years later, wearing a wig, as the owner of a chain of antique shops.'

Hardy paused for a second. 'When Kendall found out that Pattison had asked you to search for Gerry Crowther, he was afraid Thompson and Mitchell would talk. They were the only ones who knew he was behind the murder attempts. He couldn't use the old blackmail weapon. For one thing, Mitchell and Thompson were no longer in the public eye. Rather than take the risk, he decided to silence them.'

'That is so cold-blooded and calculating,' Eve remarked. 'It makes me shiver just thinking about it.'

Hardy agreed. 'That was how I felt when I listened to his confession. He said it in such a matter-of-fact way, with no more emotion than if he was buying a newspaper.'

'How did he find out that Lew had asked us to search for Gerry?' I asked. 'I take it that was Judith Lane.'

'It certainly was. She had a habit of listening in on Mr Pattison's intercom. As soon as she heard the name Crowther during a call from Miss Samuels here, she listened intently. When Mr Pattison asked her and Melissa Norton to collate all the paperwork there was about Northern Lights and anyone connected with the group, Judith Lane told Kendall immediately. He guessed that Crowther might still be alive. If that was so, the body in the Tyne was probably Carl Long's. He and Lane had accidently murdered the wrong man!'

'Was Carl Long part of the plot?' I asked.

'To a certain extent, yes. According to Kendall, Long didn't know they intended to kill Mr Crowther. As far as he was aware it was nothing more than a plot to rob him.

Long was used to lure him to the Tyne Bridge, in return for which he would receive a huge amount of money to feed his drug habit. I spoke to Carl Long's mother to tell her about her son's death and she said that her husband had booked Carl into a private sanatorium in France that dealt with people with drug addictions, but that Carl had refused to go. As a result, his father wouldn't let him have any more money until he agreed to undergo treatment. Carl was desperate, so desperate that when Kendall approached him with the idea, he jumped at it.'

Hardy winced slightly. 'Sorry, "jumped at it" is an unfortunate choice of words in the circumstances.'

'Don't worry,' Eve reassured him, 'Adam is capable of far worse puns than that.'

Hardy departed soon afterwards, but before the others followed him, Eve had a question to ask, one I suspected she had wanted to put to Crowther for some time. 'It's about that lovely song you wrote for Trudi and Sheila. Would you play it when Adam and I get married? And would Trudi sing it for us?'

'Oh,' I said. 'We are getting married then? Would you mind telling me when? My diary gets a trifle busy at times.'

Father and daughter both laughed but responded immediately, 'We'd be honoured to.'

Before they left, Trudi gave Charlie a parcel. 'That's a thank-you, from me,' she told him, 'and don't forget your promise. I want to see your castle.'

We waved them off, and as we closed the door, Eve told him, 'You should have kissed her, Charlie, there were no TV cameras pointing at you this time.'

As I'd predicted, the story had made headlines, and was still doing so when we took Charlie back to Mulgrave Castle the next day. His parents and sister had been shocked to arrive back in England and find that Charlie was something of a national hero. Tony and Harriet were justifiably proud of their son, whilst Sammy and Becky wanted to know about *that* kiss. Their curiosity about the relationship increased tenfold when Charlie showed them the photo Trudi had given him. It was a studio portrait of her, inscribed in one corner, *To Charlie Rowe. You are my hero. With love, Trudi xx.*

Life returned slowly to normal. Any sense of anti-climax was dispelled by the letter that arrived some weeks later, and the royalty cheque it contained. A celebration was definitely called for.

That evening, I had just opened a champagne bottle when the phone rang. Eve answered it, and a moment later called out, 'Adam, it's somebody called Jeremy Powell. He says you know him.' She handed me the phone, an enquiring look in her eyes.

I covered the mouthpiece. 'He's a lawyer. Used to work for the TV company I reported for.'

'Sorry to trouble you, Adam,' Powell began, 'but I want to pick your brains. Actually, it's for my kid sister, Alison. Her boyfriend's brother has been murdered, but the police don't know how. Apparently the wound was like no other they've ever come across and I wondered if you'd seen anything similar – in Africa, say. The wound was perfectly circular, like a gunshot, but when they did the post-mortem they couldn't find a bullet. In addition …' – Powell paused – 'a core of skin, flesh, tissue and bone had been removed, right the way to his heart. He'd been cored …'

The End

The Eden House Mysteries

Bill Kitson

 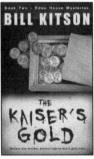 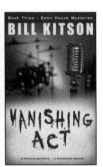

For more information about **Bill Kitson**

and other **Accent Press** titles

please visit

www.accentpress.co.uk

Lightning Source UK Ltd.
Milton Keynes UK
UKHW01f1031270618
324864UK00001B/6/P